ONCE IN A BLUE MOON

ONCE IN A BLUE MOON

Amber L. Lynch

authorHOUSE®

AuthorHouse™
1663 Liberty Drive
Bloomington, IN 47403
www.authorhouse.com
Phone: 1-800-839-8640

Published by AuthorHouse   04/29/2013

ISBN: 978-1-4817-4197-2 (sc)
ISBN: 978-1-4817-4196-5 (hc)
ISBN: 978-1-4817-4195-8 (e)

Library of Congress Control Number: 2013906929

"Space is big. You just won't believe how vastly, hugely, mind-bogglingly big it is. I mean, you may think it's a long way down to the chemist's, but that's just peanuts to space."

Douglas Adams,
Hitchhiker's Guide to the Galaxy

CHAPTER 1

Lisa was staring out the window of her science class as usual. Just looking up at the moon, still very visible in the brightening morning sky. She always did love the way it just sat up there in the mornings, as though it were sleeping. Then when night came, it would awaken with its bright white light. She felt a little like the moon at the moment. Tired and not as bright.
Someone poked her shoulder and passed a note underneath where her elbow touched the table. She used her elbow to push it onto her lap quickly before the teacher saw. When the teacher turned back toward the blackboard Lisa quickly unraveled the note and read silently.

"Meet me at my locker after class. Got something to tell you."

-D

"You're moving?" She forgot they were standing in the middle of the hallway and suddenly noticed all the weird stares everyone was giving her as they walked by.

1

So what? Let them look. It's none of their business anyway. Right now she was too upset to really care about what was going on around them.

"Mom said after this year is over. She at least wants me to finish high school." He wasn't looking at her, but she could still hear the hurt and anger in his voice.
Lisa didn't know if she should be relieved his mother was giving him more time or angry because she might be doing it on purpose. Lisa was going for the latter. When it came to her and Decker's relationship, that woman was always right there to remind them that she wouldn't make it easy. And here Lisa thought that was supposed to be *her* parent's job.

"Where?" She asked him then, hoping he would say somewhere in driving distance, or closer. But she caught his hesitation before he answered and braced herself. "Florida." He looked down.

Her chest constricted. She turned quickly and started walking away, anywhere away from where they were, in the middle of all these curious eyes. She didn't get far enough away from the crowd when the tears started streaming down her face. Good thing they clouded her vision too because she couldn't stand to see the looks on everyone's faces as she ran passed them. They were probably wondering what was wrong with her or something. How embarrassing. And with Decker chasing her, they're probably thinking they just had a fight. If only that was all it really was . . . She wouldn't want to have to look at those faces the next day in school and remember the looks they gave her while she ran down the hall crying. So much for the plan of being inconspicuous at school . . .

He grabbed her wrist and spun her around to meet him. She wanted to protest that they weren't far enough away yet, when he quickly grabbed his shades from his back jeans pocket and slipped them over her eyes.

It hadn't registered in her mind what he did until he started pulling her toward the empty hallway just around the next corner. They didn't run this time, because she didn't have to, Lisa noticed. Nobody was staring now.

Finally they rounded the corner to the long narrow hallway where nobody really passed through.

Decker pulled her into his arms tightly and let his head fall down on her shoulder.

"Lisa . . ." She heard his voice break. Forgetting what she was supposed to be upset about, she wrapped her arms around him.

On the bus ride home, Lisa sat with Decker in the back. They held each other. Hands entwined. She inched closer so she could lean her head against his chest. She would've closed her eyes and just lay there, her mind soothed by the sound of his heartbeat, all other sounds a dull murmur, when he kissed the top of her forehead and said, "I'm not gonna be there forever."

She's been telling herself that too. Anything to relieve her of the pain that was tearing at her heart. But how long could she really go without him?

"I swear I'll come back to you, love. I promise."

"You're not there yet." She said, trying to push it from her mind. They didn't need to think about it now, or talk about it. They still had time . . .

Adam poked his head up from behind the seat in front of theirs when the bus came to a stop. Him and Decker clapped hands together like they usually did and Adam got off.

She looked out and waved at him through the bus window, and he waved back. His face was sad, but accepting.

Decker rested his head on top of hers for the rest of the ride home. She tried to pretend this was them leaving . . . this was the two of them going somewhere far away.

Almost every night Lisa and her mom would sit in her parent's bedroom and watch late night news channels. Mom was a big fan of crime news. She said she once thought about being an investigator, like solving crimes and mysteries and stuff like that. Lisa wasn't really big about the crime genre, especially when it included decapitated heads and dead children, but it was fun to sit and listen to the people on the live news shows go at each other's throats with different opinions. It was more like drama than crime.

"So, anything new happen in school?" Her mom asked, not looking up from her handheld puzzle game. That was another thing mom loved, way more than the news. Video games.
"Nothing really. Oh, well besides Decker moving to Florida in nine months." Lisa felt like she wanted to slap herself for sounding so casual about it. But she knew the more she dwelled on it the worse the pain would get. And she didn't feel like crying in front of her mother because she would probably think Lisa was being overdramatic. And Lisa might believe her.

"He's moving?" Mom sounded shocked. "To Florida?"
"Yep." It was apparent that Lisa was angry about it, but hopefully that was the only thing that was apparent.

"What made them decide to up and move again?"
Lisa didn't know, but she believed it had something to do with his mother not liking Lisa one bit. When Decker's family moved here seven years ago from Philidelphia, it turned out to be a much more different scene here than over in the bustling city.

Decker had never been allowed to leave the house when he was little, not even to ride his trike out on the sidewalk. His mother's paranoia over keeping her son safe had her believing the whole world was dangerous. He told her the straw that broke the camel's back was when he was five and his mother actually let him go out front for a few minutes to kick his soccer ball around. Suddenly bullets started flying past his little head and his mother was screaming from the front door for him to come back inside. So when they moved here to New Jersey and Decker started making new friends, his mother became a lunatic about his safety. Eventually he met Lisa and didn't even bother begging his mom to go outside anymore, he would just walk out. His mother blamed Lisa for Decker's "strange behavior." And at first, Lisa tried to understand. Any good mother would want their child to be safe. It wasn't until Lisa saw for herself that Decker's home life was a lot more complicated than she first thought . . .

"Well maybe it's for the best Lisa. Maybe his father will help him out a little and get him on his feet . . ."
Lisa didn't believe that for one second.
Decker's father left when Decker was only an infant, so he never had that kind of male role model to follow by. His mother was sixteen when she had him. Their relationship took a crashing soon after, and his father promised he would never bother her again as long as she stayed away from him and his family. This was just after the crazy woman smeared peanut butter all over his truck and the guy almost died from an allergic reaction. Lisa never met Decker's father, but from what she was told, his father hadn't even wanted to be a part of Decker's life to begin with. There is only so much Lisa might believe from his mother, so she takes what the woman says with a grain of salt. Still, Lisa couldn't help but feel a kind of hatred for his father for leaving his teen girlfriend with a newborn to raise on her own, and leave Decker without a father. Decker and Lisa met seven years ago, right after he moved to New Jersey. She was fourteen and he was fifteen. They were friends at first, though Lisa dreamed of it becoming something more. She only dreamed because she never thought it would actually happen.

He was a handsome blonde. Tall, cool and a real good skateboarder, while she was just a plain -looking girl. Shy, awkward, and a real geek when it came to Japanese animation. Lisa never thought in a million years that a boy as good-looking as Decker would ever go out with a plain girl like her. Go figure.

Another year passed, and Decker was walking her home from a fun night at a friend's house. Before they got to the main road across the street from her house, he stopped her and asked if she would consider going out with him. A lightning bolt wouldn't sum up to the amount of shock she felt at that moment. Caught off guard she hesitated and started blinking her eyes as though trying to wake up from a dream. He smiled down at her. That was the night Lisa got her first kiss.

She sighed, remembering how it had felt. His lips were warm and soft, his hands reached up to cup her face. If the world was ending she wouldn't have known it. She was deaf to every outside sound, numb to the breezy night air and sounds of cars passing. All she knew right then was Decker, the boy she had had a crush on for months, was kissing *her*.

He changed her life. Soon she was out of the baggy black clothes, and started wearing lighter t-shirts and capri jeans. She still wore some of her black shirts every once in a while, but Decker never minded, he always told her that he loved her in whatever she wore. She started talking more in school. The panic attacks she had suffered from since she was five didn't happen as often. She moved her bangs out of her face so they would grow off the sides of her forehead, instead of hanging in front of her eyes. She became more confident in herself. They would spend every day together.

Seven years.
Sometimes to Lisa, it felt like they had known each other longer.

The blanket in-between Lisa and her mom started to move a little and Gustav, their pet dachshund, popped his head out from underneath.

"Hey pup." Lisa leaned down and kissed his big brown flappy ear. But Gustav didn't give her a lick back like he usually did. Something had his attention. He woofed out little barks and his ears perked up. Lisa muted the tv for a second to listen for any noise outside that he might be hearing.

Probably kids or a car or something, Lisa thought, and un-muted the tv.

Then Gustav waddled his way out of the blanket and toward the edge of the bed.

"Does he have to go maybe? Hey Gustav wait a second!" Mom yelled, thinking he was going to fall off the bed. Lisa and her dad always assured mom that he would never fall off, but she worried anyway. He was a little clumsy sometimes.

Lisa helped him down and he raced out of the room. She chuckled, amazed he could still run like that despite him being so overweight.

She slipped on her robe and sneakers.

"I'll go stand out front, I guess. Just in case he decides to wander off."

"Alright." Mom answered.

It wasn't exactly freezing cold out, but tonight's air felt a little chilly. Lisa pulled her robe closer to her body and put her hands in the pockets. Gustav went to his usual spot over near the corner where the driveway stopped near the sidewalk. Then he turned around, ears perked and tail up, and started barking madly. Lisa looked around but saw nothing. "What? What Gus?" She tried to call him back thinking he might run off after a cat or whatever it was he was barking at.

"Come here! Come!"

She didn't want to have a repeat of a few years ago, when Gustav ran after the neighbor's cat and almost got his face scratched off.

He stopped for a moment, his whole body still as a statue. Lisa heard his deep growling and backed up onto the porch, afraid there might be someone near the side of the house. She waited with her breath held. Maybe it was a cat, she told herself, and braved a step down off her porch. Huffing little barks, Gustav trotted his way up to her and nudged his head into her leg indicating that he wanted to go inside now. She lifted him up and carried him back into her mother's bedroom.

"What was he barking at?" Her mom asked as she entered.

"I don't know. But hang on a sec." If it really is a cat she better shoo it away before it gets into the backyard and goes through their trash again. Lisa was about to close the bedroom door when her mom warned, "Stay near the house alright?"

Lisa nodded.

She stepped out onto her porch again. The night air felt like it was getting more frigid. She squinted her eyes against the dark, but there wasn't anything to be seen. It was quiet save for a few passing cars out on the main road. She stepped out further to look around the sides of the house but didn't see anything. It probably would've been smart to bring a flashlight . . . Suddenly she felt a strange "booming" noise wrack her body. It vibrated through her head and down to her knees.

"Geez!" She mumbled, rubbing the sides of her temples as they throbbed. It was probably one of the neighbors revving up their car or blasting music again.

That must've been what Gustav was hearing. Relieved to know it wasn't a sneaky burglar or a trash-killing cat, Lisa stepped back into the house.

She was about to close the front door when she noticed the bright moon sitting over the top of some trees. It was a full moon tonight, her favorite to look at.

She stepped back out for a moment to get a better view. Lisa didn't know what it was about the moon that fascinated her so much. She just loved the way it glowed, not like the sun, which was so bright you couldn't look at it. The moon was beautiful, mystifying in its own way. And tonight it was a bright blue. She smirked remembering how mom always uses the saying, "Once in a blue moon." It meant something didn't happen very often.

Suddenly she was struck frozen by that loud vibrating noise again. This time it was much louder. Closer. Damn people and their stupid cars! She walked out farther onto the lawn, looking around at whomever it was that was making all this noise so late at night.

Then for whatever reason, she looked up.

All she saw now was this . . . thing. This *huge* thing . . . Her gut dropped and her face went pale.

It floated out from behind the large tree next to her house. Moving silently through the air . . . So silent that if she were blind she wouldn't know it was there. She was paralyzed by its intimidating size. It was huge, like a blimp, a metal blimp, from the way the moon's light shined on it. It sparkled red. Large sharp fins came into view from its back side. They looked so weird. Lisa felt herself want to fall back away from them, like they were moving toward her. It was the oddest shape she had ever seen on a blimp . . . or plane . . . or . . . .

What scared her the most was that it was so deathly quiet. It moved across the trees so silently . . . And before she could get out a squeak, it flew past her. Gone.

"What the—"

Lisa came bolting back into the bedroom and her mom jumped, almost throwing her game into the air. Gustav came racing out from underneath his blanket barking wildly at Lisa's frantic state. "Lisa what the hell-?!"

"I saw a . . ." She stopped to gasp for more breath, still hyperventilating. "I saw a . . . !"

CHAPTER 2

"A ufo?" Adam asked with a stupid grin on his face.
Lisa nodded her head rapidly. "I'm dead serious that's what it was!
It was just right there! Like *right the hell there*! Near my house!"
Adam and Decker exchanged looks.
"Guys no lie, the thing was huge and red and shiny!"
"Shiny?" Adam chuckled. Decker punched him in the arm.
"Well what did your mom say? Did she see it?" Decker asked.
Actually, Lisa didn't know what to make of her mom's reaction last
night. When she ran back into the house screaming, she was certain
her mom would take her seriously when she started rambling on
about seeing something outside the house. But all her mom did was
give her a confused and worried look. Hopefully the *worried* look
wasn't for Lisa's sake! That's the last thing she wanted was for her
mom to think she was crazy . . .

"Are you sure that's what it was?" Her mom asked after
Lisa had calmed down a bit.
"YES! Unless somebody around here is flying a big, *round* metal
plane!"
Damn if only she were an artist like her cousin. She would paint a
picture of what the thing looked like right now, she could still see it
vividly in her mind. Huge, round and a deep color red. Shiny. Two
shark-like red fins protruding from the top, bottom and back. But

what gave Lisa the chills more than anything was the fact that it was very, *very* quiet. It just floated there. Big and intimidating. So quiet Lisa had to question herself again if she was actually seeing something, or if she wasn't just imagining it. Then it left. Flew past her so fast she didn't even have time to blink her eyes . . .

Adam was still looking at her like she had sprouted a second head.

"Are you sure it wasn't a—"

"Oh my gosh Adam it was a freakin space ship! Can't you just believe me?" But then again, why should they? An alien space ship, really?

Decker put an arm around her shoulder.

"Ok, well maybe it was." He said.

It didn't ease her shaking. Actually she wished Decker didn't believe her story so easily. But she was sure that he was only saying that to calm her nerves.

Lisa thought maybe she didn't want them to believe her after all. Maybe then she could try to convince herself that what she saw was nothing. Maybe she *thought* she saw something, but she was just so tired that she confused it with something else. Of course that's stupid, because anybody with eyes could've seen the damn thing, it was that big. And that's another thing! How was it that she was the only one out to see it? So nobody else was outside that night? Nobody at all?

That figures. But she had to ask herself this. Why an alien space ship? Why couldn't she have thought of something else? Maybe it was because of the sci fi television show she was watching yesterday on the History channel. Maybe that was why. Whatever it was she saw, she likely won't see it again. So she'll just have to forget about it.

"Looks like we won't be having lunch milk for a while guys. Ha!" Adam laughed. "Get it? Cause if the cows get abducted then . . ." They just looked at him. "Nevermind . . ."

Well so much for forgetting it.

"Adam, promise me you won't tell anyone." Lisa begged, but it
sounded like an order. She couldn't help it. She could only imagine
what everyone would think of her if word got out that she saw an
"alien" space ship. Geez she would never hear the end of it.
"Hey don't worry, I'm not about to be made fun of for being
friends with a nut case who sees space ships." Adam joked. Lisa
playfully punched him in the arm. She already knew that she could
trust Decker not to say anything. But Adam was a little more social
than Decker was. And he was goofy. So she hoped he wouldn't
spill the beans even accidentally. She pictured all the kids coming
up to her to crack one of their dumb sarcastic humor jokes on her
about seeing aliens.
"Hey wait I got another one." Adam was laughing again. "They
must've come down to get Mr. Derbell. Ha!"
Yep. She was doomed.

To Lisa's mortification, they started a new chapter in
History class called, "Myth and Legends of the World." She
groaned and lay her head back down on her desk.
Terrific! Now everything she hears and sees is gonna be about
UFOs. Can't she just get over it and call it a day? For goodness
sakes, people see UFOs all the time. Everywhere! There are videos
on YouTube with flying saucers and weird lights in the sky. People
who actually study those things talk on tv about their theories and
"experiences." Authors who publish hundreds maybe thousands of
pages based off of extra-terrestrials.
Besides maybe it wasn't even a UFO. She'll admit she saw
something strange, but then, maybe it was some kind of top secret
government machine. *That floats around neighborhoods for the
public to see* . . . But it was dark . . . It could've been a blimp. *That
fly's close enough to the ground to touch trees*? She might've been

dreaming . . . *Yeah right*. Lisa put her head on her desk. Maybe she really was going crazy.

"Hey, is she new?" Lisa heard Adam ask. She lifted her head up off her desk to see who he was talking about. "Guess so. Never seen her before." Decker replied.

A girl stood at the front of the classroom, a book clutched to her chest, looking back and forth from the teacher to the rest of the class. She looked nervous. When the teacher urged the girl to go to her seat, the girl hesitated a moment, then walked shyly through the line of desks until she got to the very last seat in the back. She was small and thin, wearing a long sleeved green and black striped shirt with black jeans. Her oval shaped black pendant necklace hung from a thick silver chain down to her small stomach. If it weren't for her glasses, the black hat might've covered half her eyes.

Lisa had actually expected the poor girl to trip over herself with those jean flares that covered up most of her sneakers. She had short blond, curly hair that almost touched her shoulders. There was a purple strip down the one side near her ear, which was pierced with a black and purple gage.

Once she got to her seat, she rushed to open her book and start reading, her eyes looking around to see if anyone was still staring. She must be really shy. Lisa knows how that feels for sure. It was a wonder she actually made friends in middle school with how shy she was. What was really embarrassing was when the teachers would ask her mom if she had any mental problems of some kind, since she was so anti-social and rarely ever raised her hand or participated in group projects. Some even suggested going to see a doctor. Her mom would lose her cool to the point of exploding on them about how she is the mother and she would know if her daughter had any issues or not. Of course, that was only the adults. Lisa had to deal with the bullies in school herself, since she never really told her parents about the constant name calling. Yeah, she could definitely relate.

Throughout the rest of class the girl never looked up from her book.

"Accursed Bloodline," the title read, printed as though it dripped with blood. Lisa shook her head at the thought of having another vampire crazed fan girl in school. Norse High already had enough of those. And though Lisa had to admit she herself was a fan of vamps, they were in her mind, a lot hotter than the now popular ones of today's world. Lisa didn't care for mainstream. Once something got too popular, it sorta lost its uniqueness. She never understood why she thought that way, and maybe she was being a little hypocritical. After all, she did enjoy the one vampire series that was getting a lot of attention from the younger crowd. And if she were an amazing author, she would want her books known all over the world too.

"Dude, she's hot." Adam whispered next to Decker and turned in his seat to look towards the back of the room.
Decker gave him a nudge with his elbow. "So go talk to her then."
Adam mouthed a "hey" and waved at the new girl who was now looking up from her book at Adam quizzically.
"That looks a little creepy you know." Decker said, pulling him back around.
"What? Saying hi is creepy now?"
"*Saying* hi isn't as creepy."
Adam ignored the comment and looked back again. This time the new girl waved back at him with a smile.
Adam turned back in his seat and smiled proudly. "See, she doesn't think I'm creepy."
Decker shook his head.
She didn't know why, but for the rest of the class Lisa felt as though something was on her back. Like someone was watching her. She didn't want to be rude, but she must've looked over her shoulder maybe twice. But the only one sitting in the back was the new girl.

CHAPTER 3

It's been two weeks since the new girl arrived, why Lisa even bothered to think about that was a mystery to her. It's not like Norse High has never gotten a new student before, and since this is the beginning of the year they should expect to see more new faces.

It's just that this girl seemed so . . . well weird. She didn't talk to anyone. Hardly spoke up during in-class discussions. And the only indication that she actually had a working brain and wasn't just a walking fashionable zombie were the A pluses Lisa would see on all of the girl's papers as they each went up to collect theirs on the teacher's desk. They were always in alphabetical order by last name so Lisa's papers were always under the new girl's. And apparently her name was Rosalind. Rosalind Lee. Lisa didn't recall the teacher ever saying her name, nor any of the students. She would've tried to maybe go up to the girl and greet herself, but figured it might look weird that Lisa knew her name when she never told anyone of it, and that she was looking at the girl's school work. Yeah, that might be awkward. Better save the greeting for another day. This of course, wasn't the only thing on Lisa's mind. Two weeks have already passed and it's getting closer and closer to Decker's moving day.

Never in her life had Lisa wanted a school year to go by slowly. She wished she could just make it disappear from her mind altogether until it was actually time to be depressed.

She couldn't think straight, couldn't concentrate on anything. The bell at the end of every class might've been music to any other student's ears, but not her's. It was just another reminder that the clock was ticking. Everyday she wondered what he was thinking. Was he feeling it too? This horrible, weird, sick feeling? Kind of like the feeling you get when you skip breakfast. And for a while Lis thought maybe that was what it was. Her mom thought so too. "Mangia!" She would tell Lisa, which means "eat" in Italian. But the feeling never left, at least not all of it.

The tricky part was hiding it from everyone else, especially her mom. But Lisa had a feeling her mom already knew what she was feeling. Moms had that kind of intuition, the daughter in distress intuition. That would explain why she's been asking Lisa if she'd want to go to the store with her more often, and keeping her informed on the latest crime news happening around town, and asking Lisa what she thought about the new games soon to be released and if she should get them before everyone else does. Lisa smiled, knowing her mom was only trying to find out what was wrong without actually asking Lisa. Because they were so close, Lisa would sometimes just up and tell her mom anyway. Her mom stopped trying to force it out of Lisa after the age of twelve, hoping Lisa wouldn't rebel like any other teenager and instead just go to her mom willingly with whatever it was that bothered her. There was probably no reason to hide it. But Lisa couldn't help but hide it. It just felt like a personal thing, nothing that needed comfort or tending to. Decker was moving to Florida, and her heart was being taken with him. It wasn't something she would talk about with her parents, or even her close friends.

The teacher hadn't come into the class yet, so everyone was grabbing chairs to sit around desks with their friends.

16

Decker was trying to get Adam, the "chicken", to go over and talk to the new girl, all the while throwing jokes back and forth at each other like they always did.

"Alright today, man. Today!"

"C'mon you at least gotta give me some time to work my magic." Adam said, leaning his head on the palm of one hand.

"You've had a lot of time." Decker said. "Make your move already. Or someone else will." He nodded towards the group of tough guys snatching looks at the new girl. She wasn't paying them any attention, or at least trying not to, which gave Adam some confidence. He got up and took about three steps, hesitated, and then did a heel turn back to his seat, putting his head down on the desk in defeat.

"You wuss." Decker said.

"Don't rush me, man."

Lisa wished she could join in on the fun, but she was too exhausted from not getting any sleep last night. She had this crazy dream that started out with her and Decker. He was holding her against him while they sat on her porch step. It was daylight, but cloudy, and they were waiting for his grandmother to pick him up. All of a sudden the clouds grew darker, and it was no longer daylight. Wind blew the trees this way and that as the moon rose first very slowly, then it shot up into the sky, bringing blue light down on this big metal thing. The moon misted in red, its light now enveloping the shimmering ship . . . Lisa blinked her eyes open and it was over. She gave up trying to go back to sleep after an hour.

The dream was weird, sure, but what was weirder was the fact that Lisa had completely forgotten about what she saw that night. How could she forget *that*? Maybe it was because she was trying to forget. After all, she did somehow manage to convince herself that what she saw was nothing more than her imagination. So why did it end up in a dream? Lisa always believed that memories forgotten or pushed into the back of the mind would turn up in dreams, but if that's the case then was it real?

"Rosalind, would you care to solve the next problem?" The teacher spoke.

Oh wow, the teacher finally said her name?

Adam rested his chin against the palm of his hand as he watched the new girl walk up to the board.

"Dude, even her name sounds hot. Rosalind. Doesn't it sound cool? Never heard a name like that." He whispered to Decker.

"Weird is hot?" Decker asked, grinning.

"Man, with that girl, anything could be." Adam replied, watching the girl with a dreamy stare.

"You don't even know her, idiot. You can't even go and talk to her."

Adam put up a finger for Decker to be patient. "Magic, dude."

"Ms. Rosalind, I only asked you to simply solve the problem, not elaborate on it. You may sit now."

The girl blinked as though she was coming out of a trance, and then nodded and rushed back to her seat. The teacher walked over to the board, pushing his glasses up and examining the "answer" Rosalind had written. A very long and descriptive answer that had the whole class mumbling and staring with disbelief.

"Hey how about some praise for the smart young lady Mr. Dumbell?"

"Derbell, Mr. Adam. *Derbell.*" The teacher corrected and the whole class laughed.

Lisa turned around and noticed Rosalind picking up her book again and start flipping through pages, then she dipped her head behind the large novel, as though in embarrassment.

"Now that's quite enough class! Settle down!" The bell rang before Mr. Derbell could lecture any more. With a defeated sigh he said, "Now remember, five paragraphs tonight. No more and no less!" Half the kids ran out the door before he could finish.

"So are we hanging out later or what?" Adam asked, shoving his books into his messy bag.

"Maybe. We'll text you later if we are." Decker said, helping Lisa pack the rest of her things. Lisa gave Adam an apologetic look, but Adam just smiled and waved his hand as though it didn't matter.

"See ya guys." Then he was out the door.

Lisa felt bad. Adam didn't really have anybody besides the two of them, and right now Decker just wanted to be with Lisa for the remainder of time they had left with each other. Lisa felt a little guilty because she also didn't really want to be with anyone more right now than with Decker. She's just glad Adam understands.

Lisa turned her head and saw that the new girl was still sitting at her desk reading her book.

Should she say something? Thankfully Decker beat her to it. "Hey, you know the bell rang right?"

She didn't respond, just kept reading and turning pages.

"Yo, new girl."

The girl blinked and looked up now, confused.

"You're gonna be late to your next class." He said.

"Oh!" She got up quickly, her books tumbled off the desk and papers scattered all over the floor. She mumbled what might've been an apology for some reason and bent down to get them. Lisa got down to help, seeing as it would probably be rude to just walk away and leave the poor girl to pick everything up herself.

"Lisa, we're gonna be late." Decker said holding both their bags.

"Just give me a sec." She said.

He sighed impatiently.

When Lisa handed her the last of the papers they both stood up and the girl bowed her head saying, "Thanks to you so much."

"Sure." Lisa felt a little stupid giving a response like that so she said quickly. "Well, if you ever need help with getting around here or anything you can always ask us. This place is pretty big and we've been here a while so . . ."

"Yes I will ask. Thanks! Thanks to you both." The girl beamed and bowed again.

Decker gave Lisa her bag and grabbed her hand to lead her out. Lisa used her other hand to wave goodbye. The girl looked confused for a moment, and then with what looked like sudden realization, she waved back.

They were speed walking down the hallway, Decker still holding on to Lisa's hand. With a half-smile Lisa said as they reached the stairs, "Strange girl isn't she?"

"Yeah, she doesn't look too bright." Decker said.

"Well by the way she solved that problem today I would say she's pretty bright."

"She's probably a math whiz. Soon she'll be sitting with the other math geeks at lunch."

Lisa laughed. "Can you believe we actually still have those clique things?"

Decker grinned. "Well sure, I mean how long ago was it that I caught you talking with the anime club geeks? Like a week ago?"

She gave him a playful push. "Calling me a geek now huh?"

He grabbed her around the waste and pulled her in to him, kissing her along her collarbone. "Maybe." He smiled against her neck.

"But you love me." She turned around to face him.

"I do."

He leaned down and kissed her. If she knew nobody would come up or down these stairs Lisa would probably be leaning in closer, taking in his intoxicating scent, the cologne she got him for Christmas last year. And she would lose herself in his kiss, warm and passionate, not as gentle as he used to be when they first met. They parted just in time before one of the teachers started coming down the stairs.

"Hey Mr. O." Decker said, trying to catch his breath.

The teacher stopped and looked at them both suspiciously, and then chuckled. "I don't suppose you two heard the bell ring a few minutes ago?"

Oh damn. Well, at least this was only their second time being late. One more strike and they could both be looking at a lunch detention.

Mr. O nodded and continued down the stairs.

Lisa and Decker double stepped their way up the rest of the stairs and turned to give each other one last hug and kiss.

"See you later."

"Well duh." He smiled.

CHAPTER 4

"You know he's not gonna give you an A if he sees that it's not your handwriting." Lisa typed on her computer.

Adam's instant message popped up with a sad emoticon face after, "Oh come on Lisa you know I suck at essays!"

"Too bad." She typed back.

Nobody wanted to go outside today since it was freezing cold. The snow didn't even get here yet and temperatures were already dropping to below twenty. If there was one thing Lisa hated more than the blazing hot summer heat baking on her arms and face, more than the creepy crawly bugs that fly into her hair and buzz around her head, even more than all the air conditioners in the house going off at once while day turned to night and they had to sleep in the sweaty eighty degree heat . . . Lisa hated the cold. She hated having to bundle up in fifty pairs of clothes and jackets. She hated getting up early to venture out into the frigid morning cold just to go to school. She hated it.

But then again who didn't? It's so much easier to get cool during the summer than it is to get warm during the winter.

"You don't want that new girl to think you're stupid do you Adam? lol" Decker's instant message popped up then.

"Man I don't need homework to prove to her how smart I am. Magic, remember? lol" Adam typed.

"Whatever you say dude." Decker replied.

"She's a little weird though isn't she? At lunch she wouldn't stop staring at us. And I know it was her that slipped that pencil onto my desk when I reached down to pick mine up after it fell onto the floor." Lisa typed.

"Maybe she's from a weird place."

"Who cares where she's from? She's still hot." Adam typed.

Gustav started barking then and her mom called from the living room, "Lisa, one of your friends is at the door!"

A friend? Lisa sent a "brb" to the guys and jumped up from her desk chair.

When Lisa opened the front door she was stunned. The new girl from school was standing on her doorstep.

Lisa didn't know what to say at first. The girl was just standing there, smiling. She pulled her small hand out of her glove to wave at her.

Lisa put up a finger for the girl to hold on for a second. She raced back into her room and jumped onto her computer and started typing. "Omg the new girl is at my door."

"Really??" Adam replied instantly with a happy emoticon face.

"Lol" was all Decker said.

"Help me!" Lisa typed quickly.

"We'll be right over." Decker said.

"We sure will!" Adam replied.

Then their email's read "offline" and Lisa relaxed a little.

Hopefully the guys would get over here soon before it starts to get really awkward. Lisa was terrible at small talk. It was easy for her to get into an awkward situation with small talk.

She then remembered it was freezing cold out and the girl was still standing at the front door. Lisa ran back out to open the door and said quickly, "You can come in!"

But why was she here anyway?

Gustav was going crazy, as he usually did when a stranger entered the house.

Lisa saw how the girl's face brightened. "A puppy!"

"Not really." Lisa had to laugh. "But he likes to think he is."
Lisa watched, surprised that the girl actually went over to give
Gustav a pet on the head. He didn't bark or growl, just tilted his
head up into her touch and licked at her small fingers. It took
Decker years before Gustav let him even an inch close to him, but
the way he relaxed and stretched his long plump body onto the
girl's lap had Lisa thinking, *"Well how about that . . ."*
"Well well, no barking today Mr. Gustav?" Lisa's mom came up
from downstairs.
"Uh mom, this is my friend . . . Rosalind."
The girl stood quickly and bowed her head. "I thank you for letting
me into your beautiful home."
Lisa's mom laughed. "Oh hunny, I wouldn't call it beautiful the
way this wallpaper looks. But thank you."
"We'll be in my room mom."
"Alright, I'll be ordering pizza soon so let me know what you guys
want later."
Lisa led the way to her bedroom.
Rose stopped here and there to look at a few pictures hanging on
the walls in the hallway. Her eyes moved slowly over each one
with strange fascination, then she found one that seemed to grab
her interest the most and she stared at it as though it were about
to come to life. Lisa walked over and said, "Oh, that's an old one.
This is me when I was like, four or five, and this is my brother. He
was an infant."
Rose looked at Lisa, then back at the photo, then back at Lisa
again.
"Simply amazing." She murmured, running her fingers lightly up
and down the picture.
    Lisa didn't know if she should just pretend she didn't hear
anything or ask the girl what it was she found so amazing about an
old picture.

Really, it's like she's never seen one before. Maybe they don't have pictures over where she used to live, or maybe her family never took pictures.

Anyway . . . Lisa finally got Rosalind away from the pictures and to her bedroom.

Lisa walked over to her window pretending to close the blind a little when she was really looking out to see if the guys were making their way up to the front door.

Not yet. Unfortunately.

The girl was wandering around the room like she was in some other world. She spotted the bookshelf and went over immediately to look at the many volumes. She turned her head sideways to read the titles.

Now she looked like a kid in a candy shop gazing at all the delicious assortment of sweets.

Lisa suddenly remembered seeing her read a book the first day she came into class.

"You like to read?" Well at least it could be the start to a conversation. It was starting to get awkward not talking.

Her head snapped up like she had been caught red handed. "Oh! Yes, very much. I do adore your beautiful collection."

"Thanks." At least she seemed nice. A little weird, but nice.

Rosalind tapped her finger on some then picked out the book she wanted with a, "Ah ha! Here is a good one. I knew you would be most interested in this type of read."

Yeah well that surprised Lisa because she was the only teenager in school that actually liked that type of book.

It was a romance genre. An *adult* romance genre. No, she didn't read it for the "stuff" that all her classmates would mock her about for reading. Actually if it weren't for the fact that she had a real lovey-dovey relationship with Decker, she probably wouldn't be interested in that genre at all. She liked the comparison. She was in love reading about others who were also in love. Simple as that. It's not like she reads it just for the romance either, because of course that can get a little boring after a while. All of her favorite books had their share of adventure, humor and suspense. But nobody else saw it that way for some reason.

"Midnight Embrace." Rosalind read the title. "I suspect it to be associated with the fictitious creature of the night in which you call a vampire yes?"

Well . . . she probably wouldn't say it like that, but she wasn't wrong. Lisa was definitely a vamp fan. Hey, what girl wouldn't want a handsome, mysterious man with fangs and the most gorgeous eyes nobody has ever seen, who never aged and had a lonely soul acing to be loved by only one? It was maybe every woman's fantasy. Well maybe not the fang part. But no girl could resist the lonely soul.

"I must admit that I too enjoy the paranormal and romance books. There is one that I have just finished that you simply *have* to read. I must give it to you sometime."

Lisa smiled. "I'd love to read it."

Maybe she was being too judgmental earlier. Rosalind was a nice girl. There was nothing wrong with her at all. She had a smile that could light up a dark castle, and an innocence that one would assume only lived in small children. This was probably the beginning of an awesome friendship, Lisa thought happily. Usually it was only her, Decker and Adam. Now maybe they could add another member to the group.

"They are similar to windows are they not?"

Lisa looked back at her.

"Books, I mean. While we sit behind one side, we watch through the glass as a whole other world plays out right before our eyes on the other side. Though it is our eyes that are the windows and our minds that play the world."

Ok . . . Lisa was starting to wonder where it was that Rosalind had moved here from.

"Lisa! The boys are here." Her mom called from the living room.

26

Oh thank God!

"Uh, Rose, you wanna chill here for a bit? I'm just gonna go let the guys in real fast."

Rose tilted her head in confusion, and then clapped her hands together once she figured it out.

"Oh! Yes, *chill*. I will chill."

Lisa ran out to the living room to find the guys were already let in the house.

"Well it's about time you got here." She said, irritated.

"We left from Decker's house. It's not exactly a three second walk, you know." Adam said, taking off his coat.

"Besides, my stupid step dad wanted to start another argument so it took us longer." Decker said angrily.

Lisa went over to him and asked worriedly, "Are you ok?"

"I'm fine." He said, giving her a kiss on her forehead.

Adam was looking around with a grin on his face. "So where's the new girl?"

"In the room." Lisa answered, and led the way.

Rose was siting cross legged on her bed, a stack of books sitting next to her and the snow globe Decker had given Lisa for their sixth anniversary in her hands. She was fascinated by how the little confetti inside the globe swirled around every time she shook it and hung it upside down.

Noticing now that they had entered the room she looked up and waved her small hand.

"Rose, this is Decker and Adam." Lisa introduced.

"We got the same math class." Adam said to her.

Rosalind smiled. "Oh yes! I do remember you both."

"And you remember me?" Adam asked excitedly.

She nodded, "Yes, Adam. You are the funny one."

Adam nudged Decker's shoulder and said proudly, "Hear that? She thinks I'm funny."

"Funny-*looking*." Decker laughed.

"That one's old, bro." Adam said, not amused.

27

Lisa shook her head at the two. Rose stood up then and started moving around Lisa's room like she was at a museum again.

There was no question about it, the girl was weird. But Lisa just had to learn to accept the fact that everyone was different in their own way. At least this girl was nice.

"So where did you move from?" Adam asked, plopping himself down on the bed next to her.

Rose hesitated before answering, "From my home place." She smiled, seeming satisfied with her answer.

"Ok . . . So where's that?" He asked again.

"Umm . . ." She looked down nervously.

After a few moments Lisa said, "Alright no need to put her on the spot—"

"You know, you're a little weird."

"Decker!"

He just gave her a look that said, *"Well she is!"*

Decker never had a problem speaking his mind when he wanted to. But jeez!

She turned back to apologize to the poor girl for Decker' bluntness when, to her surprise, Rosalind started laughing.

"I suppose I am acting a little strangely from the behavior your society is so normally used to. My apologies." She was scratching the back of her head like she was embarrassed.

"You're fine . . ." Adam said, a little confused. He wasn't the only one.

Lisa was beginning to think the whole "new friend" thing might not be what she thought it would be. But then again maybe they just had to get to know her better. Maybe she's just from a different place that has its own lifestyle that's way different from theirs, that would make sense right?

"So Rose, I bet moving to a new place must feel strange and all. If you want, maybe later we can take you around and show you the . . . town . . ."

Rose was now too distracted by Lisa's handheld game, holding it in one hand and pushing individual buttons with her finger.

Decker gave Lisa a look that said, *"She didn't hear you . . ."*

"I know!" Lisa shot the look back.

"This is simply amazing. Such wonder . . . enjoyment even! It is as if this device is testing my coordination and thinking skills. Simply amazing."

Adam raised an eyebrow and Decker folded his arms.

"Uh, new girl, Lisa was talking to you. You could at least listen—"

Lisa gave Decker a slap to the shoulder.

"What?"

"Stop being rude! And she has a name you know."

He just looked at her as though she were hopeless. "Yeah well she could at least answer you when you're talking to her. What, does she have a mental problem or something?"

Thank goodness Rose was still too distracted with the video game to hear Decker's words. Lisa sighed.

He doesn't mean to be like this. Well, ok, maybe he does. He's actually like that with a lot of Lisa's friends.

Rose looked up from the game like a child getting caught stealing from the cookie jar. "My apologies, my mind seems to have been attracted to this small device here."

Lisa assured, "No, no its ok. I was just saying—"

"My mind gets attracted to games too. Hey look at that, we got something in common!"

Rose tilted her head to the side, confused.

Gustav scratched at Lisa's door to come in, as he often did when she had company over.

He didn't pay any mind to the guys when they stretched their arms out to pet the little plump pup, he just trotted his way over to Rose, who smiled widely when he leaped up onto the bed and into her lap.

She laughed when he looked up to give her a lick on the nose.

Lisa wasn't surprised that he would want to be in someone's lap. That was sort of his thing. What did surprise her was that Gustav felt so comfortable with Rose, who was a complete stranger really. He sees Decker and Adam all the time and still barks when they come into house, but when Rose walked in he just sat there at looked at her.

Rose turned her attention from Gustav to the window now, her eyes soft with a kind of . . . sadness? Her small hand was still petting down the pup's long back. Lisa looked to the guys but they just shrugged.

"Rose?" Lisa decided to ask. "You ok?"

Rose nodded, looking away from the window with a sigh.

They sat in silence for a few minutes. Gustav started nodding off to sleep as Rose continued to pet his back.

It was Rosalind that finally spoke. "I am truly sorry for this." She said in a low voice.

Lisa frowned. "Sorry for what?"

"For coming to your home unannounced. For leaving you to be forced to let me in. For intruding upon your life."

Intruding upon her life? Jeeze that's not really something you hear every day. But then, Lisa supposed she's never met a person like Rose before either, so maybe it was just a part of her personality. The atmosphere in the room changed all of a sudden. It felt weird. Different. Tense.

"Hey Rose, listen. It's cool alright? You're not—"

"But I am, Adam. I am . . ."

Gustav yawned and layed his head down.

Nobody really knew what to say.

Maybe she was about to tell them her life story, how she had grown up with a difficult life. That's how a lot of their friends acted when they first met them. Lisa could tell that something was wrong, but she never asked, she would wait for them to tell her themselves. She figured they would eventually say whatever it was that was on their shoulders. And they did, of course, after they got to know them a little more.

So now here was another friend with stuff on her shoulders. Well if Lisa could show Rose that they could listen to her, then maybe she wouldn't feel so burdened. Maybe that's why she was so awkward. Maybe she just needed friends to talk to.

Lisa moved to sit on the bed next to her.

"Hey if something's on your mind, you can tell us, you know."

Rose looked up at Lisa.

"Yeah." Adam nudged her gently with his arm. "If something's bugging you, just say it. We're not gonna like, kick you out or anything."

"It's not like you're the only weird one around here anyway."

Lisa smiled at Decker's attempt at being a little nicer.

Rose looked down and smiled softly when Gustav tilted his head up to give her another lick on the nose.

"I thank you all. You are much too kind to me, truly."

She lifted Gustav off her lap and laid him lightly on the fluffy pillow. He looked up at her curiously.

"I wish I had more time . . ." She took in a breath. "There is something you do not know about me . . . nor them. But I will not wait in telling you. There is not enough time."

Lisa was trying to understand what it was that Rose was saying. What exactly *was* she saying?

She hesitated. Her eyes fell to the floor when she mumbled out, "I am not from this planet."

CHAPTER 5

What?

An awkward silence fell over the room. Decker and Adam were staring at Rose like she had just lost her mind. And she just might've . . . Lisa saw how Adam was trying to stifle his laughter. Rose wasn't looking at anyone, just the floor.

Decker folded his arms across his chest and sighed.

If Lisa thought she was horrible at conversations before, she really had it bad with starting new ones out of weird subjects. Her mind was telling her to say something but what exactly was she supposed to say?

A few more moments of silence went by, and then Rose finally lifted her head to speak.

"This is all very new to me—"

"What the hell is wrong with you, are you mental or something?" Her eyes fell to the floor again.

"Decker." Lisa pushed his arm. Jeeze she wished he didn't always speak his mind whenever he felt like it. Alright, so the girl thinks she's . . . an alien. Ok. Guess there are worse things. Maybe . . . ? Well this isn't exactly a surprise to her at all actually. Lisa remembers the time one of their friends claimed they were a vampire. Must be a new craze thing Lisa didn't get the memo of. First it was wizards and witches, then vampires, then zombies, now . . . aliens?

More minutes of silence. Adam was fidgeting with his hat, probably feeling uncomfortable.

Rose didn't look up. She had a sad look on her face and Lisa felt kind of bad for her. Maybe there really was something wrong and she wanted them to help her. Was that it? Is that why she came to Lisa's house in the first place? Jeez they hardly really knew her. But what other reason would there be?

"I understand you may be shocked—"

"Shocked? Why? You think we *believe* you?" Decker snapped.

Rose didn't respond or look up.

He scowled. "I think you should go."

"Please, understand I am on a very important mission—"

"No, *you* understand. You get out of here, and you stay away from my girlfriend. Do you understand *that*?"

Rose winced at his sharp tone, but didn't say anything more.

"Hey Decker, calm down a bit alright? It's probably just a misunderstanding—"

"I speak the truth. Please, hear my words, you must believe me!" Rose pleaded, looking up now.

She then stood up and bowed her head. "I beg you to understand. This may all sound very strange and unusual but in time it will all make sense."

"You're nuts. That's all I understand. You're just like the rest of them. Crazy." Decker said.

Lisa knew he was referring to a few of their other friends, the ones that dress in trench coats and piercings. The ones who swear at their parents because they don't think anything is "fair," and hurt themselves on purpose. The ones that think they're not human and have different personalities. They're not bad people, just friends. And teenagers. That's what Lisa had tried to tell Decker hundreds of times, but he didn't see it the way she did. He didn't think they were normal, nor did he understand the whole "teenage individuality" thing, but that was because he never got to when he was a kid.

Though from the way Rose was saying it, she sounded pretty serious, desperate even.

Figures Lisa would hear talk of aliens, something that's been on her mind for weeks now.

And all because she walked outside her front door one night and thought she saw a space . . . ship . . .

"I am not from this planet."

Wait a second . . .

"Look, you're a nice girl and all, but this is just weird—"

"Hang on Decker." Lisa put a hand on his shoulder.

He looked down at her questionably.

"Let's just hear her out." Lisa winked hoping he would understand.

He got the message and sighed in defeat, walking over to sit at the computer.

Adam rolled his eyes.

"Go on Rose." Lisa encouraged.

Relief showed in her smile and she bowed her head again saying, "I thank you."

Lisa saw that the guys didn't seem so amused about letting Rose explain her "alien" story. Adam went back to fidgeting with his hat and Decker just rested his head on his upraised hand boringly as he clicked on a puzzle game to play on the computer.

"I will begin by telling you that I am here on a very important mission."

Lisa smiled and nodded to show she was listening even if the guys weren't.

It was strange though. Perhaps it was that Rose was new here and didn't know how to make friends, but to Lisa this looks like something a kid would do, make something up to describe themselves in a better way. Something crazy or unique.

Lisa remembered when she was in elementary school and she would tell all her friends that she had a "pokemon."

Oh yeah, and that she was a "super saiyn." Good times. But she was really young then.

"I want to better understand your world. I want to learn as much as I can about your kind, how you survive, how you interact, how you think and feel. Your communication and way of teaching. Your unique emotions and way of socialization. I would love to learn all about your ways."

"And take us up in your space ship so you can do experiments on us?" Adam laughed at his joking. Decker just rolled his eyes, not finding it amusing to play along with Rose's little game.

Rose laughed. "Oh goodness I would never do something like that! Besides, the act of abducting humans has been announced illegal only recently."

Adam raised an eyebrow. When he looked toward Lisa in question Lisa just shrugged.

Decker tsked.

"Oh I have so much to discuss! Alright let's see now . . . where to begin?" She tapped her finger against her chin.

Lisa could imagine what Decker might be thinking right now in his not-so-happy mood. She almost laughed.

"How about let's begin with you leaving?" Yeah that's definitely something he would say. It's probably what he's thinking right now.

"I should perhaps explain to you what it is that I am exactly." She thought about that for a little then nodded, "Yes that would be a good idea."

"Why don't you start with why you're here?" Adam asked as though that were an obvious first explanation.

"Oh well . . . no. I cannot explain that now. It is too soon."

He just looked at her.

"But I will in time." She quickly reassured. "Once you all are more comfortable around me."

That might take longer than what Rose was expecting, Lisa thought.

"This is simply amazing. I have always wanted to visit this planet, ever since I was very young. My father would always talk to us about it."

Lisa grimaced. Maybe this isn't right. They can't just let her go on like this, for goodness sakes this girl really thinks she's an alien! Should she say something? But what was she supposed to say?

It wasn't even the problem with saying anything. Lisa just didn't want to have to watch Rose's reaction. She always had problems with confronting someone's reaction, especially if it was going to be a bad reaction. Lisa would never forget the awkward time in elementary school when she turned around to the girl annoyingly braiding her hair and insisted she stop. The girl's face was both crushed and angry. Lisa felt bad.

Now she had a thing with having to word everything correctly so nobody would take anything she said the wrong way. It was a burden, but at least she didn't have to do it with Decker. She could be herself around him in that way.

"Listen Rose . . . uhh . . . " She couldn't bring herself to say it. Adam seemed to be having trouble himself. He was scratching the back of his head, as though trying to come up with something to say without being a jerk. Decker still wasn't facing them.

Lisa realized the room had gotten quiet, or maybe it's been that way for a few minutes. Rose was just sitting there patiently, gazing around the room.

Jeeze, guess it was up to her. Lisa sighed. "Uh . . . Rose." She began. Rose looked at her then with an expectant smile.

"I know you want us to believe you're an alien and all but . . ." Rose tilted her head when Lisa paused.

"What I mean is . . . umm. We don't really . . . believe you . . . when you say you're an alien." She braced herself.

A few moments went by silently. Then Rose put her finger to her lip as though thinking deeply. She murmured, "Hmmm, yes I can see why you are saying this."

"Oh, great. Uh . . . you do?"

"Yes, this would indeed be difficult for you to accept, I understand."

"Whoa wait a minute. I don't got trouble accepting nothing. It's just weird cause you're saying you're an alien and all. That's not something you hear every day." Adam said defensively.

"Ah, how interesting." She turned toward Adam and leaned in close to him.

"What?" He was leaning back further as she examined his face.

"You misunderstood my saying, "difficult for you to accept" and thought I was insulting you in some way, perhaps because I have tapped that prideful nerve that most male humans have. Very interesting . . ."

Lisa heard Decker chuckle behind the seat.

"Well I suppose I must prove to you I am what I say I am." Rose said cheerily. "Yes, that will do it. You will be more convinced when you can see it with your eyes."

They watched as Rose scouted around the room looking for something.

"Ah, perfect!" She picked up one of Lisa's old sneakers and put it in the center of the floor.

"I am not sure how well this will work, since the gravity on this planet is indeed strong. But we shall see."

She inhaled slowly, focusing her gaze intently on the shoe. Lisa looked over at Adam, who looked at Decker, who was now facing them but with his chin resting on his hand and a *"are you kidding me?"* kind of look on his face. A few moments passed. Then another few. Rose was still focusing intently.

One of her eyes twitched, and she mumbled, "Come on, come on." Another minute passed.

Nothing happened.

Decker tapped Lisa on her shoulder and whispered, "She's crazy, can we make her leave now?"

Lisa really felt bad. Rose is such a nice girl. They could still be her friends, even if she did have some kind of mental issue or

whatever. The guys would eventually get used to it just as they
got used to all their other crazy friends. Well . . . ok maybe Decker
still has a hard time accepting them, but Rose would have Lisa of
course.

Eventually they might even get used to her weirdness.

Feeling awkward from the continuing silence Lisa got up from her
spot on the floor and moved to the door. "I'll be right back guys.
I'm just going to see when mom might be ordering the pizza—"

"Oh shit guys look!" Adam exclaimed.

Lisa turned around, the blood in her face draining out as she stared
wide eyed down at the floor. The shoe was off the ground. In
midair. Floating.

Rose had her hand up, palm out. The shoe moved back and forth
slowly, up and down. It fell a little but then flew back up as Rose
forced her palm out further.

"What?!" Decker sat up straight in the chair.

"Dude are you seeing this? Are you seeing it?!" Adam jumped
down off the bed to get closer.

Lisa couldn't feel her body move, paralyzed as she was at what she
was seeing, but she felt her hand grab her head. Was she losing her
mind? Was she really seeing this? Then it hit her, like a flash of
lightning striking her memory. That thing from that one night . . .
the big, shiny *thing* . . . it drifted silently right in front of her eyes,
as silently as her shoe was moving around in mid-air. The *space
ship* she saw that night . . .

She was dizzy. Her room bounced as though she were shaking her
head up and down. Thankfully she was close enough to the desk to
lean her hand on it for support. Still holding her head, she looked
again at her floating shoe. Well, if she was losing her mind, then
she wasn't the only one, because the looks on both Decker and
Adam's faces told her they were seeing this too.

Adam reached out to move his hand over and under the shoe, like
checking for hidden wires. He pulled his hand away, realizing there
was nothing holding the shoe up.

"Well it would seem I had to use my physical energy rather than my mental because of the weight of your gravity but . . . Ta da." Rose laughed.

Was this really happening . . . ? Lisa felt like maybe she should blink her eyes, just in case she was dreaming. She did, but the shoe still floated there, no strings . . .

She gave up standing now, or maybe she felt like her legs were going to give out on her, so she sat down with the rest of them, watching the shoe float there in the middle of her room. She glanced toward Rose, who looked to be struggling to keep her concentration. She had her other eye squeezed shut like it was hurting her somehow.

"How are you doing this?" Adam wanted to know.

"Magic." Rose said simply with a grin.

Then the shoe fell to the floor with a *thud.*

"Well, now that I've got your fullest attention, I may be able to continue with what I have to say." The three of them were still staring at it. Lisa blinked a few more times. Ok, don't panic. It was just a trick, anyone can do a trick. Maybe she had some kind of invisible string thing or . . . something. Anyone could do that! Right?

"Now, I am here to study and learn more about your world. This is all very confusing for you so I should perhaps take it one step at a time."

What about that guy on tv that can do that crazy stuff like walking on water and floating across buildings? He can do tricks . . .

"Of course, it would not be fair for me to ask you questions about your home life when I am clearly the intruder. So if you wish, you may ask me any question you have. Anything at all."

Maybe she attached an invisible string to the shoe while they weren't looking . . .

"What do you mean ask you questions?"

"Just as I have said, Decker. You may ask me any question you feel curious about." When none of them said a word Rose encouraged, "Oh, come now, surely you must have something?"

Lisa was starting to fear that maybe she wasn't going insane after all. How strange is that, the fear of *not* going insane? Or maybe that was insanity taking roots in her mind. Jeez, she could use a Motrin.

"I know you have mixed feelings about my being here. But I promise I will not burden you in any way, and I will answer any questions you have."

Questions about what? Lisa was assuming she meant questions about aliens. About space. Questions every scientist in the world would kill to know the answer to.

"Oh, I forgot to mention. I will answer any question, except ones concerning your beliefs."

"Our beliefs?" Adam asked.

"It is my rule. Well not really, actually it is my father's rule. But he made it very clear to me about how important it is. I will not discuss your religion, or any other religion."

"Why?" Decker asked, suspicious.

"I do not wish to alter your beliefs in any way. Those beliefs are precious, and I was taught to respect that."

Maybe she could do with *four* Motrins . . . Lisa felt another headache coming on.

"So wait . . . just . . . what exactly *are* you anyway?" Adam asked warily.

The room was silent. The three of them all looked at Rose, waiting for her answer, but she was looking only at Adam. She had a quizzical look on her face and it made him uncomfortable. Then she said, "Oh I see. You are still trying to deny what I am telling you."

"Huh?"

"Your mind." She indicated with her finder to her temple. "It is trying to make sense of what I am saying to you. I have already told you what I am, yet your mind is still trying to grasp it all. Goodness, humans truly are complicated creatures indeed."

The pain in her head felt like it was growing with every word this strange girl was saying. Those eyes . . . alien eyes? That smile . . . an alien smile? Everything this girl is . . .

"Now then, what say we strike a deal?"

"A deal?" Adam asked.

"You will answer any and all questions I have concerning your planet, your people, your culture and yourselves. In return, I will answer any and all of *your* questions."

"Questions about what?" Decker asked skeptically.

Rose grinned. "Absolutely anything."

CHAPTER 6

A beautiful, young girl moved to the neighborhood only weeks ago. Quiet, loves to read, loves to dress fashionably, and loves to learn. Rosalind. An extremely intelligent student. A loving individual. An extraterrestrial . . .

Lisa felt like she was stuck in some kind of crazy dream, only the crazy part of it was that it wasn't a dream at all, because if it was, she would've woken by now.

Adam was still examining the shoe that had just been floating in midair a few minutes ago, which left Decker and Lisa looking at one another, waiting for one of them to ask the first question.

Lisa gulped down the lump of nervousness in her throat. Rose told them they could ask her any questions they want. But what exactly does she mean by that anyway? She was an alien, so should they ask about alien stuff? In that case Lisa did have a question she wanted to ask. But before she could Decker beat her to it.

"Why are you here?"

Rose sighed in disappointment. "Oh come now surly you have a better question than that? But wait, could this be your way of adjusting to my company? Ah, now I see. Very interesting."

"Just answer the question." Decker said impatiently.

"I may have already explained this to you all earlier, but I am here on a very important mission."

Yeah, isn't that what every alien says? Lisa continued to hold her hand to her throbbing head so she could at least hear what Rose had to say. Why she wanted to actually listen, Lisa didn't know. Maybe it was just the headache.

"I am here to study and understand more about your world. Ever since I was a little girl I have wanted to travel to this planet. Earth. Such a beautiful name. We, of course, have a different name to call this planet of yours, but Earth seems a suitable name I believe." She smiled.

"I like it because it is the name you, the people of this planet, have given it."

She pushed some of her hair out of her face and continued. "This is my first real mission, of course, so when I finally arrived on this planet I was so overwhelmed with the sights and sounds and smells that I became a little disoriented. I actually had no idea where to begin or what to do. My plans seemed to have fallen out of my memory upon taking the first step out into this place."

Adam cracked a smile at that.

"But why are you *here*?" Decker asked again.

"You mean here with the three of you?"

They all nodded like that was obvious.

"Well, you were the only ones that talked to me at school." Rose smiled.

It wouldn't have happened if she hadn't dropped her stuff on the floor. They probably wouldn't have ever talked to her any other time. She just didn't look like she wanted to be bothered.

"I see you are having trouble asking the questions aloud. You are thinking of them, but you cannot say them."

And just how did she know that? What, can she read their minds too?

"Your faces tell me of this. I am not reading your mind."

Well then what about *that* just now?!

But that doesn't make much sense. An expression doesn't tell you exactly what the person is thinking.

"I am able to guess what you are thinking based on how you react to whatever it is we are talking about, and depending on the type of person you are, I can predict what it is you might be thinking. It's actually not an alien power if that is what you are believing it to be. Anybody can do it, you just have to have an open mind and pay attention." She smiled.

Actually, now that she thought about it, it kind of made sense. Lisa's known Decker for seven years now, and she could easily guess what it is he is thinking half the time. But Rose didn't really know them all that well, so how could she have known what they were thinking so easily? Or were they all a little predictable at the moment because their expressions were so vulnerable?

Rose sighed. "I am truly sorry for intruding on your lives like this." She bowed her head.

Lisa stared down at this strange girl. Strange. That word might be the first one to come to mind now when they see Rose. That, and "alien." But how could anyone judge what is strange or abnormal? In society, we see things as a whole. So would it be strange for some of us to see things outside of society as beautiful or normal? Besides, looking at her they would never have thought she was an alien. She sure didn't look like the ones in the movies. Course, those were just movies. Was she using some kind of thing to make herself look human when she really looked like something else? There was a question Lisa could ask, though maybe another time. If Rose had another look going on under this one, Lisa didn't want to see it yet. She was still getting used to the fact that Rose was really an extraterrestrial from outer space. Jeez, she can't believe she actually believes this.

Still, when Lisa thought about it, Rose looks like any other teenage girl. She's pretty and has the best fashion sense in school. She also looks much younger than her age.

There was another question.

"Now listen, it's not that we don't like you or anything, it's just . . . well you caught us off guard is all." Adam said, probably feeling as bad as Lisa was feeling too.

Rose looked up with what looked like hope in her eyes. "So you don't hate me for telling you all of this?"

Adam half smiled and went over to sit next to Rose on the bed. Looks like he gave in, Lisa thought with a smile also. Decker still had his arms folded.

"We don't hate you. You know, you're not half bad for an alien." Rose smiled then. "You do not think so?"

"Nah. Trust me, we've seen weirder things. Take this guy over here. He's probably the weirdest thing I ever saw."

"Ha ha." Decker said dryly.

Everyone laughed except Decker.

"I thank you for accepting me. Oh you will not be disappointed friends! I will answer all of your questions, no matter the number!"

Looks like things are about to get interesting. Lisa and Adam sat down on the floor with Rose. Decker stayed in the computer seat.

"Alright then." Rose clapped her hands together. "So who would like to go first?"

Adam raised his hand right away. "I got one."

Lisa almost laughed. She felt like a kinder gardener in grade school asking questions on the ABC's floor mat.

"Very good Adam. What is your question?"

"Alright so like, you're an alien and all. So where are you from exactly? Like what planet?"

"A very good question Adam, well spoken."

He smiled proudly at the praise.

"Actually, I did not come from a planet at all. I do not have one to call home, at least not yet. You see, I am a Drifter, so I am still looking—"

"Whoa, slow down a sec. What the hell is a Drifter?" Adam interjected.

"A Drifter is a being that has no home. They drift through life, looking for a planet of their own, though it is not at all easy. A being may be a Drifter for the rest of their lives, or for a short time, depending on how long it takes them to find a planet. My family and I have been Drifters for many years. It is a difficult life, truly." She looked down, her smile fading to a frown. But after a few seconds she lifted her head and began again.

"My family and I used to live in a ship that carried us through the galaxy. Over the years we have visited many different planets, some were very generous as to provide us with the materials we needed to survive. Food is scarce for Drifters, so it is the only thing we asked for really."

"Can't you like, ask other Drifter things for food?" Decker asked, not turning around. Rose shook her head. "Drifters do not ask other Drifters for supplies of any kind. It would not be polite to ask a Drifter for food when it is so difficult to get it. If we ever made contact with other Drifters, it was only to gather information. Some help others in directing toward a planet they may have recently passed, which is the most helpful. A Drifter's goal in life is to find a planet for themselves and their families, one that they can live on peacefully."

Lisa was surprised at how intrigued she felt hearing all of this. She really thought she was going to be frightened, but now she was more curious than frightened.

"But how do you know if you found your planet? Like, do you guys get some kind of weird vibe or something?" Adam asked.

"You could say that. You see, every being in the universe has their own home planet somewhere out there. Only very few are lucky enough to have already been born or landed on their birth planet without having to be Drifters."

Rose got up to look out of Lisa's window at the sky, seeming to be off in another world as she said, "Father says you will know when you have found your home planet. The warmest feelings come over you, and suddenly you feel like you belong there, like it is calling out to you, begging for you to walk its soil, breath its air, taste its fruit. It is supposed to be the most wondrous feeling."

She sighed, turning back towards them. "But it can also be dangerous. The risk would be high to venture to an unknown planet without the right equipment. There may be poisons and hazards that we may not be aware of until we land there. That is why most Drifters tend to stay close to the Council Ship, in case they need recon assistance."

"Ok wait, before you go on, what is this Council Ship?" Decker asked.

"Oh yes, I suppose I must tell you about the High Council before I can explain about the ship. Alright, the High Council is an organization of elite alien beings. Their main goal is to provide assistance with helping others as well as bring peace to the universe. The Council recruits new members all the time, so you could imagine the amount of members they currently have now."

"Which is . . . ?" Adam asked, wondering if he really wanted to know the answer.

"Well, I cannot give an exact number, but it is certainly much larger than your own population here on Earth."

All of their jaws dropped. More than us? There has to be maybe six billion people living on Earth already. But how could all those people live on one ship? Unless it was one really, *really* big ship. Jeeze . . .

"The High Council recruits two people from each species of alien to their organization to represent their species. They choose one, and then that chosen being will choose another as their Second Seat. The job of the Second Seat is to assist their partner in any way they can, and to also provide some company. Usually Second Seats are close family members or mates. They do not help in making the decisions with the others at the meetings, but they do aid in providing valuable information to the Council Elders. The information may be, for example, about a vacant planet somewhere close by. The Council then sends out messages to every single

Drifter in the universe who may be close by the planet. Once a recon mission is completed, the data information on the planet is put through a computer, which then compares the data with those of Drifters whose information is also put into the computer. If there is an absolute match between a Drifter and the planet, then the Elders will announce the great news to the Drifter ships, along with the coordinates so they may begin the journey to their home planet."

Lisa had to switch her siting position again for the tenth time, so did Decker. They were so intrigued by what they were hearing. Adam listened with his chin leaning on his upright palm.

"So you see, the High Council aid tremendously in helping Drifters search for their homes. They also visit past Drifters who have by now colonized greatly on their planet thanks to the Council's help. In return for the Council's services the planet's people gift the Council with food and supplies for their ship."

"And that's why the Drifters stay close to the Council Ship? Because if they ever pass a planet that they think might be theirs, they got the Council there to help them see if it really is their planet."

Rose smiled brightly. "Exactly. I am impressed Lisa, you are a fast learner indeed."

"Hey me too right? I asked all the questions."

Rose laughed. "You are also very smart Adam."

He shrugged and smiled back. "I try."

There was something else that had her wondering.

"But Rose . . ."

Rose looked to her then with a big smile on her face, happy to see that they were asking more questions. "Yes Lisa?"

"How is it that all those people can fit on one ship? I mean, if the numbers of members are double the amount of people that we have here on Earth, then the ship would have to be bigger than this planet."

The guys looked at her then with realization, like they hadn't
thought of that, but now that they did it sounded incredible.
"Oh well the Council of course have more ships. You would know
right away if you were looking at a Council ship. They are long
and extend widely into almost a flat diamond shape. Drifter ships
are smaller, and are usually oval shaped, though some have been
made to resemble a cube, it depends on how many family members
there are to one group of Drifters. But only the main Council Ship
holds all the Council Elders. The High Council provides Drifters
with ships if they are in need of any, or some Drifters will build
their own with materials gathered from a non-planet that they may
have been living on."
"And a non-planet is . . . what now?" Decker asked.
"A non planet is what we call a large mass of rock, like an asteroid
or something that is as large as a planet, or smaller, but does not
have the right resources for someone to live on. Many Drifters who
live on these non-planets usually die within a few years."
"That's messed up.
"There are Drifters who have taken in other fellow Drifters who
were at the brink of death, but important supplies could run out
quickly, so as much as someone may want to help another family,
one must also think of their own family and what might be best.
Another problem would be the possible hazards that a family
taken in would have to face while being transported to another
planet that is not their own. A species cannot live with another
species on the same planet without there being consequences or
risks. The air may grow toxic, and the environment could decay.
One species may try to harm the other. These are just a few of the
many consequences. Although it sounds as though it would work,
the truth is no being would take the risk of putting their own in
danger like that, even if it was to help another species that was near
extinction."
Lisa thought about that for a moment.

"But hang on. We live with animals here, and they're a different species than us right? So how is it that we're able to live with them?"

"Look at what happens though. We take their homes from them. Eat them. And they can retaliate back." Decker said.

"What's your point?" Adam asked.

"My point is that those are the consequences. Sure we got some people that actually want to save them instead of kill them, but that's not everyone."

"I don't get it." Adam said.

Decker sighed impatiently. "Ok, you know how we got cows? You really think we could live with them and not want to turn them into hamburgers?"

Adam nodded when he finally understood.

"But why is it that one species can't live with another? That sounds a little ridiculous doesn't it? I mean, its not like we can distance ourselves from all the animals on this planet by going up in a space ship with the aliens. We just can't do that. Besides, not everyone would want to go vegan just because—"

"I can hear the frustration in your voice, Lisa. You are wondering why it is that your kind could be so unlike ours, so imperfect. Even now, as I say the word, "imperfect" you are assuming that I am deliberately calling humans imperfect."

"Well that's kinda what you're broadcasting." Adam said, a little frustrated himself.

Rose nodded. "I apologize." Then she chuckled. "That is what I adore so much about your kind, the human race. You are all so very emotional. Any word I say could sound like praise. Or a threat."

Lisa then remembered something Rose said that had her curious. "Oh yeah, I forgot to ask. If you're here on Earth, then is your family here too?"

Rose tilted her head like she was confused by the question.

"I mean because I saw your ship one night, and it was so big, and then you mentioned that all Drifters have ships and all, I was just wondering—"

Rose gasped. "You saw my ship?"

"Well yeah, I saw it right outside my house the one night. I didn't even know what it was at first—

"Oh! I knew I should've had that darn thing fixed!" She stood up and paced the room in a panic.

"Hey calm down Rose, what's the problem?" Adam asked.

"The cloaking device has been malfunctioning lately. I sent a signal message out to my Father to see if he could tell me what to do, but I haven't received his reply yet. He told me before I left to make sure it was working. Oh but I was so excited to be on my way I completely forgot about it!"

"Wow, so you aliens got text messaging too huh? How long do you think they've had that?" He asked Decker. Decker just shrugged.

"Hang on a sec Rose. You're making me dizzy." Lisa tugged her gently to stop her pacing.

"Now if it calms your nerves, I was the only one outside that night to see it."

Rose looked at her desperately. "Truly?"

"Really . . . or yeah *truly*. Besides if anyone else around here saw it we'd know, trust me." Not just them, the whole world would know if someone sent the story over to the news or worse, got it all on tape and put it up on the internet. But that didn't happen yet, and it's been a few weeks now since Lisa saw it so she's assuming she was the only one. She won't tell Rose that she's only assuming, but chances are nobody else saw it. Hopefully.

Rose put a hand up to her chest to calm her racing heart. "Oh, thank goodness."

"So you were really serious about seeing that thing Lisa?" Adam asked.

She gave him an annoyed look because he would, of course, believe her *now*.

51

"But to answer your question Lisa, I am actually here by myself on this mission. The ship you saw was a small borrowed vessel. It was only given to me to take for the journey here."

That was a *small* vessel?! If that was considered small then what did a big vessel like the Council ship look like? Jeeze. Here comes that headache again . . .

"How many people do you have in your family?" Adam asked.

"I actually do not have a large family. Not anymore. Many of my close relatives died."

The room was silent as they waited for Rose to tell them more.

"I will explain. We were living on a non-planet at the time, and we were running out of valuable resources. The planet's food supply had grown un-edible about a year after we arrived. And the liquid dried to dust. It started out as maybe two hundred of us, but soon it came down to just the four of us, and we were waiting for the next tragedy. We believed that because my sister was the youngest and weakest of the four of us, she would be next. Mother held her close every night. Illness was a constant worry, because my younger sister was prone to the worst kind, and it would take her longer to recover."

Lisa could just picture all of this. Imagine the fear they had to go through, wondering how much time they had left. Must've been hell.

"Drifters normally move from one non-planet to another if they have to, especially when resources become scarce. But our travel ship had been damaged during the landing. The planet's gravity pulled some of the wiring out of the ship's main control system and we couldn't get it to start up again. Father tried everything he could, and after a few days he did get the control system to work again, but it still couldn't fly. Father told us he needed more material, but the planet did not produce the material he needed. We really believed we were going to die there."

Rose smiled softly then.

"And just when we thought we were lost, we see this large ship looming over our heads. There was no doubt in my mind that it was a Council Ship. Something I had only heard Father tell me in stories. It was perhaps the greatest relief we had ever felt, so much so that we didn't think it was really happening. But it wasn't just another Drifter ship. It was indeed a Council ship, the main Council Ship. They inspected the dry non-planet and noted the many bodies buried in its soil. We told them that our numbers were great, until famine and illness consumed us. My Father spoke brilliantly and boldly to the Elders when they stepped out of the beautiful silver ship, their long arms folded inside their blue robes. Mother told me that she at first feared he was being too bold as to ask if the Council would take us in. All four of us.

Nobody ever asked such a favor before from the High Council. After examining our broken ship and having my father explain to the Elders how he only managed to restart the ships controls, they all looked surprised. I was still very young so I could not exactly read their expressions very well, but now that I look back they seemed, well, impressed in a way.

The Elder stared down at my father and grinned. When he began to walk back towards the Council ship our hopes left us briefly, until he stopped at the doorway and turned to look back at us. He said, "Well do not stand there in a daze, boy. Bring your family onto the ship so that they may fill their empty bellies."

I lifted my head out of my mother's arms then, shocked at what I had just heard. Father bowed to the Elder. He bowed down to his knees, something I had never seen him do, and he led us onto the massive ship. There we stayed. We were so overjoyed, our gratefulness never enough to repay the Council for their kindness. Father said this to the Elder who had let them on that ship, and he put a hand on my father's shoulder and said, "Then join us at the next meeting, boy. I know a way you can repay us for our kindness." So Father did. After that our days with the High Council turned into months, then years."

Lisa found herself smiling for Rose and her family. After everything they went through they finally found help. She could only imagine what she would do if she were in her position. She would be pretty happy too.

"So how come you guys got to stay on the Council Ship? I thought you had to be a member to be on it?" Adam asked.

Lisa's smile brightened, already knowing what Rose was going to say next, and Rose said with the very same smile, "You are right Adam, we would not have been able to stay on the ship, which is why they chose my father to join the organization."

The amazement on Adam and Decker's faces was priceless. Lisa couldn't help but laugh as they sat there with their mouths hanging open.

Rose laughed too.

"That's freakin awesome!" Adam said.

"So you're in the Council too?" Decker asked.

"No, just my parents. And you've probably realized that my mother was chosen to be his Second Seat. She usually didn't have the time that she wanted to spend with me and my sister, but we understood. It's her job after all, and we do owe the High Council for all they have done for us."

"How old is your sister anyway?" Lisa asked.

"She's three."

Lisa smiled but it surprised her a little. Rose's sister must've been an infant when they were still living on that non-planet, yet she miraculously survived, even while all of her older relatives passed away.

"So then your mom is watching your little sister right now while you're here I'm guessing." Decker said.

"Oh no, Elizabeth is by herself at the moment." She said it so casually that her words didn't really sink in until Lisa played them back over in her mind. She gasped and exclaimed, "She's *alone*? By herself? With nobody *watching her*?!"

"It's ok Lisa, its ok! Elizabeth is quite capable of taking care of herself."

"But . . . you said she's only three!"

"Yes, she's a little late in her development, but that was due to her illness, and at least now she has learned to operate the ship's control panels and the eatery compartments. Though I must boast that I was much younger than she was when I learned how to get my own food." Rose scratched her head, laughing.

Now Lisa's jaw dropped.

"Oh, I may have forgotten to mention that. Our life development is very different from yours."

Well that figures . . . No wonder everyone says aliens are intellectually smarter than us. It's because they are.

"So, did you all realize something?" Rose asked them, but they just looked at each other and shook their heads.

"Realize what?" Decker asked.

Rose smiled. "Not too long ago you didn't believe I was an alien, but now you are all asking questions and listening to my stories." It's true, they've gotten a lot more comfortable around Rose, it seemed. And in such short a time. Lisa admitted she may have been skeptical in the beginning . . . no, she *wanted* to be skeptical, because it sounded too crazy to believe that aliens were real. But then again why should it sound crazy? Because we didn't know anything about them and so we just said we didn't believe them? Because we are afraid? But then why is it that people can believe in something that they've never seen before, but they won't believe in aliens? Do they believe in something because they think they have to? Or is it because they are afraid and so they are forced to believe it? Why do we always need to have proof to believe in something? Why can't we just . . . imagine?

"Alright I got a question." Adam said. "So is Rosalind your real name? Or is that like a secret alien spy name or something?"

Rose laughed. "Rosalind is indeed my real name. But that is something I have just recently studied upon. Humans use names to indicate in a conversation who or what it is you are talking about, and for sentimental reasons. But if you had what we have, you wouldn't really have any use for names except for those sentimental reasons."

"And what do you have?" Decker asked, but it sounded like he knew the answer already.

Rose smiled. "*You* call it Telepathy."

CHAPTER 7

The rain outside seems to have stopped now because they no longer heard the downpour against the window, but nobody was really paying attention to it anyway. Usually, when the rain stopped, they would go outside and do their usual walk around the neighborhood. But today they were more interested in their little alien friend here. And pizza. Lisa's mom called for everyone to come get pizza out in the kitchen and the guys, the two black holes that they are, sprang up instantly, leaving Lisa and Rose to talk to each other. Lisa had to admit that she really did feel more comfortable around Rose now, and it was weird because a little while ago she was as nervous as a mouse in a cat's cage.

While the boys went to get the pizza and soda, Rose and Lisa got to talk about other things.

"I can see the love you and Decker share with each other. It circles around you both like a visible aura, pure and beautiful."

Lisa's face turned red and she said, "Thanks." Trying to turn the subject away from her she then asks, "Do you have a boyfriend Rose?"

Rose smiled softly and grabbed hold of her pendant necklace. "I do. I love him more than words could describe."

Lisa could see it on Rose's face that she was thinking of him right now, and missing him.

"How long have you two been together?"

Rose looked to be counting in her head. "About five thousand years . . . I believe." She started to laugh. "Oh how silly of me, all these years and I cannot even give you an exact number."

Lisa sat frozen, face pale. She couldn't even get out a *"what?!"*

Did she really just say *about five thousand years*?!

"Oh, are you alright Lisa? You look petrified."

Lisa shook her head to get the look of shock off her face.

"I-I'm ok."

Rose was still looking at her with concern.

"You just threw me off there." Lisa laughed nervously. "I thought you said five thousand years or something."

"I did." Rose said.

She did?!

"Oh! I see. You are surprised that I gave you such a high number." She nodded in understanding. "I have forgotten that your people have very short life spans compared to us. But five thousand years is really not a lot at all, it's almost like five years down here on Earth." The surprise left Lisa now, replaced with curiosity and amazement. "So in other words, you and your boyfriend have only been in a relationship for five years?"

"Five years Earth time." Rose corrected, winking.

It sounded like something really far-fetched. Lisa knew there had to be something out there about time and space and whatever it is that defines "age." Of course we all go by a certain time and day here on Earth, heck, not even all of Earth goes by the same time all at once. How complicated would it be then to track time in space?

The guys came back in with the plates of pizza. Decker handed Lisa and Rose their sodas first then Adam gave out the pizza plates. Rose picked up her glass of soda and looked at it strangely. She lifted up her glasses and examined the bottom of the glass, then turned it in her hands, watching the little bubbles fizz to the top.

"Something wrong?" Lisa asked her.

Rose held the glass up to examine the bottom again, then blinked and held it up to her ear.

"Interesting. What is this?"

"It's soda . . ." Decker said dryly.

"Soda? And you . . . consume this?" She watched as Adam chugged down some of his.

"Yeah. It's good, try it." Adam said, taking another chug.

"But it is making strange noises. Is it supposed to do that?"

Decker sighed. "It's not gonna kill you, trust me."

Rose lifted the glass slowly to her lips cautiously and took a small sip. She squeezed her eyes shut and winced.

"You alright?" Adam chuckled.

"Et bunt ma tongue."

"What?" Lisa asked her, trying not to laugh.

"It burnt my tongue" Rose said when the stinging feeling left her mouth. She stuck her tongue out to fan it with her hand.

All of them laughed, even Decker chuckled a bit. He tried to play it off that he was coughing rather than laughing when Lisa looked over at him. But he wasn't so good at pretending.

"But it's good right?" Adam asked Rose, and the girl shook her head in disagreement.

"So what were you saying before about telepathy?" Decker asked, biting into his slice.

Rose picked up her slice of pizza. She looked at it the same way she looked at her soda and set it back down on the plate, picking at a small piece of cheese off the top.

"Well, rather than use our vocal cords, sometimes we revert back to communicating telepathically. It's an older style, but much easier to communicate with.

But the Council does not use telepathy because they enjoy talking at their meetings. It is what makes the meetings more interesting."

Adam nodded. "So you guys don't talk you just . . . ?" He rotated his hands around his head.

Rose laughed. "Oh, no, we do indeed talk. But say for example, I was to run up to Lisa with urgent information that had to be passed on quickly because time was of the essence. Instead of vocally communicating, which could take much longer, I would send my thoughts into her mind, and she would receive the information-" she snapped her fingers. "Like that."

"That's pretty cool." Lisa had to admit.

"Dude, so you can send messages and stuff to our minds?" Adam asked excitedly.

Rose smiled apologetically. "Unfortunately, I can only communicate that way with my people."

Adam's shoulders drooped and he sighed. "Man! I wanna be all telepathic."

"Well you ca—I mean . . . umm . . . you could if you were like us, I suppose."

Lisa saw that Decker was now looking at Rose suspiciously.

"Pff! Yeah well we're not as cool as you aliens are with your telepathy and making things float and flying all around space with your space ships and stuff." Adam pouted.

Rose smiled and put a hand on his shoulder. "You are equally as cool Adam. Perhaps you do not possess the ability of telepathy, but that has not stopped your people from advancing in communication.

"What do you mean?" Adam asked.

"She means like phones and texting and stuff." Decker answered.

"Exactly." Rose nodded.

"But c'mon guys, telepathy is way cooler than texting don't you think?"

Decker shrugged. "I guess. If you like that sort of thing."

"So then you can read each other's minds too?" Lisa asked.

"No, we can only send messages. If however, someone were to leave their mind open to view, then I suppose we could read their mind, but they must be willing or vulnerable enough to not realize their thoughts are open."

"This is some crazy shit." Adam shook his head.

Rose laughed. "Oh but we've only just begun."

CHAPTER 8

They had just gone through two boxes of pizza by the time seven o clock rolled around. Normally this would be about the time that the guys would head home and get some sleep for the school day tomorrow, but they were so lost in conversation they didn't even realize the time, and they were *really* into conversation now. Even Decker was opening up more and asking his own questions. Lisa thought it was cute how he tried to hide his growing curiosity by asking in a firm tone of voice, as though he was suspicious in believing Rose when she gave him her answers. He was total opposite to Adam, who was spewing out questions like a kid asking about the wonders of the world, which in a way, he kind of was.

"So you wish to know about the . . . what was it you called them?"

"The dinosaurs! I heard they found ancient carvings on Egyptian walls and stuff about how the dinosaurs were still around and the aliens were taking their heads and putting them on human bodies. Oh! And the whole thing with the asteroid wiping them out was just a cover-up. I always knew that anyway."

Lisa thought it hard to believe the dinosaurs had anything to do with aliens, but after everything else they've heard so far, anything seemed to be possible.

"You are quite the observant one Adam, I admire that truly." Rose commented.

"Actually he just saw it on tv."

Adam shot Decker a look. "Yeah well for your information I turned that episode off just before they got to the part about the cover-up."

"So how come you know about it?" Decker challenged.

"Look man, I just know things ok? I'm awesome like that."

"Alright Adam I will answer your question, but before I give you my answer, explain to me this: Why is it that the dinosaurs are no longer alive?"

Lisa looked at Rose quizzically.

"That's kinda what we're trying to ask you . . ." Adam said.

"But think about it. Why would it be strange for these creatures to no longer be walking on this planet? Such strong and powerful creatures, how were they destroyed so easily?"

"Can't you just tell us the answer and not beat around the bush with it?" Decker was irritated.

Lisa tried to think about this one. Why is it that the dinosaurs are no longer around? For one thing, *we* certainly wouldn't be as heavily populated as we are now if there were still man eating T-rexes hanging about. Maybe they were just wiped out for a purpose . . .

Lisa was about to voice what she was thinking when Decker beat her to it. As usual.

"What, did you guys kill them off or something?"

Rose looked hesitant, but she quickly gave a smile and said, "Well observed Decker.

I believe that answers the question then."

"No it doesn't. We still don't know *what* it was that killed them off." Decker said.

Rose seemed to be thinking about it for a minute, as though wondering if she should tell them or not. Then she said with a sigh, "There is still much to be discussed. If I were to tell you—

"Was it aliens or a meteor?" Decker asked firmly now, his patience gone.

She paused. But she said, "Yes. It was us."

"Why?" Lisa asked her.

She shook her head. "I cannot explain at the moment. There is too much that needs to be discussed. But fret not friends. You will know the answers eventually."

CHAPTER 9

Lisa woke with a deep breath in. She felt the fan's air on her face and she could tell then that she was sweating. Sitting up slowly she looked back at her clock and saw that it was only 5 a.m. In another two hours she would have to get up for school. Laying her head back down she thought of the crazy dream she just woke from. It felt like such a rush of things racing around in her mind all at once, too much at once. Aliens . . . dinosaurs . . . It was too much. She sighed, trying to calm her nerves. She wished it was a dream . . . Rosalind, the new girl in school. They hardly even knew her, and then she comes to Lisa's house out of nowhere and starts telling them about how she's an alien from outer space. An alien for goodness sakes. At first, Lisa didn't really believe her, not even when she made the shoe float. She figured maybe this new girl didn't know how to make friends and maybe this was her way of doing it. In her weird way . . . But how did she even know where Lisa's lived anyway? Right now it all just felt like a blur. Lisa remembers Rose telling them to ask her questions. Questions about anything in the world. After that it all went crazy. Lisa pulled the covers up to her shoulders and turned on her side uncomfortably. Everything that happened yesterday really happened, she felt she had to admit to herself. She grabbed her cell off the drawer desk behind her head and opened the texts she had apparently missed two hours ago. "What do we do about this? Should we really believe her?" This from Adam. The other from Decker read, "I'm thinking about it now Lisa and I don't think we should get involved with this girl anymore. She could be nuts." Rather than answer back, Lisa laid the phone back on top of the desk and closed her eyes, hoping for it to all just be some crazy dream . . . But it wasn't.

The next day they were all back at Lisa's house again. Eating leftover pizza. Rose was here again, and talking more about alien stuff . . . again. After the first few hours of awkward silence, they started to ask their questions. Slowly, cautiously, they moved back into this strange new rhythm they've become accustomed to. They ask the questions, listen, and then discuss them. Sort of like the way the three of them did when they went on one of their walks around the neighborhood, only this was different . . .

"Alright I got a question." Adam raised his hand like he was in school.

Rose smiled. "Yes Adam, and what is your question?"

He took a big bite out of his fifth slice of pizza, swallowed and said, "Ok, I always wanted to know about this, so don't call me weird or anything but . . . Do you know anything about the Bermuda triangle?"

That was actually a really good question, Lisa thought. She was curious too. They say the Bermuda Triangle is haunted by the ghost ships and planes that it took down in the past, and when you venture straight through it, you can see the ships sailing out in the foggy distance and then disappear the second you blink your eyes. Sailors have said their clocks and mechanical devices go crazy, that their compasses spin in every direction. Pilots reported flying through weird cloud tunnels and jumping through time, believing they had only been in the air for a few minutes when it was actually hours. Some have even said that the triangle threw them into another dimension and that they were the luckiest souls in the world to have come back to tell the tale. Basically, you don't mess with the Bermuda triangle.

"Ah yes, the Bermuda Triangle." Rose said, reminiscing. "One of Father's most favored inventions."

Now they were all looking at Rose with confusion and interest. "You see, upon learning that the humans were making an incredible leap out of primitive living and into a more intelligent way of thinking, the High Council began coming up with ideas on how to better study them. They wanted to watch the humans grow more, seeing as how they missed a few hundred years of precious evolution. They didn't want to miss any more. During a meeting the topic was brought up and Father announced that he had an idea on how they could have a way to study the humans more closely." Rose smiled proudly. "He told the Council, who were eager to hear his words, that they could hold a secret base on Earth that they could travel back and forth to without the humans ever knowing of it—

"I knew it! I knew it was some kind of alien thing going on down in the ocean." Adam said.

"Wait, it gets better." Rose said excitedly. "Eventually Father had found a perfect place to put the base, now all they needed was a way to get to and from it from the Council Ship. Father spoke once again to the Council that he could invent a teleportation system. A unique system that would enable anybody to travel from the Council Ship to this base. The system would be invisible to human eyes, and stretch diagonally. They could travel to and from the base in a heartbeat. It was a genius idea, and the Council was pleased. However, Father had not thought that the humans would advance so much as to make their own vessels to carry them out to sea, so far out that they would come into contact with the system."

"But wait, I thought you said it was invisible?" Decker said.

"To human eyes, yes. But it was still very much there, like a creature who is simply camouflaged into its surroundings. Anyone traveling horizontally through the system would interrupt its electrical waves. You're only supposed to travel straight down not straight through. Over the years the system has brought down many of your sea ships and air crafts."

"Holy shit. So it's a teleportation thing that's been messing us up this whole time? That's why people have gone missing?" Adam asked.

"But what about the clocks and the compasses?" Decker asked.

"The electrical, as well as our very own energy may cause your machines to lose their functions."

"But what about people saying that they saw ghost ships and stuff?"

"Ghost ships?" Rose asked confused.

"Yeah, you know . . . ships that sunk a long time ago. Dead sailors . . ."

Rose was shaking her head at Adam's every word.

"You don't know what a ghost ships is." Decker said dryly.

Rose shook her head again.

"Hold up. Do you at least know what a ghost is?" Adam jumped in.

Rose shook her head for the third time. The guys just looked at her. Lisa was a little surprised, but then, Rose *is* an alien from outer space. Maybe they don't have ghosts up there.

"Based on the way you separated "ghost" and "ship" and then asked me if I knew what a ghost was I am assuming they are both different?

"Uh yeah, like really different." Decker said.

"A ghost is like a dead person or animal . . . It's kinda hard to explain, but when they die, their soul gets stuck here or something. They're all see-through and can float and disappear and stuff. And they haunt places and freak people out." Adam tried to explain.

"I see." Rose said, mentally picturing this "ghost."

"And they can possess you. That's probably the scariest thing they can do." He went on.

"How interesting. But to answer your question about the "ghost ships" I will tell you that the electrical energy surrounding the Teleporter could cause a Replay of some kind."

"A Replay?" Lisa asked.

"Yes. A Replay is a phenomenon we have recently discovered while observing Earth. Past movements are recorded in time, and then replayed over and over. For example, the supposed "ghost ships" you see may be Replays of past ships. Their energy is still connected to time, and because this energy is mixing with the Teleporter's energy, the object's energy then becomes visible to see. It is trapped forever in time."

Wow . . . that actually makes sense. Then does that mean that ghosts are Replays too?

"Hold up though. Now that might be true with the ships, but you can't tell me that ghosts are not real. I watch those haunting shows all the time. There's no way that stuff is fake." Adam was convinced.

"Well, I am really not so sure about these "ghosts" in which you speak of. However, if it has anything to do with death than I must politely remind you that I cannot speak of religion or anything that has to do with it."

"What's the big deal anyway? If you got something to tell us than you can tell us, I mean whatever it is we can handle it." Decker said.

It was the first time Lisa saw Rose with a scowl on her face. "So you speak for Lisa and Adam as well? You know they can "handle" it like you can?"

It was also the first time Lisa saw Decker silenced by someone other than her.

"I admire your curiosity and willing to speak of the subject Decker, but I wish for you to respect my disapproval. As I have said before, I will not alter your beliefs in any way, for they are special and precious to all of you."

He tested Rose when he said angrily, "Oh yeah? Well what about you coming down here and telling us that you're an alien huh? You don't think *that's* mind altering? I *believed* that we were the only living things in the universe until you came here spewing all this nonsense."

"Decker." Lisa chastised. He didn't look at her though, only at Rose, waiting for her to give him the answer he was asking for. Lisa didn't think even Decker realized he was asking it. But Rose did. She gave him a "nice try" smile and said, "If it wouldn't have a risky effect on your mental health, then I would be happy to talk about it."

"The same effect you had on us when you told us you were an alien?!" Decker kept at it.

"You are feeling some negative mental effect Decker?" Rose threw back, clearly trying to tease him now.

"Maybe." He responded, still angry.

"Alright man, you can stop with all this political correctness crap. You're starting to sound like Josh."

Decker grabbed Adam by the front of his shirt, which shocked Lisa into grabbing his arm and yelling at him to let Adam go. What's gotten into him? Decker and Adam play around all the time with each other but nothing ever got this bad.

"Don't *ever* compare me to him." He shook him once then pushed him back.

Lisa slapped his arm yelling, "Calm down! What the hell is wrong with you?"

He was quiet then as his eyes went to the floor. He must've realized what he had done because he looked to Adam with an apologetic expression. Adam just looked away.

Rose was looking down at the floor as well, probably not wanting to get in the way of Decker's anger lest she be next. Even though Lisa knew Decker would never do something like that to a girl, in fact he only did it to Adam because they were so used to being rough with each other. And Lisa knew Josh was definitely a subject they always avoided.

It was that one summer day that changed the way Lisa thought of Adam, when he got into an argument with Josh. They and a couple of their other friends were just hanging at the field like they always did. Josh was a friend to one of Lisa's friends. A stranger really. He's the kind of guy that always has something to complain about . . .

He was telling them all the story on how his dad treats him like dirt, and his mom does nothing to help him, or stop his father when he gets into his drunken fits. Adam got annoyed and told the guy to stop with his complaining because it was starting to get annoying, that, and his cigarette smoke was depleting all the oxygen in the air. "Besides, at least you got a mom." Adam told him.

Josh shot back saying, "You know, just because you're mom is dead doesn't mean you gotta have something to say about—"

"Shut up!" Adam snapped. He would've gone for Josh's throat if Decker didn't jump in time to hold him back.

"Just let it go man. He's not worth your time."

Adam was fuming so much he actually pushed Decker aside so he could walk away . . .

What made it worse was that Josh refused to even apologize for what he said, which only deepened Adam's hatred for him. Decker didn't care much for Josh either, but that was only because Decker thought the kid had a cocky personality. And Decker always thought of Adam as his little brother, so he liked to stick up for him when he needed to.

After that day, they didn't really see Josh or the rest of the group for a while, and maybe it was meant.

"Dude what was it we were talking about again?" Adam laughed then, trying to lift the awkward silence. Lisa laughed too, hoping they could get back to what they were talking about. Decker shook his head but grinned. "Don't even remember."

"By the way Rose, what made the High Council want to watch over the humans anyway?" Lisa asked.

Rose didn't answer right away, but rather than try to avoid the question she decided to say, "I will explain in good time."

The guys both sighed. "C'mon Rose why can't you just tell us?" Adam whined.

"All in good time." She winked.

Lisa was a little disappointed herself that Rose wouldn't tell them, but she'll just be patient for now, probably best to let things sink in one shocker at a time.

"Hey, isn't that new movie out yet?" Decker asked.

Rose tilted her head and Lisa asked, "Which one?"

"The alien one." Adam looked to Rose with a grin. Rose didn't get the joke.

"You should come with us. You'll like it. We go to the movies all the time. It's like watching tv only on a really big screen." Lisa said.

Rose agreed to go, curious to see this "movie" thing.

CHAPTER 10

They went to the five o clock showing of "Cowboys vs. Aliens." Lisa sat in between Decker and Rose, and Adam sat on Rose's other side. Their friend, Joe, came along too because he said he's been dying to see this movie. Lisa forgot to mention to Rose that the theater would get a little loud with all the speakers, and she was holding her ears closed as the beginning features came on. They were always the loudest because they wanted you to know what else was coming out, and Lisa told her after they were done that she wouldn't have to hold her ears closed for the rest of the movie. She didn't put them down until they got to the action parts, then she was reaching over to grab some popcorn out of Lisa's bucket, never taking her eyes off the screen.
Lisa laughed when she reached over blindly for the bottle of soda and Lisa had to hand it to her.

At one part in the movie the actor got thrown down and knocked out cold, so there was a long silent scene. Everyone in the theater was quiet, waiting to see if the actor would get back up again. Adam took a nacho chip up to his mouth slowly, looked around and bit down on it, not wanting to make any noise.
Of course, the loud "crunch!" of the chip broke through the silence of the scene. They all had to shush each other when they broke out into laughter. Lisa even heard the other people in front of them

laugh too. Poor Adam ducked his head hoping nobody would turn around and scold him for his loud chip eating.

The funniest part was probably a few seconds after Adam bit the chip, the actor in the movie sprang up out of his knocked out state.

CHAPTER 11

Rose was so excited Lisa thought she was going to jump out the car window. She gazed out at the large building as they pulled into the mall parking lot. She was the first one out of the car. "Is this it? Are we here?"

"Yup, this is it." Adam said, putting his arm over her shoulder. Lisa laughed when Rose yanked him forward, so eager was she to get a look at this so called "mall" they always go to.

When they walked in Rose gasped at how large the place actually was.

She looked around like a child at an amusement park.

Her eyes grew big behind her round glasses. Decker had to grab her hand to stop her from wandering away. "Just stay with us alright? It can be easy to get lost in here." He warned.

She nodded, still looking around in amazement.

"Well where to first?" Lisa asked.

"Gamestop." Both the guys said at once.

They took the escalator upstairs. Lisa had to hold onto Rose before she leaned too far off the side. "How amazing! It is exactly like walking onto a ship, only these platforms have steps to hold one's balance. Humans are so clever." She said.

They got to the game store but Rose stopped just before entering. Lisa turned around and asked. "Coming in?"

"Are we not supposed to ask permission first before entering another's home?"

Lisa laughed. "It's not someone's home. Well, I guess it could be if you're really into games like those two." She looked over at the guys as they searched the same rack for their favorite games. "But trust me, we're allowed in." She reached out her hand for Rose to go in with her. Rose took it and walked in slowly.

They joined the guys over by the Xbox games rack. Rose looked around and asked in confusion. "And what is the purpose of walking into these places?"

"To buy games." Adam said. He then found something that he liked and said, "Hah! Told you they had it dude. Check it out." He held the game up for Decker to see but Decker just tsked. "That one sucks."

Adam slumped his shoulders. "What?! Dude are you kidding? This is the best one."

Lisa laughed at the two.

"How interesting. And what do you use to trade for these . . . games?"

"Uh money . . . ?" Decker said, taking one game up to the register. Rose nodded in understanding. "Oh, I see. Very interesting."

They left the store shortly after with Lisa insisting that Rose would love Hot Topic instead. So they walked over to the rock store. Rose immediately went over to the clothes on the far right and started skimming through a few. She got real excited when she found some that she liked.

"This clothing looks exactly like the ones I have at home. Amazing!" Lisa laughed at her excitement. If Rose lived here on Earth this would probably be her favorite store to shop at. It was certainly Lisa's, actually it was the only store in the whole mall she liked other than the Gamestop. Sometimes she had to practically drag the guys away from the games every time they came here.

It wasn't until the two saw the funny shirts over on the left wall that they finally stopped their complaining that they wanted to go back to Gamestop. Lisa decided to leave them to that and go over to Rose. She was still looking through all the clothes, putting a few shirts up to herself and turning to Lisa asking, "What do you think of this one Lisa? Too dark? I do admit that the color is not exactly my favorite but oh I do love these stripes."

Lisa smiled. "It looks cool. You know, they have a dressing room in the back. You can try them on if you like before buying them."

Her eyes lit up. "Truly? Oh now I must do so right away." She gathered her huge pile of clothes and raced for the changing room. Lisa laughed following behind her. Hey, who says aliens can't be fashionable? She looked at herself in one of the mirrors. Maybe Rose could even give her a few pointers, Lisa thought, thinking now that she might want to step out of her comfort zone of black t-shirts and jeans. Lisa wasn't much into clothes or fashion, but it wouldn't hurt to have a little fun while they were here. She searched through the one rack of clothes until she found a cute little purple striped shirt and ripped jeans. She grinned and took them back to the dressing room.

The guys were now checking out the belts when Lisa and Rose walked up in their new clothes.

They both just stared at the girls with blank faces at first.

"Well? What do you think?" Lisa asked looking at Decker.

He smiled at her. "You look beautiful."

She blushed. "You don't think it's a little . . . ?"

He chuckled and went up to kiss her on her forehead. "You know I think anything looks good on you."

Adam couldn't stop staring at Rose in her long-sleeved forest green sweatshirt with black jeans.

"The girls look good don't they Adam?" Decker threw a hand on his back to snap him out of his trance.

"Yeah, yeah." He stuttered out. "You guys look awesome."

Lisa led Rose up to the cash register with their pile of clothes.

Decker burst out laughing then as the girls walked away. "Hey man you alright?"

Adam just nodded his head still staring at Rose. "Yeah I'm good."
Decker was still laughing. "Dude only you would fall in love with
an alien."

They all left the store then, Lisa and Rose carrying two
bag loads of clothes as they led the way up in front, while the guys
followed behind.

They decided to stop by the food court to grab a bite to eat.
After they all sat down at a table Adam said, "So I'm guessing you
don't have malls up there in space."
Rose took a bite of her sandwich awkwardly, some of the food
coming out the other side of her bread, before answering. "Well,
we obtain different materials from different planets by trade. Father
has many allies with a variety of species that used to be Drifters
but have received the help of the High Council in finding their
planet. Each planet produces certain materials, and the people of
that planet trade those materials with the High Council in exchange
for technology, information, or just as appreciation for helping
them."
"Cool." Adam said taking another bite of his big sandwich, but it
actually sounded like "Crvool," with his face stuffed.
"Do you guys have a money system of some kind like we do?"
Lisa asked.
"No. Although the Council did hold a meeting about creating
currency like the humans have on Earth, but after some studying
they have decided to deny the proposal. Such a system would
likely destroy their gracious trading and breed much greed,
something that is under good control at the moment and does not
need to be tampered with."
"There is a reason we have it though, it's just really complicated."
Decker said.
"We would not be able to create such a limited system anyway
because we trade with a very large variety of species everywhere
all the time. It simply wouldn't work." She took another awkward
bite of her sandwich.

Lisa figured that made sense. Most of their countries have their own money that cannot be used in another country, so in a way, it is limited.

"That's crazy to think about though. You guys deal with so many aliens that you can't even make a money system. Makes you feel so small, you know? Being a human on this little Earth?" Adam said.

"Perhaps you have created such a system in order to have control. It is one of the many interesting things about your kind. You cannot venture out as far as we can, so your world is actually very small, even though to you, it might seem big. We have the whole universe. There is nothing that is too big or too small for us. We accept and accommodate to whatever we have to in order to survive, though to be truthful, we would much rather learn."

She looked out the long window then at the small bird that perched itself on the ledge of the glass.

"This may sound strange, but surviving is not so much a first priority anymore but rather something that we take for granted. Unless of course, you are a Drifter and everything you do you do to survive. But when you live for as long as we do, life can become a little boring. We love to learn about new things. It is what makes life more interesting."

They finished their lunch and headed downstairs to check out the rest of the mall. Rose stopped in front of one store and smiled brightly. "Lisa, look there! This store has clothes of only one color, isn't that unique? It seems to be an all-female store of some sort. Oh we simply must go in!"

"Oh no we must not." Adam walked ahead of them with his hood over his head.

Decker laughed and yelled out to him, "What's the matter Adam, chicken?"

Adam turned around and yelled back, "Sticks and stones!"

Lisa caught the red in his face as he pulled the hood back down over his head.

78

CHAPTER 12

Rose was laughing.

"Oh c'mon you gotta know something about this." Adam begged. She wiped at her eyes from laughing so much. "Oh indeed I do, but do you really wish to know? It is quite embarrassing."

"C'mon Rose pleeeaaase?" He begged again. Then he grabbed Gustav and held him up to her.

"Look, see this face? How can you resist this face?" Gustav tilted his head at Rose, and then attempted to lick her cheek. She smiled and gave the pup a pat on the head.

"Oh I suppose it couldn't hurt." She caved in. "But the answer may surprise you."

"Pff! You don't have to warn us anymore. I think we're already used to the whole surprise thing by now." He said.

That's what they think, Lisa shook her head.

They all huddled on the floor in their little circle around Rose. Gustav waddled over to lay right next to her, something he did often now. It still amazed Lisa that he wouldn't bark when Rose would come up to the door, that's how Lisa knew it was her knocking. And when she walks in, the first thing he does is run over to her, tail wagging. Of course, when Decker or Adam would walk in he would just bark, even though he sees them almost every day.

"Alright. So you want to know about your . . . what did you call it? Stonehenge?"
They all nodded.
"Very well. Hmm. I suppose I should begin with how it all happened . . ."

She sat very still, her one small hand gripping his and the other balled into a tight fist on her lap. He noticed her nervousness and gave her hand a gentle squeeze. "Don't worry. You'll do fine."
"But what if I cannot? What if I am just not capable of controlling it?" She turned away, looking out the small window at the many stars as they passed them. She leaned her head against the glass, watching as the blue from the galaxy they were drifting through dust the outer window. Every shade, every cluster and swirl she saw followed them. Over in the distance, a red galaxy rotated vertically. She never really cared for the color red. Blue was what she preferred, which is why her father chose to drift through this galaxy instead. He looked back at her, one hand on the control panel, and he smiled. But his smile quickly faded when he saw the look of worry and sadness on her face.
"Something wrong, Rosie? I thought you liked the Blue galaxy."
She sighed. "If I must be honest, father, I am not in a very confident mind. What if I cannot do this?" Her pleading look tore at his heart. He switched the controls to auto pilot and went over to her. Bending down on one knee he said, "Rosie, my sweet one, you must believe that you can do this."
"But I don't believe." She said in a low voice.
He pulled her into his arms. "Now, now do not fret. I know you will do a fine job. We will practice and practice until you are confident enough to control it on your own."
She looked up. "I am not so sure, father. I am not as brave as you believe me to be."
"You are brave, Rosalind." Her betrothed and best friend, Cornelius, reassured her. "The bravest I have ever known. Do you

not remember when I told you of my constant failure when I first practiced my lessons? Oh I can assure you that nobody took as long as I to get it right."

She smiled at that.

They landed the ship on an empty flat land of green and brown. Rose looked curiously out her window and asked. "Father, where are we?"

"I thought you might want to practice in peace, away from judgmental onlookers and an extremely cautious mother." He winked.

They followed her father off the ship, Cornelius still holding her hand. She shut her eyes against a cool breeze that blew some of her hair off her shoulders. At first, it was brisk, then it turned warm. The heat on her head seemed to be coming from the large non-planet just above them, and strangely this planet only had one. Every other planet she'd ever been to had at least two or three.

What lay before them was a pile of very large stones. She gulped down the rest of her nervousness and looked up to her father.

"I'm ready." She said with more confidence now.

He nodded. "Good. We will begin then."

Wrapping a metal chain around his wrist, he extended his hand out to the ship. The chain snaked around each finger and up his arm, shading from a dull grey to a brilliant red. The top of the ship lifted off slowly, and a smaller ship floated out. It was beautiful. The metal glistened with polished blue. It landed right in front of them, and Rose looked it over in awe at its unique design. It was a much smaller ship, about five feet tall, but Rose could not help running her fingers along the metal, its designs beautifully painted with black.

Her father put a hand on her shoulder and smiled. "Shined it up for you."

And shined it did. A beautiful creation. Her father's creation. Rose didn't expect she would be practicing in something so . . .

"Magnificent, Marius, truly this is."

"Thank you, Cornelius. But then, I wouldn't have anything less for my precious daughter."

"Father, this ship . . . it's so . . ."

He laughed. "That is because this will be your ship to practice with my dear. You will not have you're real ship until you can successfully control this one."

She was shocked. "But father, this ship, it's—"

"Do not worry Rose. This ship will see many dents and breakings. It was built only for practice purposes." She still felt unsure. Her father was an amazing architect and designer. He loved all his creations. Even if this ship is for practice purposes, she couldn't risk destroying it. She could only imagine the amount of time it took him to build something such as this.

She looked back up at him, unsure, but he had a confident smile on his face.

The ship's top opened up, and Cornelius helped her step in. Two constraint straps slipped over her head and around her waist. If only the entire ship had a protective constraint belt . . . She gulped down another lump of nervousness.

"Now listen Rosie, the ship's controls are very sensitive. Be careful not to overthink anything, and turn on the tracer after you get in the air."

She nodded. Cornelius gave her a smile and a thumb up.

"Ok Rose, you can do this." She told herself. She laid her hand on the control panel and a green light passed back and forth across the bottom of her palm. She almost pulled away until the screen changed to black, then two green lines came up from the bottom of the screen and branched out into what looked like two round circles, then more lines. They reached out and stopped. Now they resembled two . . . hands. Her hands, she realized when she moved her hands and the lines moved with her. She waved her right hand back and forth across the screen, and the lined hand following her movement.

"Amazing . . ."

"Rose." Her father tapped on the top of the ship's glass. "Push the button on your right to get the ship in the air."

"Button on my right? Button on my right . . ." She searched among the many buttons, then she found one that said "Anti-gravity" *This one?*

She pushed it and the ship started to vibrate and pulse. She yanked her hand away from the button quickly. There was the sound of electricity and suddenly the vibrations stopped. At first she thought she might've done something wrong and she looked up to ask her father when she noticed that he was no longer there. All she saw was sky. She leaned her face against the glass and saw that she was high above both their heads!

Goodness . . .

In a panic she whipped back to the controls to look for something to make the ship stop floating. But she couldn't find one that said "gravity" or something of the sort. She looked back down and saw that now she was even higher than before.

What do I do?! She sent the message telepathically to her father.

Hit the brakes! Cornelius's voice rang.

"The brakes?" She looked around, but couldn't seem to find a button that said "brakes." So there was a button to start the ship but not to stop it?!

"Cornelius!" She yelled and hit against the glass for the top to open up, but it was locked shut.

He bolted for the main ship, but Marius grabbed his arm. "Slow down boy, let her do this."

"But sir—"

"She needs to learn how to control the ship."

Cornelius looked up worriedly as Rose's ship floated higher and higher.

Panic made her heart race as Rose tapped on the screen again but nothing came up. She tapped twice. Three times. Nothing!

"Get me out!" She screamed.

She looked down and could see that the ship was taking her too high, much too high. Her father and Cornelius were getting smaller and smaller. Oh now what was she to do? How would she escape? And why wasn't she being rescued?!
She held her fingers to her temples desperately, thinking, thinking of anything. Maybe if she tried to search for a latch on the roof . . .
She twisted in her seat to reach her arms up and just as she did, the ship suddenly took a plummet back down. Adrenaline raced through her veins and almost froze her hands from reaching for the "anti-gravity" button. She braced herself for the impact.
And just before the ship could hit the ground . . . it stopped abruptly.

The top of the ship lifted up and Rose scrambled to finally get out of it. Cornelius caught her when she jumped into his arms.

"Are you alright?" He asked, holding her head to his chest.
"I'm fine." She breathed.
"Rose, you have to know where the most important controls are to the ship. One mishap could cause disaster." Her father said, walking over to them.
"Father I've changed my mind. I can't do this. Can we just go home now?"
He looked surprised, but sighed and put his hand on her head, the same way he would whenever she was upset or worried. And he could clearly see her worry.
"Rosie, you mustn't give up so easily. Think of how well you will do once you are able to—"
"And if I am not able to?"
He stared into her big round eyes, eyes that started to glaze with unshed tears. He shrugged. "Then you are not able to."
She frowned.
"But." He tilted her chin up. "How will you know unless you try?"

She could try. She knows this. Even if she were to fail, she knows her father will still love her. She just didn't want to disappoint him, or anyone for that matter. What would all the

Council Members say if they found out Marius's only daughter couldn't even fly a Tracer ship? He would be humiliated. She just didn't want to risk that. Let them taunt and tease her until the end of her days, but leave her father be.

"I am afraid of your expectations, father. I am afraid that I will never be able to do this. And I truly do not think I can. Please understand."

"I only understand that you are afraid." He said. "But Rose, explain this to me. If you truly cannot do something because you believe you can't, then would you only need to believe you could so you can?"

She looked up at him. Her father has always been there for her and always will be. For her to even have the slightest worry that he would just shun her over something like this sounded ridiculous. She smiled now, ready to finally believe she can do this.

Three hours into practice and she had finally mastered the movement controls. Forward, backward, up and down. She flew through the sky, shot into aerial turns and flips, spins and whirls. Her confidence turned into thrill-full courage and in midair she turned off the anti-gravity system. She chuckled wondering what her father and Cornelius must be thinking down below, and just for fun she opened her mind to their thoughts, seeming vulnerable to be heard through their worried looks.

"What's going on? Why did she turn off the system?!"
"Rosalind!"

She laughed now. Putting her hand back on the screen the system rebooted once again and she was back flying through the air.
"Whooohooo!"

On the ground, Marius and Cornelius both sighed in absolute relief.

In all her excitement she almost didn't see her father waving up at her to come back down. She opened her thoughts to him.

"Goodness child, you nearly gave me a heart malfunction."
She smiled. *"But I did well?"*

85

"You did extraordinary, as I knew you would. Well done daughter."

The ship lowered easily back down to the ground and the top lifted off. Cornelius rushed over to Rose and scooped her into his arms.

"That was amazing!" He said, spinning her around. "But please don't ever do that again." She laughed and kissed his cheek. "Oh I will definitely be doing that again."

Her father shook his head but smiled. Clearing his throat he said, "Very good Rosalind, you have excelled at learning to control the ship's movement, now comes the challenging part."

She still felt pretty confident, but a little knob of nervousness jumped back into her throat when her father walked over to the pile of rocks. She looked at Cornelius and he just gave her a wink.

"These ships are built for more than just the purpose of transportation. They are also tools. The Council uses these ships to aid in construction."

"Construction?" Rose asked her father.

"Say for example, a species was in need of building or rebuilding their homes for whatever reason. If the material is too heavy for them to lift, they would need the help of the Council's Tracer ships to help lift them." Cornelius said.

"The system will activate only when you need it to." Her father finished.

Rose was told that the Tracer system will allow the driver to trace any object, all she had to do was bring her surroundings up on the screen, then with her finger, trace around the object she wanted to lift, then tap the screen to make it weightless. With that, she was able to trace one of the larger stones and stand it up.

She carefully moved the ship to the left and with it the stone, then to her right.

After a few minutes, she had all the stones stacked and standing. She lowered the ship back down and smiled at her masterpiece she had created . . .

Lisa was still in awe over what she had just heard. The guys had their jaws hanging open.

Rose chuckled at their shocked faces.

"No way. So it was *you* that built Stonehenge?" Adam asked, stunned.

She nodded and smiled with pride. "And I do say it is a beautiful work of art wouldn't you agree?"

"Uh yeah. You know how popular that place is? People think it's some place of worship or something." Decker said.

"Oh, yes. Father did mention the way later humans used it as a sacred place. I offered to take it down but he thought it couldn't hurt leaving it up. After all, the humans seemed to have a fascination with it, and it is sort of a reminder of the first day I had my ship flying lessons."

Lisa shook her head. If the world knew about this it would probably be all over the news. She could see it now, "Truth about famous Stonehenge and teen alien driving lessons."

CHAPTER 13

It's been two weeks now since Rose has become a part of their lives, and after all the strangeness with floating shoes, aliens and truths of the universe, Lisa's noticed that nothing really seems all that different. She would've thought that she'd be looking at life in a whole new way, especially considering the fact that only the three of them knew about it all. But it's the same old life. They go to school, go home and procrastinate on homework, hang out, go places, talk about the latest news or gossip, who's dating who or posted this on Facebook, which movies look awesome enough to go see, which one's don't. The usual stuff.

Even the guys don't seem to be thinking much about it. Of course, it's probably killing Adam not to impress anyone with his "incredible knowledge" of every wonder anybody has ever questioned. But then again, Lisa shouldn't be so surprised. If they weren't told about aliens or the Bermuda triangle or any of that, then their lives would still go on as they do every day. It's just now Lisa felt a little strange. She was sitting in a classroom, in a world, where only she held the answers to some of Earth's greatest mysteries. What would happen if somebody were to find out that she knew? What would happen to her, to them?

"So, who can come up and write in the definition to this vocabulary word? Anyone? Someone?"

"Rose wants to do it Mr. O." One wise-mouth student spoke out and the other kids laughed.

Rose looked around at them all and started to laugh too, not understanding the kid's sarcasm. Then the laughter stopped, but Rose was still laughing.

Decker was shaking his head and Lisa could see he looked irritated.

Mr. O gave the wise-mouth student a look of warning.

"Oh I suppose I could do this one."

Rose stood up and walked to the front of the room. Taking the chalk from the teacher's hand she started right away at defining the word, "Author."

Actually she defined it in many different ways. And in many different languages . . . It only took her a few minutes to completely fill the whole board up with writing. When she was done she handed Mr. O the chalk and bowed.

Mr. O bowed back and said proudly, "Well done Ms. Rosalind. Well done."

The whole class mumbled and stared at the board. Somebody whispered a "what the hell?" to one of their friends.

Decker grinned. Adam put out his hand for Rose to give him a high five. She hesitated at first, probably not familiar with that kind of gesture, and held her hand up. Adam clapped it with his.

"Someone want to erase the board for me while I get the out the quizzes?"

"I'll do it Mr. O." Adam volunteered.

As he was passing the front desks he turned to the wise-mouth student before grabbing the eraser and grinned. "You mad?"

Mr. wise-mouth just looked at Adam, not really knowing what to say.

Decker did laugh this time. So did Lisa.

She thought she heard the teacher chuckle too.

They went for one of their daily walks after school that day. The boys just got done arguing about the gun law thing, and

Decker was opposing it, while Adam was agreeing that everyone should have the right to protect themselves. Decker shot back, no pun intended, that more people use guns to rob and kill other people than to protect themselves. Adam countered that it was in their constitution, the Right to Bear Arms, so there was nothing anyone could do about it. Lisa told Rose earlier that when they get onto a sticky subject to just let them talk it out. It's more fun to hear them argue. Rose just smiled warily watching the guys go at each other's throats with another controversial topic, which game is better, Call of Duty or Halo?

This is the result of soda, junk food and random bored-ness.

CHAPTER 14

A few days later they decided to go on another one of their walks since it was Friday and the weekend was finally here. They just got done talking about the Mayan Calendar and how the world is supposed to end on December 21st of 2012. Decker brought it up first and quickly gave his opinion on how ridiculous the whole thing is. Adam had to agree that it was just another attempt at making people go crazy for nothing. When they turned to Rose to see if she knew anything about it she reminded them that she would not go into detail because a lot of the subject revolved around religious beliefs, but she could tell them that the world would not be ending any time soon, at least not the entire world anyway. She went on to say that the "world ending" could hold many different definitions. The entire Earth could end for everyone, or just an individual's world could end.

Now they were on a different topic. The pyramids.

"You can't convince me that we made them. I mean, c'mon, how did they carry those heavy stone blocks? And how are they so perfectly aligned with the Orion's belt?" Adam brought up how he was watching a television show about the suspicions surrounding the pyramids, how odd it is that some of the stone blocks they found were cut clean down, no jagged edges like you would expect to see from using a primitive carving tool. They looked as if someone had used a sharp blade. Rose was waiting patiently for Adam to finish talking.

"It was just crazy cause it got me thinking you know? Like, the way they explained how the people would've had to lift the blocks and stack them, that just didn't sound right. Did they really have that kind of manpower?"

"Maybe. I mean, how can you just assume it was aliens?" Decker asked.

"Cause man, they showed these stones that were just too neatly cut to be from those chisels they used to have back in the day, and those blocks weigh a ton! Nope, too fishy if you ask me."

"Well let's just ask our little alien friend here." Decker looked down at Rose, who was trying to appear distracted with Lisa's handheld game she was playing with.

"Way to put her on the spot like that dude."

"No, it's quite alright." She looked up now, her face red with embarrassment. "It is true that your ancient people had help in building your great pyramids. It is also true that they were not able to produce enough manpower. The intense heat temperatures made it difficult to perform such a task at all. And in order to *almost* have enough manpower, every single person had to have been strong and healthy, yet there were many women, children, and elderly who would not have been able to lift even a scraping tool."

Lisa thought that sounded legit. And all those strong, healthy people would eventually grow old and frail. They would have to live healthy and strong for the rest of their lives if they wanted to get all three pyramids done.

Rose hesitated before saying, "My kind indeed aided in providing help with building these structures, only because we could see how difficult the task was becoming of your primitive people."

"Hah! I knew it!" Adam said.

"So in other words, you felt bad for us." Decker grinned.

". . . Yes." Rose nodded.

"But why?" Adam asked then.

Rose didn't respond immediately, more like she was thinking on what to say.

Adam was about to ask her again when Rose blurted, "Well we couldn't just stand by and watch your people suffer so. We are not that way . . ."

"So you were watching us the whole time? Even back then?" Decker asked suspiciously.

Rose looked nervous.

Even now it was pretty obvious she was trying to hide something, the way she bit her bottom lip and hesitated again on answering Decker's question.

"That's no news to me. Of course aliens would be spying on us. They abduct people don't they?"

"As I have said before the act of abducting is illegal . . ." Rose mumbled.

"I guess. But then how did the aliens help them anyway?" Decker asked.

"My people used Tracer ships. These machines are capable of lifting even the heaviest of objects. Someone pilots the machine the same way you pilot a plane, only the person inside the Tracer is sitting in front of a large screen. The screen is turned on to reveal the outside. When you find what it is you want to pick up, you lock onto the object, then send out a laser that traces around the object. Once the object is traced, the pilot can then send out anti gravity energy, and then you can lift the object. Tracers can run on land, sea and air, which made it easier to lift the cut blocks onto the next set, thus stacking them in the way you see them now."

"So that ship you said you were practicing your flying lessons in was a Tracer ship?"

"Correct, Adam. Though I believe I might've mentioned the name while I was telling the story . . ."

"And the blocks? How were they cut?" Decker asked.

"Really big silver slicers." Rose tried to show the length by stretching out her arms.

"Father used the rarest silver in the entire galaxy to make them. Silver that was gifted to him by previous Drifters who he saved. Apparently their home planet is rich in silver."

That would explain how they got to stack the blocks in such a way. That would explain the perfectly cut blocks. That would explain a lot of things . . .

"I knew it. I totally knew it. Those shows don't lie man."

"You wouldn't have even known if you didn't watch those shows, idiot."

"Hey, I got a brain, I can think for myself. I already knew aliens helped to build the pyramids. That show just proved I was right." Adam beamed.

Decker rolled his eyes.

Lisa knew this was really off topic, but she figured, what the hell, they were already asking questions.

"Hey Rose, I don't think you ever told us how old you were."

She looked surprised. "No? Hmm . . . no I suppose I didn't. Well to your eyes I may seem very young don't I? As young as the three of you."

They all waited. None of them even realized they had stopped walking.

She shocked them all when she said, "I am indeed the same age as the three of you."

They were quiet. Lisa was thinking maybe they were all expecting what she was expecting . . .

Adam started to laugh. "You know, I thought you were gonna say you were like, a million or something."

Rose chuckled. "Well, I do not age as quickly as you do, so if you were to count the years I have been alive, it would be much longer than your normal human existence."

So she *is* old.

"Then you're like, what, eighteen, nineteen?" Decker asked.

"Yes, on Earth. We do not usually keep track of our life years but if I had to make an estimate, I would say . . ." She counted using her fingers. "I would be about nineteen thousand. Well about, maybe more."

All their jaws dropped open.

"Damn! Nineteen thousand?!" Adam exclaimed.

"About." She corrected.

"Well hell." Decker was just as surprised.

Lisa actually wanted to laugh. She had completely forgotten Rose telling them that she and her boyfriend had been together for over five thousand years, so of course they had to expect her to be at least over one thousand. Really, how does anyone forget hearing *that*?

"Well then, any other questions?" Rose asked cheerfully.

"This is just crazy." Adam sat down on the curb putting his face in his hands. Decker folded his arms and shook his head chuckling.

"I apologize if I may have shocked you a little." Rose blushed, scratching the back of her head. "Though I have to admit even to me such years aren't nearly as length-full as those of the great Council Elders."

Adam looked over at Rose and said dryly, "Let me guess, they're like, a billion and a half right?"

"You could say that." She nodded.

He put his face back in his hands.

Lisa's cell phone began to ring and she answered, "Hello?"

Rose tilted her head, watching Lisa talk into this strange black square. Lisa almost laughed, Rose looked so funny.

"Yeah . . . tonight? I'll ask them . . . Alright, we'll call you back. See ya." She hung up.

"Who was that?" Decker asked?

"Joe. He wants to know if we wanna go galactic tonight."

"Cool! I've been wanting to go galactic for forever." Adam said.

"What is this galactic you speak about Lisa? Is it a form of space travel? My goodness, have your people advanced to that level already?" Rose asked.

"It's bowling." Adam told her.

"Yeah, it's just a game." Decker said.

"A game?" She looked down at the handheld game in her hands. "Interesting. May I join you all?"

"Of course." Lisa smiled. "Two of our other friends will be there too, so it should be a fun time."

Rose smiled, excited to go now.

Decker asked Adam if he could borrow his phone so he could let his mom know that he was going to be home late tonight.

"So must we travel to the . . . what was it again? Oh! The "mall" and purchase this game in which you call galactic?"

Lisa laughed. Trying to explain the simplest things to Rose was like trying to explain the purpose of human behavior to a dog. Sometimes Lisa forgot that Rose was actually an alien from space. You really wouldn't know it just by looking at her.

"No, we go to the bowling alley to play bowling not the mall. I'll show you when we get there—"

Lisa heard Decker raising his voice over by where he and Adam were standing. He was holding the phone a few inches away from his ear like someone was screaming into it.

"Alright mom I got it . . . No I don't have homework, it's Friday . . . No it's not that cold out I'll be fine . . . Yeah well you can forget it cause he's not my responsibility!" He clicked a button on the phone to end the call and handed it back to Adam.

"Everything alright Decker?" Lisa asked him.

"Yeah it's just my mom having another freak out. She wanted me to stay home tonight to watch my step brother while she goes out to a friend's house."

"Dude what if she locks you out of the house again?" Adam asked, remembering how Decker had to crash at his place a few weeks ago because his mom kicked him out for not taking out the trash.

"Then I'll climb through the window." Decker said like he didn't have any other choice.

Lisa wished Decker could stay at her house whenever he wanted but her parents would never go for that. Besides, her house wasn't big at all so there would be nowhere for him to sleep. Except her bed . . . but Lisa knew better than to ask her parents about that.

"Well, we gonna bowl or what?" Adam asked.

"We're bowling." Decker confirmed, knowing he wasn't about to be stuck at home on a Friday night.

CHAPTER 15

It was around nine thirty when Joe came by to pick them up. Lisa introduced a shy Rose to their other two friends Alexandria and Marie.

Joe took an immediate liking to Rose, but then, Joe liked everybody. He was just that social, outgoing kind of guy.

Marie was probably more outgoing than Joe, so when Rose finally squeaked out a "hi . . ." after Marie had just introduced herself personally to her with a wave to the back seat, Marie laughed. "You are so adorable!"

Rose gave a half smile.

Alex didn't say anything, but she hardly ever did. She was more of an observer, liked to get used to everyone around her before letting her real personality show. Lisa understands why. When her and Alex were in middle school, they were constantly picked on. Whether it was because of their interest in Japanese anime, which of course was considered something only "geeks" would like, or because they just didn't talk much, Lisa couldn't say. But Alex let it all go in one ear and out the other, while Lisa would get pretty upset by the teasing. She always thought that out of the two of them, Alex was the bravest, and the smartest. She wouldn't just ignore the bullies, she would shoot clever comebacks at them.

Being judged was a fear they both shared, though Alex is probably better at dealing with judgment than Lisa is. Looking

back now, Lisa wonders what judgment both Alex and Marie
gave her when Lisa started hanging out with only Decker in the
beginning years of their relationship. Not once did Lisa think she
was hurting their feelings when she would tell them she would be
hanging out with Decker for the day, for the week. Not once did
she think about how it would affect their friendship. She's just
happy they've forgiven her for it.

"So Rose, you like it around here so far?" Joe asked, looking in his
rearview mirror.

Rose nodded shyly. "It's nice."

"Aww she's so shy! You remind me of my little sister." Marie said.
It might be that Lisa is already used to being around Rose to really
notice, but she probably looks way younger than the rest of them.
Yeah, if they only knew!

"So," Marie's head popped up from behind the seat in front
of them. "Where're you from Rose?"

Lisa felt like a cold ball of ice dropped into her stomach. She
looked at Decker, who thankfully started talking about a new
video game coming out, and Rose listened in, making it look like
she didn't hear Marie's question. Then Lisa had to think quickly
because Marie suddenly looked to her like she was going to answer
for Rose. *Uhhhhhhhh—*

"Japan! Yeah, right Rose? Japan?"

Rose was frozen, probably not knowing what Japan even was.

Lisa mentally face palmed herself.

"Are you serious?" Marie asked in disbelief.

Lisa held her breath.

"That's so awesome!"

She sighed in relief.

When they finally got to the bowling alley, Rose stepped out of the
car and stared wide eyed at the place as though she were a kid in
Disney world. Lisa almost laughed at her excitement.

"This is the bowling alley?" She asked getting out of the car.

"Yep. We come here at night because that's when galactic starts. They play music and there's disco lights and . . ." Lisa noticed Rose giving her a really confused look and just said, "Well you'll see."

They walked in and were met with the blasting base of the music and the sounds of bowling balls crashing into pins and lots of people talking.

If it weren't for all the different colored lights the place would be pitch dark. There were people everywhere, mostly teens probably around their age. Food and drinks on every table. The computer screens that hung from the ceiling above every lane showed the music video to whatever song they were playing.

Adam threw his arm around Rose's shoulder. "Bet you guys don't have places like this up there in space."

The guys led Rose ahead to the front desk while Lisa hung back with the girls.

"So she's new huh?" Marie asked.

"Yeah . . ."

The guys were now staring at Rose and Lisa guessed it was because she didn't know what to answer for her shoe size. Decker lifted her up so Adam could take off a shoe to find out.

"From Japan." Lisa turned back to their conversation.

"Duh we got that already. What I want to know is why we haven't seen her around school. Did she start her enrollment yet?"

"You haven't seen her?" Lisa asked.

"No. We didn't know who she was until you introduced her in the car."

Decker was now bending down to tie up Rose's shoes for her. She laughed with the guys at whatever it was Joe was telling them.

"Something wrong Lisa?" Alex asked.

No, but she had to remember to ask Rose later about the school thing. How could they not have seen her? She's been going to Norse High for almost three months now.

"Lisa!" Rose came running up to them. "What do you think of my *awesome* new shoes? They are awesome are they not?"

The guys came walking up then and Lisa grinned, "You taught her awesome?"

"Yeah! Awesome is *awesome*." Adam beamed.

Lisa rolled her eyes but smiled at the way Rose was sliding across the floor in her bowling shoes.

Decker and Adam started tabbing in their names on the computer board when they got to their table. Rose was still looking around in fascination at the different lights, and at the way the colors danced on her white sweatshirt.

"This place reminds me so much of the dark nebula my father once took me to."

Lisa froze. She looked at the girls and sighed with relief when she saw that they were more focused on deciding with the guys on who would bowl first.

The list went by Adam, Decker, Lisa, Rose, Alex, Marie and Joe.

Everyone laughed when Adam went up to take his turn and hit only one pin. He slumped his shoulders and went back to his seat.

Decker got a strike, and Lisa gave him a smile. He went over to her and decided to give her a kiss rather than a smile, a deep kiss that left her a little dizzy and she almost didn't hear Marie say, "You're turn Lisa."

She didn't get a strike, but she knocked a few pins down, getting a cheer from the girls and a smile from Decker.

After her second bowl she went back to her seat and said to Rose, "It's your turn now."

Rose looked at the computer screen where it had her name highlighted in red, then at everyone else. She got up shakily and looked to Lisa, who smiled encouragingly. But Rose asked nervously, "What is it that I am supposed to do again?"

"They don't have bowling alleys over there in Japan?" Marie whispered to Alex, who just shrugged.

Lisa stood up to show her. She handed Rose the lightest ball to start with and instructed, "Just roll the ball down the lane and try to hit those pins. It's easy."

Rose nodded and focused all her attention on the pins. She was about to use both hands but decided on using just one and swung her arm back lightly. Rather than rolling the ball underhand, she released it with a pull back of her wrist.

The ball flew down the lane and hit every pin. A perfect strike. Lisa gasped. Decker and Adam looked at each other with open mouths, and the girls cheered from behind.

"Way to go Rose!" Marie yelled.

The guys were still gaping. Rose turned around to walk back and looked at Lisa. She gave her a thumbs-up and Rose started to smile, guessing that she had done a good job.

"I did it?" She asked coming back to her seat.

"You did." Lisa said.

A half hour had already passed, though nobody was really paying attention to time. The game turned from "simple" bowling to a hard core challenge between Rose and the guys, who were determined to beat her. Lisa, Alex and Marie cheered when she made another strike. Her fifth one in a row.

The guy's already looked beaten, but Adam still felt strong-minded.

He made his way up to the lane with his bowling ball and after some seconds of concentration, he finally got a strike.

"Ha! You mad?" He did a little dance back to his seat.

"You wish, you geek." Decker nudged him on his way up to take his turn. Adam was still laughing. Lisa was too at the way the guys suddenly turned their competitive attention on each other, seeing as they weren't likely to defeat Rose.

Decker ended up hitting all the pins in the middle leaving two on both ends.

Concentrating hard he took a step back only to take a fast step forward and throw the ball into a curve. It hit only one pin.

"You failed! Ha!" Adam said.

"Shut up." He tried to look serious but ended up grinning and walked back to slouch in his seat.

Lisa took her turn quickly so she could let the guys get their chances to show off their supposed "skills" some more, seeing as how Decker was tapping his foot impatiently waiting for his turn again.

It was Rose's turn next and Adam was saying, "There she goes. Man, she's kicking our butts!"

"Well what did you expect?" Decker said.

Lisa looked toward him with concern but he gave her reassuring eyes and said, "Beginners luck right?"

She sighed in relief.

"Man that's no beginners luck." Joe sat back in his seat in defeat, knowing he wasn't winning this game like a planned to.

"Lisa! Watch this one!" Rose waved from the lane, nearly dropping her ball but catching it just in time.

Lisa smiled. She felt Decker come up behind her and lay his hands on her shoulders.

"Are we gonna have enough time to go back to your house later?" He grinned against her cheek. She turned to meet his kiss and that painful ache came back to stab her in the chest. They only had until the end of this year . . . then Decker would leave. How could she have forgotten about that? Guilt gave her a knot in her throat. He pulled away to ask her, "What's wrong love?"

She knew he would ask. They were connected in that way, that strange way where one couldn't be without the other. Where one knew what the other was feeling. One day apart could feel like months, and a week like years. How will it be when they are no longer a block apart, but a state? It won't take long for a black emptiness to spread through her. She will try to hide it from her parents, and her friends. Looking over at Alex and Marie, another knot of guilt clogged in her throat and almost made her choke. She won't see then as often, and they will try to get her out, try to convince her that she can't live a life indoors and away from everybody. But she won't be living indoors at all. She just won't be living. And they'll think she's being overdramatic and probably shun her. She would understand. Mom would know that something is wrong, but she won't ask. At least there is that one ray of light. Lisa could always count on her mom for support, and maybe, eventually, Lisa will slowly come out of that darkness . . .

"isa . . . Lisa." She blinked. Decker was holding her face in his hands. "Lisa, I said are you ok?"

She nodded.

He sighed. "My love, I don't want you thinking about it so much. I promise you that I'll come back." He leaned down and kissed her lips. "That's a promise I intend to keep."

"I know." She felt a little silly now dwelling on it. Maybe she really was being overdramatic.

Rose had her ball held up to her face with determination. She swung her arm back and the ball went rolling down the lane with unbelievable speed. Another strike.

The girls cheered and the guys clapped, Joe was smiling but shaking his head. "This girl is something else, man." He mumbled.

Rose was trying to mimic Adam's little dance back to her seat but stopped when her hand suddenly came up and knocked her glasses of her face.

She froze in her spot.

Everyone looked at each other and Lisa called from her seat, "You ok Rose?"

Rose didn't answer. Lisa was about to ask again when suddenly they heard screams coming from someone two lanes down from them. Everyone in the bowling alley stopped dancing and laughing just to see what was going on. Lisa paled when she saw a man convulsing violently on the floor.

"Nine one one! Nine one one!" Someone called out hysterically. Another person yelled. "Somebody help him!"

The man twisted and gasped on the floor, his hands grabbing hold of his hair and scratching at his face. He was sobbing and screaming and it all sounded garbled in his clenched throat.

"Someone help!" The lady next to him screamed.

A moment later, the managers came running towards the scene with a police officer right behind them. The officer yelled into his walkie-talkie to get an ambulance at once.

Rose staggered to grab up her glasses from the floor and ran back towards the group, huddling behind Lisa and trying to put her glasses back on shakily.

It took another twenty minutes for an ambulance to arrive.

The music went off and all the lights changed back to white. More officers arrived and started ushering everyone away from the scene.

"C'mon let's get out of here." Decker grabbed hold of Lisa's hand and led them all out of the crowded bowling alley to the parking lot. Lisa felt Rose grip her arm and she was going to turn and tell her it was going to be ok but decided not to, seeing as how Rose looked absolutely petrified. She'll tell her once they were in the car.

"What the hell just happened?" Joe asked.

"That guy was having a seizure dude, that's what happened." Adam said obviously.

"I know that Adam." Joe said hotly.

"Alright guys cool it." Marie said.

"Yeah, maybe we should get out of here and head home." Alex said.

The paramedics wheeled the guy out on a gurney while the police separated the crowds to give them room. The guy wasn't convulsing now, but he was moaning and pulling at his hair. One of the paramedics tried to restrain his arms.

They all walked back to the car and Lisa had Rose get in first so she could be near the window, figuring she might need some air during the ride back. Lisa got in next to her and asked, "You alright Rose?"

Rose nodded but didn't look at her.

The girls got in the front. Marie turned around in her seat.

"Hey it's ok." She soothed. "Don't be scared, everything's ok now."

Rose swallowed hard but nodded. They all watched the emergency paramedic truck leave with its sirens blaring.

It was quiet in the car on the way home. Lisa was holding Rose under her arm like a frightened child, which she was in a way. Joe decided to turn the radio on but keep it at low volume.

"Yo that was inane." Adam exclaimed. "I mean I just look over and there's a guy on the floor having a seizure."

"Maybe it was from the flashing lights." Decker said and added, "That can happen you know, to people who have epilepsy."

Everyone nodded thinking that was the likely cause.

"I never saw something that crazy in all my life, like . . . damn." Adam said, leaning his head back against the seat.

Everyone was quiet the rest of the way, probably wanting to just put it all out of mind.

Lisa, Rose, Adam and Decker were dropped off at Lisa's house. The back window rolled down and Alex said to Lisa, "I'll text you."

"Yeah." She waved as the car drove off.

Lisa looked over at Rose and saw that she was still shaking a little.

"You sure you're ok?" Decker asked her then.

Rose crouched down slowly and sat on the concrete sidewalk.

The three of them crouched down with her and looked at her with concern.

"Rose?" Lisa asked softly. She was really shaken up. Maybe she's just not used to seeing something like that. Then again, none of them were really.

Suddenly Rose pulled her knees to her chest and started sobbing. Lisa put her hand on her shoulder, more concerned now. "Rose, what's wro—"

"It was me . . ." She said on a sob.

They were all looking at her confused and then Rose choked out another gasp.

"I did it." She cried.

CHAPTER 16

"Slow down Rose, take it easy." Adam soothed while Lisa rubbed her back. The poor girl was so upset she was gasping for breath. Lisa moved some of her hair off her wet face.

"He saw me . . . He saw me!" She sobbed.

"What do you mean he saw you?" Decker asked.

"He saw!" She cried, sniffing and gasping.

Lisa looked at the boys knowing this wasn't going to be easy with her so upset like this. And they had to get her somewhere more private, Lisa thought, seeing that some of the neighbors were outside on their front porches now, probably trying to get a smoke or talk with the other neighbors. Too many people around.

"Let's go to the field." Lisa said, grabbing Rose's hand and lifting her up off the ground.

"Good idea." Decker agreed.

They all walked down the end of the street where there was a gate that separated the field to the community. There was a large hole in the fence on one side and they slipped through.

They settled down over on the benches and Rose accepted a tissue Lisa pulled out of her bag.

"So what were you saying? He saw you?" Adam asked.

Rose sniffed and dropped her head in shame and embarrassment.

"The man in the bowling alley saw me. He saw my eyes." She said in between sobs. She blew again into her tissue.

"You're eyes?" Lisa asked, confused.

Rose nodded and sniffed.

"These glasses shield away the color of my eyes from humans. Father told me to keep them on at all times while I was down here on Earth. He told me it was crucial that I not take them off while around any humans." She looked to Lisa for another tissue and Lisa searched her bag and handed one to her.

Rose nodded thanks and continued. "You see, humans have a spectrum of colors that they are used to seeing every day. Light casts off like a mirror here on earth to reflect those colors. Red, blue, green, yellow, orange, purple, black. You see these colors every day."

Rose lifted a finger to trace the outer rim of her round glasses. "But my people do not see just these colors. We see many, many different colors that humans cannot see. Our spectrum of light changes."

Lisa and the guys were silent, trying to absorb this information. "So you have different colored eyes?" Adam asked, understanding dawning.

Rose leaned away as if she feared he might try to see for himself. "Yes. It is a color you have never seen before. That man witnessed something his mind could not understand. His brain knew it was a color, but as it was trying to remember what kind of color it was, his memory neurons collapsed."

Rose let more tears fall down her face before she said almost in a murmur, "He may never recuperate."

That sent a chill down Lisa's back. What exactly will his life be like now? Will he always think of what it was he saw, and will he continue to have convulsing episodes like that? Will his brain ever adapt? But it wasn't Rose's fault. It was a complete accident.

"You didn't do it on purpose." Decker said before Lisa could. Adam added, "Yeah, it's not like you knew your glasses were gonna fly off like that."

"But I was careless. I should have been more aware. I
should've—"

"You didn't know." Lisa said.

"That's no excuse . . ." She sobbed again.

"Rose, listen, things happen. Accidents. Sometimes you can't
control it and there's no use dwelling on it."

Rose looked at her now.

"You didn't know it would happen, and you can't go back in time
to change it. So there's no use blaming yourself."

Lisa couldn't stand it, seeing her like this. Rose was usually so
bubbly and happy.

Adam decided to add in with a grin. "What, you're
supposed to be on guard with everything all the time and not be
yourself?"

Rose looked back down at the ground but she seemed to have
calmed down a bit.

"So, the glasses show off a different color to us. Then your eyes
aren't really hazel." Decker said.

Rose nodded. "My irises do indeed contain a small amount of the
color hazel. The glasses simply enhance this color to cover the rest,
so you are only seeing this one color."

"Weird." Adam said.

"I think it's pretty cool." Lisa smiled. "And clever."

Rose smiled, still sniffing.

"You know, it is the weekend. We can stay out late tonight."
Decker mentioned.

So they stayed at the field for the next few hours, almost into the
very early morning, asking strange questions and receiving even
stranger answers. Rose even asked a few questions herself.

"And how is it that you capture these evil villains, but then release
them later? Do you not fear that they will continue their crimes?"

Decker was the first to jump onto that one. "Yeah well our justice
system is so messed up that we can't even give you a good answer

on why that is. It pisses me off so much, like how are you gonna let a guy out of jail after he killed people? Does that make any sense?"

"Well you gotta think that these people might not do those crimes again after they get out. I mean, everyone deserves a second chance right?"

"A second chance for what? To kill more people?"

"I'm not saying that dude. All I'm saying is that people go to jail for a lot of reasons and what if it was like, someone who killed someone else out of self-defense?"

Decker threw his arms in the air and gave up then, seeing as how he wasn't winning this argument with Adam.

"You know, that might've been the first question you really asked us in a while." Lisa said to Rose.

She shrugged. "I suppose it is."

"But why? You don't have any other questions for us like about Earth or our lives or anything?"

Rose told them before that the deal was she would answer any of their questions so long as they answered hers, but they haven't heard Rose really ask a lot of questions.

Rose smiled. "I receive many answers just by being around the three of you. The way you communicate amongst others, and each other. Your curiosity, opinions, predictions . . . I have analyzed it all."

"So wait, you only hang around with us to analyze us?"

She chuckled. "Oh goodness you humans take offense to everything don't you? No, no Adam. I am merely saying that I do not need to ask so many questions when *your* questions give me all the answers I need."

"Right . . . guess that makes sense, I think . . ."

"Don't pull a brain muscle now Adam." Decker joked.

"Shut up dude."

Lisa saw that Rose was getting back to her bubbly self. This definitely was an experience she probably wouldn't forget, and neither would they. So there are more colors out there that they still don't know about . . .

Rose was twirling her necklace around her fingers as she listened to Decker and Adam talk. That brought up a question in Lisa's mind.

"Hey, I know I might be getting off topic here but I forgot to ask you before."

Rose tilted her head up at Lisa.

"I wanted to ask where you got that necklace from. It's beautiful." Rose looked down at her black pendant and smiled softly. She took hold of it in her palm and held it to her chest.

"This is my special treasure. Cornelius gave it to me."

"Your boyfriend?" Adam asked.

Rose blushed. "Yes, my betrothed."

She looked up into the night sky, lit by the full moon and millions of tiny stars.

"How I miss him. We have never been apart for so long. Every time I look at this necklace, I think of him, and the first time he gave it to me . . ."

I was very young, and my father toured me through the Council's ship to show me everything, all his creations. He got permission from the Elders only because they favored my father. The Secret Weapons room, the Prison walls, the Gift Ships and Tracer ships, the energy fuel pods, and even the furniture for the Elder's Hall were all crafted from my father's hands. I was impressed greatly.

Then my father received a call to join the Elders in the Control Room. They had spotted something.

I followed behind him quickly. He kneeled down and ruffled my hair, telling me to stay behind the glass door while he spoke with the others. The door closed but I could still see everything that was going on in that other room. My telepathic skills were weak at the time, so I could not hear what they were saying. But as I searched

around the room I noticed an air vent just above the book shelf.
I fell clumsily the first time, but quickly got myself together and
made it up onto the shelf, and I listened closely . . .

"We made contact, sir. They are not hostile."

"Good. Then let us see what we can do, shall we?" The men
nodded and left the room.

The door opened and I nearly took a terrible plunge to the floor,
but father caught me just in time.

I smiled but the guilt was written all over my face.

He lowered me down and said to me, "I need you to wait here for
me to return."

I frowned. "Is something wrong father?"

He grinned and shook his head. "Not at all, my dearest one. Just
some business that needs to be taken care of."

He lifted me up onto the large seat in front of the control panel.
I leaned up against the glass and looked out across the barren
non-planet the ship was sitting on. It was huge, like a normal
planet, only there was nothing there, just craters. I saw the
beautiful colors clusters of stars were making in the sky. It was like
watching a dance. They swirled and waved and changed shades.
The blackness of the universe was no longer black. Dust star
clusters formed and moved through the sky in all different ways.
I was entranced. So entranced that I hardly heard the door close
behind me. Father had left, and as I looked out again I could see
he was following the Elders behind as they walked off the ship and
onto the planet.

They met with a small group of beings who were holding each
other closely. They looked to be frightened.

The beings bowed their heads in respect to the Elders as they
neared.

Looking at the group my eyes immediately spotted a young
boy. He looked to be my age. For some reason I couldn't take
my gaze away from him. Unlike the rest of his group, who had
short . . . well I perhaps could not tell you the color I saw but he

did not possess it, rather, he had black hair, and it waved down to the nape of his neck.

They talked for a really long time. Father handed one of the Elders a transporting glove to summon a small Gift Ship off of the Council Ship. The orange glove burst into a bright flame that encircled up the Elder's arm and with a forceful tightening of his fist the Council Ship opened up to reveal a newly designed Gift Ship, a model my father had just recently created for safer travel.

The crowd of huddling beings straightened and stared at this magnificent craft. Confused, but relieved. Then when the Elder removed the glove from his wrinkled hand and presented the ship to the beings they cheered and bowed. The boy was smiling too. He had a really nice smile.

The ship would provide the beings with everything they needed to survive out in the never-ending universe. Eventually they would have to have their own planet to live on, but the Gift ship was better than living on a desolate non-planet.

I was happy for them, but a part of me was sad too. I didn't know why at the time, but now I know it was because I didn't get the chance to even talk to that boy . . ."

"Then you guys met somewhere else?" Adam asked.

Rose shook her head, a blush still on her face.

"The High Council decided to continue wandering around that part of the universe, to see if there were other Drifters also in need. I was glad we didn't leave. Every time I woke up from my sleep, I would beg my father to lift me up onto the big chair, so I could see outside. He would smile and take me to the control room. I loved looking at the outside. It was so beautiful and I sometimes wouldn't even leave the room. Father told me he would find me there asleep against the window.

Sometime later, the Council received a visit from the small ship they recently gave away.

Three people from the Drifter group boarded the Council ship to give the Elders their thanks for all that they had done for them. Giving them the ship was like a miracle for them, because now they no longer had to wonder if their home was really out there, now they could go and find it.

I looked shyly out from behind my father's leg to see the people who had visited. When I saw the boy standing there, my heart must've leapt in my chest, because I felt it suddenly beating faster. I thought it was strange, of course, so I got scared and tugged on my father's sleeve.

"What is it my sweet?"

"My chest feels funny."

He looked confused when I told him this, but then one of the Elders started speaking and that grabbed his attention for the moment.

I looked again at the boy, who was now looking at me. His eyes were of a most beautiful color. One I have only seen perhaps twice in my lifetime. They held mine and my mind felt hazy.

"And this is my son." The man who was standing next to the boy introduced and he put his hand on the boy's shoulder.

"Ah, yes. Another generation to carry the name, well done." One of the Elders commented to the boy's father, who bowed his thanks. The boy bowed his head too, but I noticed his eyes never left mine. It was like staring into . . . I thought of the gifts Father bought for Mother the one time I was very little, he said he crafted them from materials he received from ally aliens.

Diamonds, he called them. That's what I thought I was looking at. Black diamonds. Diamond shards. I don't really know how to describe it, but it was beautiful.

My father had insisted that I show the boy around the Council ship. I was excited that I was finally going to talk to this boy.

I showed him everything, from the prison cells to the Gift ship chamber. I smiled at the look of pure amazement on his face.

"I cannot believe what I am seeing. This is truly remarkable." He said. "And your father made all of this?"

"Yes. All of it. After the Council took us in, my father insisted that he build them an entirely new ship, with new gadgets and ships and communication systems. The Elders really like him."

"As they should, he is a very nice and generous man."

I hope I said something back to him, but now I cannot even remember. All I could think about were his eyes, and how relaxed I felt just standing next to him.

"I must thank him myself when I see him again later. He and the rest of the High Council have helped my people in a way that I cannot express enough gratitude for."

I wanted to ask him about his family, but I didn't know if it would be rude of me. Mother always told me I should never intrude on another person's life, especially if I knew they didn't wish to share anything. But I didn't know then if this boy wanted to share or not. I was overly curious. So I took the risk of asking him anyway.

"So . . . what was it like? Living on that non-planet . . . Was it scary?"

I expected him to tell me to mind my own business and to not worry about it, but instead he smiled down softly at me and said, "Yes, very scary. The non-planet had very little resources available, and the food had shriveled away as quickly as it had grown.

He lowered his head then, staring at the floor with a sad look.

"I was mostly afraid for my mother . . . She was so sick, I did not know if she would make it."

It reminded me of how my family felt when we were living on a non-planet and we didn't think my younger sister would live. It is a terrible feeling. At times when I saw her suffering the most I almost wished that she would . . . pass away. Just so the pain would end. So she wouldn't have to suffer anymore.

"I was born on that non-planet, so for a long time I thought it was our home. My mother eventually told me that it was not our home after all. She told me that our real home was out there somewhere just waiting for us. I didn't really understand at the time, but I reassured her that I wasn't angry or upset." He chuckled. "Actually I was relieved. That non-planet was filthy. We never had enough to eat or drink and one of us would always come down ill. The sky was never lit with stars, just brown dust. When I thought about how our real planet would look it gave me hope. My father told me stories of the High Council, how they were named the "saviors of life," because they rescued Drifters. I asked when it would be our turn to be rescued, but my father never answered me, perhaps because he did not want for me to have high hopes. The Council may be strong, but they travel all over, and the chances of them finding us were slim to none. I dreamed about our real home, our real planet. I imagined how happy and healthy my mother would be."

His words tore at my heart. My eyes became cloudy and I swiped at them annoyingly so I could still see him as he spoke. His look of sadness faded then, replaced with a soft smile.

"When we saw the High Council ship, our hopes flared once again inside us. I could hardly believe that we were finally being saved." He looked down at me and put his hand on my head. His hand was so warm.

"You saved us all." He said.

I wanted to correct him because it was not me who had really saved them, but he bent down and kissed me on my forehead. I was so still I thought I had frozen to ice.

I remember seeing Mother and Father kiss each other before, but I only thought that was something mates did. I didn't really know him too well, so at first I felt a little uncomfortable. But after a while of spending time together, I got more and more used to him being there, like he was meant to be there at my side.

Eventually our time together had come to an end when his mother and father announced their departure. I was sad that he was leaving, because I didn't think I would ever see him again. Before he left, he gave me this pendant.

"My mother's ancestor gave this to me. She told me to gift it to someone I treasured the most."

I couldn't think of what to say as he was putting it around my neck. I lifted it in my hand and noticed it resembled the color of his eyes. Black shards. But then I looked closer at it, and my eyes widened at what I saw. It was the star clusters, the beautiful colors dancing around like they did in the sky. I wanted to ask how it was doing that, but he said, "When you look at it, remember this promise. I *will* see you again, one I care for the most."

He kissed my forehead again. And then he was gone. I grew older and still held onto that promise, never doubting his words.

He returned to me again a few years later . . .

"So what happened with his family? Did they ever find their planet?" Decker asked.

"Actually yes they did. Beautiful place, absolutely gorgeous I must say. It was everything he had ever dreamed of and more. At first I was confused when he announced that he would not be staying there with them . . ."

"Your father has asked permission from the Elders for me to be a part of the High Council." He must've seen the shock on my face because he laughed then and ruffled my hair, the way father always did.

"I knew that would surprise you. Isn't it fantastic?"

"But what about your family, do you not wish to live with them? And your planet . . ."

He silenced me then with a kiss, and this time it was not on my forehead but my lips. I had never known such warmth in all my years of existence. It was intoxicating.

"What I was truly waiting for all those years was not a planet to call my home, only a love that I can share with another, someone that I can call my real home. I am at peace with the knowledge that they will forever be safe and happy. This planet will provide them with anything they need."

"Except you. What will your dear mother think when she learns of her precious son leaving?"

I admit that I was a little mad with him. He was leaving his family, a family that loved him more than anything, just to be a part of the High Council. True this would sound like a glorious achievement for many. After all, not everyone can be in the High Council. It is the Elders that recruit only those who they find useful or acceptable. But then a spark of . . . well I did not know it at the time, but a spark of excitement raced around my heart, and I felt it beat wildly like it had those years ago when I first stared into those eyes of his.

Still, I did not expect him to say, "They understand that I too have to live my life. If we were still living on that non-planet I would never have left, knowing the sickness and sadness that penetrated us even when we were at our greatest would be back again to claim a life. My mother knows this. She has known ever since we saw your Council Ship land down before us."

Those black diamonds glistened, and I couldn't take my gaze away, not even to hide the red that I could feel was staining my cheeks.

He stared back into mine and I could see the strong will he possessed, his determination to keep us together and to always be by my side. But then that made me think of more serious matters. Beings do not separate from their own group to mate with other beings of a different species. One could not bring the other back to their home planet without the fear of rejection and rebellion. Those born from different species of parents will have to be categorized into a different group, and the Council would have to be notified of the birth immediately to make changes to the system. And those children would not be allowed to breed, because then their mixed genes will continue down the line. Conflict would arise if I were to ever bring children into this universe, and I could not bear to deny them of anything, especially their freedom and pride.

But the decision was made, and we have decided there on to continue our relationship without the regard of other's opinions. Though I may never be able to produce children, at least I could spend the rest of my life with the one I loved. My father of course was in complete denial at first, but after realizing how much Cornelius cared for me, he gave in. Eventually he had come to accept Cornelius like his own son, despite some complaints from other Council members. What surprised us the most was how all the Elders willingly accepted our coupling . . .

"So your boyfriend is a member of the High Council?" Adam asked.
"In a way, yes. But he is more of a soldier rather than a member who attends frequent meetings like my father. He does have incredible skill and strength in combat, which is what I believe, is the reason for the Elder's quick acceptance."

"Hey, how come *you* don't wear any of the necklaces I buy you?" Decker leaned down to ask Lisa, a grin on his face.
"I'm just afraid of something happening to them. What if one of those chains accidently breaks off without me knowing it?"
"Then I'll have to get you one you can wear all the time." He nuzzled her cheek.
"Decker. Another time, love." She warned, feeling a blush creep into her face.
"Yeah, really, before I loose my lunch." Adam said and Decker gave him a scowl. Rose put her hand to her mouth to keep from laughing.
Decker traced a finger down Lisa's neck grinning, "Then again, sometimes it's better to have nothing on at all."
"Decker!" She protested.

"Dude seriously?" Adam complained.

"Jealous?" Decker teased.

"Yeah man! I need a girlfriend . . ." He pouted. "This sucks."

"Do not fret Adam, perhaps one day you too will find a lovely woman to nuzzle and say romantic things to." Rose smiled.

"Hopefully you won't be walking with a cane by the time it happens either." Decker teased.

Adam scowled. "Shut up dude."

CHAPTER 17

The boys came over early the next day. So did Rose. It looked like it was going to rain and thunder, with the way the dark clouds swirled and the breeze picked up. Lisa didn't want to bug her parents with asking if they could all hang inside, so she threw on her shoes and ran out the door.

When she stepped outside, she immediately noticed Rose dressed in her own fashionable style of clothing. She was wearing a long sleeved blue and black striped top with a v-neck, and dark blue jeans with cuts that zigzagged down the knees. The rims of her glasses were a dark blue to match her jacket with beautifully drawn white flowers stretching back to the earpieces, and the large black pendant that hung on a dark blue chain.

Lisa was almost jealous she couldn't be that fashionable. They started to walk down the right end street to the town homes. For some odd reason Rose didn't look like her bubbly self today. Actually she looked kind of down.

"So dude, how about next time I stop over, you lock Thunder up in the closet or something, man."
"Thunder?" Rose looked up to Adam.
He rolled his eyes. "Yeah, Decker's crazy psycho dog from hell."
"Hey man, don't blame me if he sees you as a lean cut steak."
Decker laughed.
"Do I *look* like a steak dude?!"

Lisa was shaking her head.

They were almost toward the end of the street when they saw a group of young boys playing basketball. Lisa recognized two of her little brother's friends out of the six of them.

"Hey check it out man, the pipsqueak crew." Adam nudged Decker. This was sort of a thing whenever they passed a group of kids. Adam would always be the one to mess around with them, not in a bullying way, just in a big brother kind of way. Lisa assumed it was because Adam didn't have any siblings.

"Yo why aren't you home doing your homework boy?" Adam said to one of the smaller kids they knew.

Lisa sighed.

"You got school tomorrow son. Ha!"

Yeah Adam *was* laughing until the kid jumped onto his back and put him in a headlock. Lisa's mouth dropped open and she heard Rose gasp beside her. Decker burst into laughter next to them . . .

"See what happens when you try to be big and bad Adam?" He was laughing so hard now he was kneeling over.

"Dude! Help me out here!" Adam was running in circles trying to pry the kid off his back. But Decker was laughing too hard to even hear him.

"Oh dear, is he going to be alright?" Rose asked her.

"Don't worry, he'll live." Lisa said trying to stifle a laugh herself.

They continued their walk when Adam finally got his head back and made a run for it. Decker was still laughing at him when they rounded the next corner past the school.

"Yo, that kid's benching one sixty dude." Adam said, rolling his one shoulder to get out the kinks.

"You know I'm never gonna let you forget this!" Decker said when he got control over his laughing.

Adam rolled his eyes.

"Hey man, that kid is probably stronger than both of us. Well, *you* anyway." Decker taunted.

"Uh, no, I think you mean *you*."

"Do they always argue like this?" Rose asked Lisa while the guys went at each other with insults.

Lisa chuckled. "They're just messing around, but yeah, they always do this."

They walked for another hour before heading towards the field where they sat in their usual spot over by the front benches. Surprisingly it didn't rain at all, even though the sky was still dark. The sun could be seen from behind the clouds as just a ball of grey light, and it was still breezy out. Lisa didn't mind this kind of weather when it wasn't too cold or too hot.

"So . . . other than you giving that guy a seizure and all, did you like bowling—ooff!"

Adam scowled at Decker when he jabbed him in the rib.

Lisa mentally face palmed herself for Adam being such a goof as to bring up *that* at a time like this. She looked at Rose, who instead of frowning, was actually smiling.

"Yes, I enjoyed the bowling with you all last night. It was fun, indeed. Thank you for inviting me."

Lisa was still wondering what it was that was bugging Rose. Something had to be bugging her by the way she twirled her necklace around her finger and stared down at it with a sad look. But what was it?

Decker reached over and ruffled the girl's hair. And Adam gave her a playful push.

"Hey, you don't gotta be thanking us."

"Yeah, it's what we do, you know? How about going to see this movie with us next weekend?" Decker mentioned and Adam asked. "The super hero one?"

"Yeah, I think she'll like it."

Lisa noticed that while the guys were talking, Rose had a weird kind of look in her eyes.

"I can't wait to see it, it's supposed to be really good cause they got new . . . people."

He paused when he looked down and saw Rose's face.

"Rose? You alright?" Adam asked.

Rose looked up with that soft smile of hers and said, "You truly are the best of friends. I couldn't ask for anything more." That caught Lisa off guard for a second, only because she had a feeling something not-so-good was going to come up next.

"I feel that I have become so close to you all . . . it's almost as if I have always known you, even though we only met just recently." It was uncomfortably silent. Lisa was wondering if maybe Rose still felt bad about what happened back at the bowling alley. She seemed alright a few minutes ago.

"I just hope that you will always want to be my friends . . ."

Lisa saw that the guys were as confused as she was. What was Rose saying? Of course they would still be her friends, why wouldn't they?

"Ok, is this some type of alien "thank you" or something? Cause down here on Earth, when someone starts talking like that it usually means something's up. Is something up?" Adam asked her with concern.

Rose shrugged. "I guess I am a little troubled."

"Yeah we can see that." Decker said.

Then Rose stood up and announced, "I have something else I wish to share with you all. I believe it is important that you know. It is your right to . . ."

A shiver went up Lisa's spine. Whatever it was Rose had to say, it didn't sound good . . .

CHAPTER 18

Rose took a deep breath in before beginning . . .

They were all standing now, the tension too much to be sitting for. Adam had his hands in his pockets and Decker folded his arms, ready for whatever it was they were about to hear. Lisa wasn't so ready herself. Actually for some reason she felt afraid.

"As I have explained before, the High Council collects and creates data about every planet and every alien species they come into contact with, in order to maintain peace and build onto their society."

She paused for a moment, then continued.

"I have also explained that every species in the universe has a home planet somewhere, whether it be ten billion light years away or farther, ever species has one. Why this is, we do not know. But my father made it his mission in life to help other Drifters in need. Joining the High Council gave him an opportunity like none he would ever see in all his life."

She paused again, then asked, "Do you remember the story I told you all about my first flying lessons?"

They nodded.

"And the many answers I gave you when you asked about your planet Earth?"

They looked at each other, but nodded.

"It was many years ago, almost a year after the Council took us in, that the High Council spotted a strange planet while they were making their usual trips around the Warm Galaxy, the galaxy which holds some of the Drifter peoples that they have helped in the past. The people provide the Council with minerals and some of the finest stone material in gratefulness for the Council's help. The strange planet they found orbited around a large mass of heat that the Council had before dismissed because no life could ever survive on such a non-planet.

My father was the one who took notice of this planet, and proposed they send for data to be collected. The Elders were very curious as to what sort of planet this was, so they sent out special drones to collect any kind of data they could. The process took about six days.

Only the High Council's special military teams are allowed to go out on recon missions, to investigate unknown planets, in case the environment may be poisonous in some way. They normally wear protective suits for safety. But one person had sent their own team to inspect the planet, without the High Council's permission . . ."

$\mathcal{M}$arius was taken aside by one of the High Elders and was told about the situation. He was both outraged and terrified. Never in all of time would he believe his comrade, his one true friend, would be so bold as to go against the High Council. Truly the man had to be mad! Marius went to confront him immediately for his recklessness, but a meeting was called just then, so he had no choice but to wait until later.

After the meeting, it was his friend that pulled him aside to talk. Marius was still fuming after sitting through an entire meeting, all the while shooting warning daggers at his friend as he sat on the other side of the seating rows. Now here he was. And Marius was more than ready to speak his mind.

"This is it Marius! I have finally found it. I have finally found my home!"

Marius grabbed a hold of his friend's shoulders and said, "This is madness, do you know what would happen if the Council knew you had gone behind their backs?"

"Hear me, friend. There is edible vegetation, the air is tantalizingly fresh and clean, the minerals in the ground soothing and rich! The system matches our physiological needs exactly, perfectly. Don't you see? This is my planet. This is what my people have been searching for all these years! A miracle is it not?"

Marius was so full of confusion he did not know where he wanted to begin, so he said, almost pleading, "My good friend, whom I have known for so long and cared for like the brother I never had, please hear my words. What you have done is strictly forbidden."

"Do you not believe me?"

"I do! Truly, friend, I do."

"Than speak of my findings! Tell the High Council Elders of my amazing discovery so that I may announce to my people that we have found a place to live."

Marius saw the look in Hadrian's eyes, a look of courage and self will, of determination. But Hadrian saw the hesitation in Marius's eyes, and he said more seriously, "Or perhaps I should announce it myself."

"No! You will be punished!"

"But it is *my home*! This I am certain of!"

Marius was taken aback at his friend's sudden anger. He never, in all the years he had known him, seen such stubbornness, such boldness. Hadrian truly believed that this planet was his home. How absurd! How senseless! How . . . And what if it was? Could he really deny Hadrian of his own home planet? The only goal that every Drifter in the universe strives to discover?

Marius knew what it was like to live as a Drifter. If not for the High Council he and his family would still be isolated on that dreaded non-planet, and no doubt, his wife and youngest daughter would've surely died. But Hadrian was also an important member of the High Council, though he had never really spoken to Marius about where he and his family had come from exactly. Hadrian is the only one on this ship that could think up the best procedures for tackling a problem. Often his plans were used to figure out how to approach an unknown species of alien or collect data from a discovered planet. Such a brilliant mind. What would make him think up such a foolish idea?

True, the Elders were also very intelligent beings, but Hadrian had a gift. That is why they had chosen him to be a part of the High Council. He could predict almost precise outcomes to every idea, calculate ten billion thoughts and sums all at once. Still, even at the cost of his life, at the cost of his people, he would go against the High Council in such a way?

"Why are you so eager to present this to the Elders? If you are certain this planet belongs to you than why do you not wait for the other families to be scanned—"

"I have waited too long! Much too long, my friend."

Marius was stricken. He was battling so many thoughts as to what he should do.

His friend pleaded to him, "Give me this chance, Marius. Give my people this chance."

Marius was torn. But Hadrian was now facing two very real consequences for his actions. He could be in-prisoned for life, or killed. Though the High Council rarely ever killed, for they thought it a barbaric thing to take away a life for a crime so little, and none of the recon soldiers died from the data collection mission Hadrian had sent them on, so perhaps the Elders will be kind. But Hadrian also searched through the Species Data Base only to compare the planet's data with his own, an action that is absolutely forbidden to even the High Elders without permission. When a new planet is found, every species is scanned with its data and a grand announcement is made to all Drifters in search for their home. Hadrian must have hacked the system secretly . . .

"This Hadrian guy sounds like bad news to me." Adam said.
Rose lowered her eyes, a kind of sadness and disappointment
filling them. "He was never perceived to be a foe in any way. I
had known him and his wife ever since they were brought onto the
Council Ship, and I had seen the look of pure love in his eyes when
he was told by Maria that they were with child. Nobody expected
he would turn against everyone . . .

"*I* have news." Hadrian stood to announce at the next meeting.
Marius froze in his seat, but dared not speak a word.
"This planet we have recently discovered is mine as well as my
families. This I am certain of!"
Whispers and murmurs sounded around the room. All the Elder's
eyes narrowed on the man standing. One of the Elders asked,
suspicion dripping off his lips, "And what makes you so certain of
this Hadrian?"
Father held a clenched fist up to his chin, hoping, praying, his
friend would not be so stupid as to say—
"I have sent my own team to investigate the planet."
Then again, maybe he would . . .
Everyone gasped and whispered in shock to each other on what
they just heard.
Another of the Elder's bent forward to stand up slowly. He rasped
out angrily, "You have acted on a forbidden mission?"
"Please hear me—"
"And you endangered those people!?"
"But I must tell you—"
"Seize this man! Take him out of my sight!"
Guards surrounded and took hold of Hadrian as he struggled to get
free of their tight grasp. "No! Please High Elders hear my words, it
is my planet! It is!"
With a wave of his frail, bony hand, the Elder said, "Take him
away."
"Wait!" Marius yelled from his seat.

Everyone looked towards him now, even the Elders looked over at him.

"This man's mind is clouded. He knows not what he is getting himself into, so desperate is he. I am asking you to listen to what he has to say."

Marius looked to the Elders and bowed his head.

The Elders looked at each other slowly, speaking to each other in their minds, until one of them said, "Very well. Release him."

The guards dropped Hadrian back onto his feet and un-cuffed the hard steel braces from his wrists.

"You may have your time to speak, one who disobeys greatly."

And so Hadrian spoke of what his team found during their mission. He spoke of the luscious landscape, the many different colors, vibrant and free. Bodies of liquid that covered almost the entire planet, its color reflected off the planet's provider, the large mass of heat it orbits. How the planet is uniquely nursed by its heat, for it is what creates the life.

Marius listened with interest as Hadrian told of the different life phases the planet goes through. For a short period of time the temperature is warm and comforting. The vegetation grows quietly from the ground, feeding on the nutritious minerals in the soil. Liquid will fall from its sky's, quenching the land when it is parched. And the growing will continue to grow full and strong. Ooohs and Aaahs sounded around the room as everyone pictured in their minds everything he was saying, as though it were happening right in front of their eyes.

Then, he spoke of how the short period of warmth fades to a cooler climate. The green colors begin to change to other beautiful colors. Red, orange, brown and yellow. Colors limited to our own spectrum of light, but beautiful still.

Then it gets cooler and cooler, until all green dries to a dull pale. The liquid freezes from the dropped temperature, and instead of what had once splashed to the ground, now lightly sprinkles down in white crystals, blanketing the land in a thick covering. And the grey non-planet that sits opposite to the heated one will rise as the heated one falls, and shed its own light down on the land. Though not as bright as the heated one's light, it is just as marvelous, for only then can you witness how the white blanket sparkles in the blue light. It dances. A beautiful scene, truly.

Marius had to admit to himself that he was indeed impressed. It sounded like nothing they had ever seen before. Such wonder and beauty. What else awaits them on this interesting planet?

His words captured much attention, but now Hadrian faces the Council Elders.

All settled to a silence as one Elder stood and raised his frail hand to speak.

Then, to Marius's absolute shock, the Elder said to Hadrian for all to hear, "You say you are certain that this planet is your home. I believe I speak for everyone when I say that a more thorough investigation must be carried out before we take any more action. We have many Drifters without homes in this universe, and a new planet is always a spark of hope. So long as you do not disobey anymore, Hadrian, you will not be punished for your act. However . . . You. Must. Be. Patient. We will scan all Drifters and compare the results to the planet's own data collection. If there is a match, we will discuss all preparations in the next meeting. In the meantime I ask that everyone not get their hopes too high. One's mind can indeed grow clouded in desperation, as Marius has said."

The meeting was dismissed then. Marius made his way over to Hadrian, who was now wrapping his arms around his overjoyed mate and young daughter. She was a beautiful woman, who always saw past the stubborn side of Hadrian and loved him for who he truly was.

A mate was something truly special. Someone who could love and cherish you through good and bad, and forgive or see past all your faults and sins. Marius laughed during the times he and Hadrian would just sit together and talk, meaning to talk about the Council and new developments of any sort, but Hadrian would instead talk of how his mate's eye's entrance him, and how her cute little laugh fills his heart with joy, how her kiss makes his knees weak and his mind a blur.

Marius stopped and decided perhaps now was not the time for conversation, though it would've been more like a scolding than a conversation.

He would give Hadrian time with his mate, and they would talk later . . .

"So he has a daughter?" Lisa asked, surprised.

"Yes." Rose smiled. "Valerie. She is a few years younger than me, but she has the outstanding intelligence of her father, and beauty like her mother. We used to play together many years ago."

Lisa could hear it in Rose's voice that it was a deeply treasured memory. But if a guy like Hadrian could have enough love in his heart to give to a wife and child, then he couldn't be that bad, could he?

"Now I know you got more for us Rose." Decker said, and she nodded. "Indeed. There is much more . . ."

Soon after the discovery of the new planet, another discovery was made. Two strange life forms were found sitting together on a small non-planet just outside the Red Galaxy.

The Council decided to make a quick landing on the non-planet to see if they could communicate with these strange beings.

But after a quick scan the Council was shocked to find out that these beings were the only two on this non-planet. A very rare situation, indeed. Usually Drifters are found in at least a group of ten or twenty, but rarely two or three. The Elders assumed it was because these beings had been living on this non-planet for such a long time that their numbers faded down.

One Council member, who was gifted in many tongues of communication, asked for the beings to come closer to the ship.

But they were frightened and would not move. So the Council member moved toward them.

Eventually the Council member was able to lead the two beings onto the ship. He said that they did not give any hint of a language, and they did not know telepathic communication. So the only way for the Council member to communicate with them was to make body movements. He first waved his hand slowly back and forth in the air, and to his surprise and interest, the beings mimicked the action. Then he opened both his arms out wide, and the beings smiled and moved toward him. He believed that the beings communicated through a combination of body language and emotional expression, and when he opened his arms out to them, they saw that as an inviting welcome.

An Elder stepped down from the ship and walked over to the Councilmen and Drifter beings.

The Council member bowed his head and the two beings mimicked the act. The Elder raised a grey eyebrow. One of the beings looked back and forth from the Elder to the other being, then tried to raise their bushy eyebrow too.

The Elder smiled, quite amused. He pulled a silver glove out of his long robe and slipped it onto his frail hand. The beings looked with fascination at the glove and then at their own hands. The Elder turned and faced the ship, extending his arm out, pulling back the sleeve. The glove sparkled and burst up his arm in a long coating of silver ice, then with a squeeze of his fist, the top of the ship opened up and out rose a Gift Ship.

The two beings moved back when the ship landed in front of them. But then they slowly moved toward it, and one of them ran a hand along the smooth blue metal. The other touched it with a figure and immediately jumped back.

The Council member cleared his throat and said to the Elder, "Sir, forgive my observations but the Drifters do not seem to be of the same intelligence that we are."

The Elder stroked his long grey beard. "You do not believe they have the capabilities of flying a Gift Ship?"

The Council member shook his head. "I do not believe they possess any kind of abilities sir."

This would indeed be a problem then. Never before had the Council encountered such a primitive species.

"Do you think they are still in early stages of development?" The Elder asked.

The Council member shook his head again with a sigh. "I do not know, sir. This seems to be an entirely new species."

They were stranded with two options. Leave the beings here on this non-planet where they will surely die, or . . .

"May I be so bold as to propose an idea?" Marius approached them from the ship.

He bowed his head to the Elder and the Elder said to him, "You may."

"Could we not bring the two beings with us on the Council ship?" Both the Elder's grey eyebrows rose and the Council member next to him stammered out, "That is much too bold a question to ask Marius, much too bold! We do not know anything about these Drifters and you wish for us to take them into our company?"

"Don't you see? It is because we do not know anything about them that the opportunity couldn't be greater. Here is a species we know nothing about, and now we get the chance to learn from them. Wise Elder," He bowed again. "I will take all responsibility in caring for the beings."

The Elder stroked his beard, thinking. His Council member beside him still questioned Marius about his proposal. Then the Elder said, "Very well, Marius. You have my trust."

As time passed, so did the hope of finding the family of the two strange beings. It was becoming clear to Marius, as he studied the beings endlessly and with the granted permission of the Elders, searched through the database for any similar connections to a planet or another species, that wherever they came from, it had not been close by.

One of the elders spotted Marius near the planet control station, still searching through every planet they had ever met. He also sent out messages to ally planets and Drifter ships to see if anyone was missing two members of their family. When he turned to find one of the Elders enter the room, he immediately bowed his head in respect.

"I know you wish to help these beings, one whose heart is good, but they cannot live with us forever." Marius thought the Elder sounded sad when he told him this. But he was right. The beings could not live on the Council ship. There were limited resources available as it was, and they still did not know a whole lot about them.

"I do not wish to abandon them." Marius admitted.

"Nor do I. Perhaps we can get another's opinion on what we should do."

A day later, a meeting was called. They were to discuss the situation with the two strange beings.

"Is there no one who suggests an idea for their survival?" One Elder proclaimed.

The room was silent, so silent it took Marius by surprise. The room was never silent. There were always people eager to put their own opinions out on the table, always ready for an argument or a conversation.

"Nobody?" The Elder asked again.

Oh, he knows he should not do this. He thought about Hadrian, and his mate and their little girl. He thought about what Hadrian would think when he hears this . . . But then, the results did not get back yet. They were still scanning all the Drifters. The results may not come back with any matches at all, and if that were the case then perhaps . . .

Marius rose from his seat slowly. All eyes turned toward him now, waiting for whatever he was going to say. Oh, he shouldn't do this . . .

"These are beings we still do not know anything about, and I would love the chance to learn more about them. I would also love to see them survive happily, to create their own world, where there will be more beings like themselves."

Some people looked to each other and nodded.

"Listen well to my words. Could we not give them that world? What if we could provide them with what they needed to begin with, and watch them grow, watch them develop and thrive. Would that not be the greatest experiment? Imagine this, friends. These small life forms will grow in numbers, and we may track their every move. We can aid in their survival, or we could simply watch as they survive on their own." His voice grew with enthusiasm.

"Can you not see it? A world we have helped to create! One we can care for and learn about, and there is much we can learn from these beings. This I am certain of."

More people nodded their heads in agreement and some could be heard yelling, "Yes!"

"Agreed!"

"It might actually work."

Marius continued. "I say we scan the beings and compare them to the planet's data. The new planet we had just recently discovered." He paused, but then continued. "So that we may better know if it is possible. Are you not as curious as I to know more about them? I say an opportunity such as this is something we may never see again. We should take advantage of it."

More people applauded.

"Who agrees?" He asked the room, and everyone replied with a united, "I!"

He didn't expect it to go this well, if anything he expect more arguments than cheers. Actually he expected a big argument to erupt from Hadrian more than anyone. He had waited for his friend to interrupt him during his little speech but was surprised when he heard nothing, except for shouts of approval from the other council members. Now that he thought, he didn't even see Hadrian walk in. He looked around the room now at all the people still cheering, encouraged greatly from his words. But he saw no Hadrian. Where was he?

"I congratulate you on your effort to help the beings, one whose heart is pure."

"Thank you sir." He bowed to the Elder.

"You are a natural born leader Marius. Hopefully this trait will be passed on to a new generation of leaders." The Elder winked his wrinkled eye, and Marius grinned.

"You're hopes are mine as well, sir."

"Oh ho!" The Elder caught the hint. "And when should we be expecting this wondrous event?"

Marius laughed at the Elder's choice of words. "In another year or so maybe. She is having difficulty breeding. But we have faith."

"As you should." The Elder said with a soft smile. "The universe would be committing a terrible crime not to give you two the happiness you both deserve."

Marius smiled back and bowed his head before he left.

It took some time for the results to come back. They needed to add both the being's data to the system in order to make the comparison between themselves and the planet. The process took longer than Marius had expected. The data would read "inconclusive" or "error." So they had to keep uploading the data. Finally, after much uploading, the results were received.

There were levels of toxicity within some areas of the planet where it would be harmful to the beings, but the rest came back positive. That means a lot of the environment on the planet suited well with the being's data collection. An almost perfect match.

Marius was disappointed. How would he be able to move forward with this plan if there was even a small amount of danger to the beings? And everyone had been so excited about it too. Now he was both disappointed and guilty for raising everyone's hopes. Even though the Elder had told everyone not to get their hopes too high, still, Marius felt as though he had failed them in a way. Letting loose a sigh and raking his hand back through his hair, he decided the best thing he could do now was to give everyone what they were waiting for, and to see what would happen from there.

So another meeting had been announced and Marius stood up to speak first.

"The results are clear."

The whole room erupted with cheers and Marius said quickly before they got too excited, "Almost."

The cheers died slowly and there were some murmurs of confusion that circulated now around the room.

"There are small areas of toxicity found in the results."

He listened to the gasps and whispers. Looking around he could also see the looks of disappointment on everyone's face. Oh, he should not do this . . . He cleared his throat and said, "However . . . These small areas could be easily restricted."

Some of the Elders looked to him now with eyebrows raised.

"With our help, we could easily lead the beings into this environment and teach them all they should know before growing their own population. Educate them on how to survive. They would be the wise elders to their people, and they will guide *them* into succession, just as we guided them."

Now instead of whispers and gasps there were nodding heads.

"They are not as intelligent as us, this is true. But when I saw these beings for the very first time, with my own eyes, I saw their future. And there were two outcomes. One, we would leave them to fend for themselves, unknowing of what lies ahead of them they would soon wither and die. Or . . . we could lend them our help, and they would flourish. Their intelligence would grow and grow until no more would they need our assistance. And there we would watch them mature and develop into . . . well we do not know yet. But I would like to see, would you?"

More nodding heads and some "Yes!" and "*I* want to see!"

One of the Elders stood up to give his opinion. "Marius, would our interference truly make any sense? After all, you wish to see these beings populate on their own. What would be the point in watching this as an experiment if we lend our hands?"

Marius nodded and bowed his head to the Elder.

"I hear your words, Elder. And I say it may sound dim to call this an experiment. Otherwise, why not do for all? But these beings are not of any species we have ever found, and of all my years of being a respected member of the High Council, I have never found any species so much on the very brink of death. We have learned that survival increases when there are more to be involved in the fight, and there are only two of them, let us not forget."

"But what if there are others? What if they are far off but still alive?" Another Elder asked.

"Perhaps that may be a possibility, but how long will we wait to find them?"

The Elder seemed to be pondering it, but shook his head as he realized it would not work after all. They cannot keep the beings with them on the ship.

"I cannot promise this planet will be peaceful to the beings, nor can I promise their survival. But if we do not give them a chance to live now, than they will have a greater challenge to face. Surviving without a planet. They cannot even fly a Gift Ship, for whatever reason they are incapable of doing this."

The room began murmuring again as people were both shocked and confused as to how anyone would be unable to fly such a ship. The murmuring died down as Marius said his final words.

"Perhaps in time . . . we may show ourselves to them, and educate them on how their civilization had begun. And perhaps," He looked back to the row of Elders. "We will have two more members to the Society."

That had the crowd cheering once more. The chance to teach and create was something all of the Council took deeply to heart. Everyone wanted to be the wise to someone, and everyone wanted to learn something new. The Council Elders also always looked for new members from different species to add to their council, it was the chance to get new fresh minds into social conversations and debates.

"I do have one concern." One of the Elders said from his seat. "There are only two of these beings. How long would it take for them to populate?"

Marius had not really thought about that, and he was at a loss of words.

Another Elder stood and raised his one bony hand, then lowered it slowly for everyone to calm their talking.

"To move on to the experiment as quickly as possible, perhaps we could clone the beings. The process would not take long."

Marius turned to look at the Elder speaking and he turned to look down at Marius. "I understand that you wish for this to be as natural a process as possible, Marius. But it would be much faster."

He bowed his head, not wanting to disagree with one of the Elders. Besides, maybe it would help. Their cloning devises would not change anything in the being's DNA, it was more of a reproduction process than cloning, only they were taking the exact DNA from the beings and mixing it.

"Then we shall begin with the experiment at once." One Elder announced.

And so after some cloning the beings were landed on the planet. All areas of danger to them were sealed off using special barrier technology Marius had developed himself.

Some society members were asked to live with the beings for a while on the planet, to observe how they develop and thrive. They were to lend no help, just their studying eyes.

After their mission was complete, the members returned to the ship to announce what they had learned about the beings.

"Their life spans are short." One member said.

"And reproduction is a risky task for the females."

"The infants need great support and much nutrition, otherwise they are vulnerable to anything, and they are unaware to the danger around them. They are more curious than cautious."

"Truly?" The Elder asked, stroking his long silver beard. "How interesting. Our newborns adapt quickly to the environment and know right away where threat lurks."

"Yes, Elder, it would seem the being's intellect is small compared to that of our people's."

"Then this may prove to be a more difficult experiment than we had thought. I will speak with Marius."

The members bowed their heads and left the room.

Marius paced back and forth across the satin rug in the Elders room. He was mumbling incoherently.

"Ease yourself, Marius. We will think of something." The Elder soothed gently in his old voice. But Marius did not stop his pacing.

"That is just it, Elder. It should not be "we" but "I." This is my responsibility. *I* must come up with a plan."

"You truly are a born leader Marius. But a leader knows when to ask others for help, if he needs to."

"I do not want to trouble you in this." Marius said. His pacing slowed to a stop. He sighed. "I did not think the beings would be in such need of assistance."

"None of us did." The Elder said gently.

Marius stood silently to go over the situation in his mind. So the beings lacked the survival capabilities they needed. Then there is no other choice . . .

"Elder, I ask for your opinion on what I am about to suggest."

The Elder nodded for Marius to continue.

"Perhaps we should provide the beings with our knowledge."
The Elder paused to look Marius in the eye directly. "Are you
certain of this, Marius? This will no longer be considered an
experiment if we interfere."
Marius nodded his final decision. "I understand, Elder."
"Your heart is great, Marius. I could tell right from the beginning
that your sole purpose was not to please everyone with attempting
to make this into an experiment. I knew you wanted to see those
creatures live. I saw the look in your eyes when you helped them
on board the ship, that excitement and nurturing look."
Marius smiled at the Elder's compliment.
"I will follow you on this plan, Marius. I too, wish to see the
beings live in happiness."
Marius could no longer fool himself. He really didn't want to use
the beings as an experiment. When he said that at the meeting, he
grimaced at the thought. Life was not an experiment. Life was life.
One lived life the way one chose, and it should not be to please
anyone else. A life was precious.
He thought about his mate then, and the precious life they would
be bringing into the world someday.
"Come, there is much to be done." The Elder said, and led the way
out of the room, and into the meeting hall.

The new plans to help the beings had been discussed,
and like Marius expected, everyone seemed confused. Only he
knew that this was more than just a means of discovery, it was a
mission of life and death of an entirely new species. It was during
the middle of the discussion that Marius had noticed something.
Hadrian was absent. Again.

He tried to push his wandering thoughts about where his
friend might be to the side when one of the Elders called him
suddenly to explain the plans. Marius spoke of what they could do,
and after a long speech, he had the crowd applauding once more.
They had unanimously made the decision to extract volunteer DNA
from any member of the Council and mix it with the beings DNA,

to perhaps give the beings an extra boost in case their survival depended on it in the end. From what the studies have shown, the beings were weak, very weak. With their DNA the beings might have a better chance, that is, if mixing such different DNA together will prove to be harmless. One Council member uniquely skilled in the sciences have spoken on the podium about certain side effects. The mixing could alter the beings view of reality and disorient them, or they could develop unnatural growths. Worse yet, they could develop the ability to read each other's minds. Such a power cannot be taken very lightly. The Council member also spoke about unknown developments, meaning some beings may be more gifted than others, and that would surely cause confusion and disagreement. But these were all *possible* side effects. Nothing was guaranteed.

Marius was growing more anxious by the minute, so after the scientist had spoken he finally got his chance at the podium once more, ready to assure everyone that the experiment would still prove to be a success. The Council accepted his words, to Marius's relief. He nodded and sat back in his seat, pleased at how the meeting went. He glanced over his shoulder at the Elders, who were nodding their heads at him in approval.

After the meeting, Marius caught up with one of the Elders before they descended into the Elder's Hall.

The Elder turned and smiled when he saw him approach. "Ah, Marius, forgive me for I have not told you how well you did at the meeting. Once again, you have shown us how much of a true leader you are."

Marius bowed his head. "I thank you for your compliment, Wise Elder. But there is something I must ask you."

"And what would that be?"

"It has come to my attention that Hadrian has not been with us at any of the last three meetings. Would you happen to know where he is?"

The Elder looked down, his wrinkled face sagging into a frown. "Hadrian is in the Council's prison."

"What?" Marius asked in disbelief.

"Yes, I'm afraid his mind is truly clouded like you said. Our guards caught him rounding up another team to investigate the planet, only this time he meant to bring back samples."

Marius couldn't believe what he was hearing. How could Hadrian act so foolishly? Had he not learned what his actions would result in the first time?

"May I go see him?"

The Elder nodded. "You know you do not need to ask, one whose strength is great. Of all the members of the High Council, you are the most respected."

Marius bowed before storming away. If Hadrian would not see the error of his ways through punishment, then perhaps a good firm talk would better suit.

He walked carefully down the winding silver staircase down to the Council Prison. Two guards standing in front of a large door that led to the cell rooms immediately let him through when they saw who he was. The cells hallway was just that, a long, narrow hallway with doors to rooms where they kept prisoners. The doors were crafted by Marius's own hands. Indestructible black steel, two feet thick, strong enough to block out sound. The steel was collected from a planet now inhabited by the Iron Workers species. They were once Drifters before the High Council found them their planet. They in return, gifted the Council metals and building irons to work with in case they wanted to expand their ship, which they did. The Prison took the longest to build out of everything else. At the time, Marius was the only available person who had a skill of working with his hands.

He walked down the long hallway before coming to a door that had its red light turned on above, indicating someone was in there. He tapped in the door's code and some of the steel melted to the side revealing a small open rectangle inside the door, just large enough for Marius to see in only with his eyes.

Hadrian was lying against the corner of the wall, chained from his neck to his wrists, his ankles bound to the floor. He looked up with one eye while the other was covered by his black hair. He looked to be in the worst mood, but Marius didn't care.

Hadrian grinned then and said, "Well, if it isn't the great speaker." Marius scowled.

"I would graciously bow my head before you but as you can see I'm a little . . ." He rattled his brace and chains.

"Sarcasm ill suits you friend."

"I am no friend of yours!" Marius was taken aback by Hadrian's loud voice.

"And you should know why I am in here." He turned his head away.

"I do know. But I must ask you this question, why *are* you in here?"

Hadrian laughed as though it were obvious.

"I am not going to let you be difficult with me Hadrian." Marius said firmly, losing his patience quickly. "Now tell me why—"

"You betrayed me!" Hadrian snapped.

Marius was stunned.

"Oh do not pretend you do not know, *friend*! The recon soldiers told me everything about your little plan to save those pathetic creatures. You and everyone else will go out of your way to not only save them but protect them! That planet is not even theirs and you know it, otherwise there would be no toxicity."

"Please Hadrian, try to understand—"

"Why should I try to understand?! You did not understand *me*! You did not hear *me* when I asked you to hear *me*!"

Marius could see now the anger and hurt in his friend's eyes. He sighed, raking his hand through his hair, trying to come up with something to say. But he couldn't. He felt the guilt pang inside him, and perhaps he deserved it.

"You betrayed me . . ." He said again, this time his voice broke with emotion, and he slumped back against the wall.

Marius just looked at his friend's wretched state. He looked beaten and worn, his face scratched and bloodied from fighting with the guards.

"I had finally found a home for my family . . ." He said in a low voice. Broken.

"Friend, please I—"

"And you took it from us!"

"I took nothing!" Marius yelled.

Hadrian just stared at Marius through the small window opening in the door, his gaze piercing.

"I had to do something, if I didn't they would die."

"And what about me?! What about my family? If we do not find a home for ourselves we too will die! Does that not matter to you, Marius? I believed we were friends . . ."

"We are!" He was growing tired of this, he didn't want to argue. He just wanted to scold Hadrian for his foolish actions. But now it seemed he was the one being scolded. The guilt grew and could've choked the life out of him. Hadrian had been Marius's friend for so many years. How it would be like, if it were him in Hadrian's place. Chained, beaten . . . the hope for finally finding their home planet ripped away from him as though ripped from his soul? Would he act the same way?

"You took my planet from me. But I *will* get it back." That warning in his voice caused every alarm in Marius's body to go off then. Hadrian chuckled. "You should see the look on your face. It is fear isn't it? The Great Marius. Afraid."

"You are a fool if you think you will escape these walls."

"Oh but that is the most amusing part, Marius. You, the Gifted Creator underestimate me, the Strategist."

Marius scowled.

"And unlike you, I have something *worth* protecting!" He leaned his head back hard against the wall. And Marius was done talking.

It seemed nothing would get through to Hadrian at the moment. He just had to be patient and wait for a better time. He tapped in the code to close the window, but paused when he heard the wretch actually laugh. Marius slammed on the button to shut out the wicked sound, but it was already in his head.

Not much long after, only a few years and Marius was hearing that his greatest fear had become a reality. Hadrian had escaped. There was no sign of him or his family. That evil laugh sounded once again in his head, echoing whatever dreaded future they would have to eventually face . . .

"Damn." Adam breathed.

"That really sucks." Decker said, shaking his head.

"Yeah, but you know, I kind of feel bad for the guy. I mean, how would you feel if you had your home taken away from you?"

"But that wasn't really his home cause the data thing didn't match them with that planet, so technically Rose's dad didn't do anything wrong. Right . . . ?" Decker didn't seem so sure himself.

"So you guys don't know where he went? Like . . . you have no idea at all?" Adam asked Rose, a little worry in his voice.

Rose shook her head. "We know only that he stole one of the emergency deployment ships and took his wife and daughter with him. Father had insisted that the Elders send out contact calls to every ally they had in case anyone should spot him, but sadly nobody has confirmed any sightings."

"Damn." Adam repeated.

"But don't you think it's weird that his family would just up and go with him like that? I mean, didn't they think he was a bit crazy?" Decker asked.

"Hadrian could be the craziest being in the universe and Maria would love him still."

Lisa couldn't help but think that was probably the greatest love out there. To love somebody through all their faults, even if they put them both in danger. It certainly wasn't a safe kind of love, but then love is never safe.

She thought about all the times her mom warned her about how crazy and unstable Decker's family is, but all Lisa could really do was reassure her mom that everything was ok, and try not to tell her about anything else that goes on over there at that house. It was hard, of course, because Lisa told her mom everything. But she loved Decker too much to walk away from him, even if he did have a crazy family. It isn't his fault.

"Well, that really sucks for that planet that he was so hell bent on getting to. Maybe he's there right now taking it over with some alien army or something." Decker grinned at his joke. But Lisa suddenly noticed the look of seriousness on Rose's face.

Rose gulped so loud they all heard it. She was looking down, and her hair fell in front of her face so they couldn't see her eyes, just the rim of her glasses. Lisa reached forward with concern.

"Rose . . . ?"

She didn't lift her head up to meet them, but with a shaky voice she said, "There is no reason for you to fear, the Council has taken extreme precautions to protect this planet and—"

"*This* planet . . . ?" Adam asked, his face going pale.

There was silence as it all sank in.

"Earth?" Lisa felt like she was going to faint, no wait . . . going to be sick. She made a dash behind the big yellow building.

Decker told everyone to wait while he went to check on her.

She heaved the last of her guts up before standing up straight to face Decker. He opened the cap off his water bottle and put it to her mouth. "Are you ok, love?"

She nodded, guzzling down the water.

When she finally stopped to take a breath she gasped out.

"Yeah . . . I think I'm alright . . ." He walked her back to the benches. Adam was sitting with his knees up to his chest, looking up at the sky as though it was going to fall on him. Rose had her head down.

Decker lifted Lisa to sit back on the bench and she said to Rose, "Hey, listen." Rose lifted her head slowly to meet Lisa's eyes. "It's ok. It's ok right guys?"

"The hell it is! You mean all that crap happened over us? Over this planet?! That's crazy!" Adam exclaimed.

Yeah, and not only that, but now we got this nut that wants to wipe us all out." Decker said.

"My father rebuilt every tracking system on the Council Ship for the very purpose of protecting this planet. I can assure you that if Hadrian were anywhere close to Earth we would know. We will not let anything happen to any of you."

Decker rolled his eyes like he didn't believe that for a second.

"Hey now hold up, if that whole story you just told us was about Earth, then does that mean those two beings you guys found were—?"

"I'm sorry Adam but we are not going to get into that. Do you not remember my rule?"

"Doesn't matter, cause that's who they were and that's what happened. We know now Rose, so you don't have to beat around the bush about it anymore." Decker said, the anger clear in his voice.

"Do you?" Rose asked, appearing like she was surprised at that. "And how do you know those two beings were who you believe they were?" She asked with a grin.

"Because . . . You said those were the first two "beings" and Earth was uninhabited. So that must mean that's who it's supposed to be."

"Are you sure?" Rose challenged.

Decker was silent because he knew he probably wasn't winning this one.

"So wait . . ." Adam was holding his head trying to think of what to say first. "There's so much now . . . So the dinosaurs?"

"We wanted to exterminate the dinosaur species to make room for the human species here on Earth. Father did not believe that your kind would be able to live with such creatures. But interestingly enough, you ended up finding a way after all. You see? You truly are clever beings."

"Wait, slow down a second Rose. What are you saying?" Lisa asked.

"Father built special bombing devices that would go off when they hit the ground. However, some of those creatures managed to escape their destruction and ended up living for thousands of years. When we scanned this planet, we knew there were other life forms that lived here, but we had no idea they were dinosaurs, so small were they in numbers. Eventually your people came into contact with them and we would've destroyed them right away if one of the Elder's hadn't intervened.

He didn't want us to interfere anymore, so we watched as your early ancestors interacted with these creatures, and to our surprise, there was no conflict. Somehow your early people had managed to tame these wild creatures, even the most threatening ones."

Lisa just couldn't believe what she was hearing. Well, yes she could, actually.

"So you're saying we had *dinosaurs* as pets?" Adam asked.

Rose nodded.

"Dude could you see me coming down the street with a pet T-rex? I'd call him Rex." He said to Decker, who couldn't help but laugh with him. The tension from earlier gone now.

"But how were they able to tame them? I mean, it's not like taming a wild dog. These things were colossal size, and had rows of sharp teeth." Lisa said.

"We still do not know how your people were able to control these beasts, but it impressed everyone in the Council truly. They used them to catch food, carry materials to and from long distances, and for protection against other creatures that we assume were not as easy to tame. Humans truly are remarkable beings indeed."

"My dinosaur would totally kick your dinosaur's butt."

"Adam, if I had a dinosaur he would eat your puny little Rex."

"Dude I would have a T-rex, you wouldn't beat me."

"I would if my T-rex was stronger, which he would be."

Lisa shook her head at the two. Knuckleheads.

"I still can't believe it was Earth that you were talking about the whole time. How come you didn't tell us before?" Adam asked.

Rose shrugged. "I feared your reaction." The guys looked at her like that was stupid to fear since they reacted just the same as they would've if she had just told them before the story.

"I know the Council has this whole protection thing going on right now up there but don't you think Hadrian is a little smarter than that? I bet he's waiting for a specific day to come down here and annihilate us."

Decker folded his arms. "Yeah, it'd be like freakin Independence Day."

Lisa thought about how real that could be and saw past Decker's sarcastic joke. What if Hadrian really was waiting?

"Well, I think I've had enough learning for one day." Adam stood to stretch. "I'm out, guys. I'll text you all tomorrow."

They waved as he left.

It was getting late, so Lisa and Decker decided to head home too. They waved to Rose as they were leaving.

Lisa looked up into the sky then before they left the field. So many stars out. The sky looked beautiful with all those stars. She imagined where Hadrian might be right now . . .

CHAPTER 19

It was the most boring day they had ever had. Well, maybe not the *most* boring. They've had plenty of those to know what the very definition of *boring* meant. But it was just one of those days. The four of them sat on Lisa's front steps, slouched over, Lisa leaning up against Decker's shoulder, Adam leaning back on both hands, and Rose . . . well she was upside down. Literally. She was showing them the other day some of her "magic" a.k.a. alien powers, and told them excitedly that she finally mastered the skill of controlling our gravity.

They were amazed the first ten times.

Lisa was so bored and out of it she couldn't really care less if the neighbors were outside wide eyed and gasping at what they were seeing.

Actually she was more stressed than bored. She couldn't get her mind off of Decker leaving for Florida soon. It was bothering her so much she hardly slept. Mr. O asked her a few times at school if she wanted to go to the nurse's office, but she told him she just had a cold.

It was weird because she never got stressed. It was such a horrible feeling she actually thought at first that she really was coming under the weather. That is, until her mom confirmed it was stress the second she looked at her. How was it that moms knew everything that was wrong?

God, she felt like one of those stupid, emotionally train wrecked teenagers. This just wasn't like her.

"Uh Rose, you can stop with your little floating trick now. It's old." Decker said.

She frowned and floated back down to the ground.

Adam chuckled. "Think anyone saw?"

Lisa had to laugh at how none of them seemed to care whether someone saw Rose floating in midair or not.

An idea popped into her head then and she told everyone to wait while she went to get something inside. She came back out with white pieces of paper. Everyone looked confused until Lisa began trying at folding a paper airplane. The guys went right at taking some paper and making their own, challenging each other at who could make the best one. Rose just watched as Decker threw his into the air first, only to have it come crashing down. Adam laughed at his failed attempt.

"Let's see yours then." He scoffed.

Adam threw his and the plane flew over the roof of the house and landed smoothly back down to the lawn.

This eventually got old too and Adam was suggesting a better idea.

"We should go get a frisbee."

It was agreed, and they drove up to the closest store and bought a blue one.

"So you just swing your arm back like this, and let it go, like this." Adam was showing Rose how to throw it when they got to the field.

"Like this?" She swung her one arm back real fast and flung it forward. It scraped across the grass only a few feet away from her.

"Don't feel bad, I'm not much of a frisbee thrower either." Lisa laughed.

"Oh, I'll get used to it." Rose said with determination and picked it up to give it another try. This time it went straight up into the air and crash landed on her head.

"Jeez, you're not supposed to just look at it silly." Decker went over to make sure she was ok.

Rose just smiled wryly as she rubbed her head.

They spent the next hour tossing and catching. Lisa noticed a small group of people over by the benches but decided to ignore them. One of them was yelling, "Hey guys I got a drink right now! I'm trying to get wasted!"

Decker said something foul back to them and one of them threw him the bird. He almost tossed the frisbee aside to go over to the laughing group but Lisa caught his arm. "Just ignore them Decker, they're not even worth your time."

She thought she heard him growl under his breath. They all knew at least three of the people in that group and they were not at all friends with either of them.

"Yo, let him come over here and try something!" Adam fumed.

The "him" Adam was talking about was Josh, the guy that did everything under the sun.

Rose hid behind Lisa's back saying, "I don't like that human over there Lisa."

Lisa just assured her softly, "It's fine Rose, he's not going to do anything."

"I am not speaking of the one you call Josh, I am speaking of the other human next to him. His eyes are frightful."

That kind of surprised her. The guy walking next to Josh was someone who they only met a few times. Lisa doesn't even remember his name.

Adam picked up the frisbee to throw to Decker. "Don't worry about him Rose. He's just a punk."

"A punk who's got guts enough to throw me the finger. Little asshole. If I ever get my hands around his throat he'll be sorry he ever met me." Decker threw the Frisbee back to Adam.

The group stayed on the other side of the fence dancing with their cigarettes and bottles in the air, yelling and making all kinds of ridiculous noises. Decker was slowly losing his cool.

"You gonna go home and cry to your mom Adam?" One of them yelled and gave a high five to Josh.

Adam just turned without saying anything and started walking towards them, his eyes and silence screaming his intent on murdering the kid. But Decker was quick to get in his way. "He's not worth it man." He was trying to push him back but Adam was getting more aggressive with his growing anger. "Just move, man. I got this. Just get out of the way."

"Adam, he's not worth—"

"Get the hell out of my way!" Decker was wrestling with him to the ground just to keep him in place.

Rose had her hands up to her mouth while Lisa was yelling for Adam to get a hold of himself.

The group behind the fence just kept laughing. Now Lisa was the one fuming. They had a hell of a nerve to just come over here and start trouble. What did they ever do to them anyway? All they were doing was playing some Frisbee . . . Rose moved out from behind Lisa and lifted the Frisbee off the ground slowly. The guys were still wrestling on the ground, and Lisa was looking at her, confused now.

She lay the Frisbee on her upraised palm. Lisa saw how calm her face looked, and within seconds the Frisbee was above her hand, still, floating there in a tilted way. Then it started spinning. Fast. It shot up into the air spinning so fast they could actually hear the wind catching on the outer blue rim. The group behind the fence still laughed and cheered while Decker and Adam turned their heads, looking up at the spinning disk. It sat up there for a few minutes, Rose looking over at the arrogant group flicking their cigarettes over the fence and breaking their bottles on the concrete.

Then suddenly it flew past them over towards the laughing idiots who were now not laughing but trying to protect themselves from the disk as it came down on their heads and smacked them in their faces.

Lisa's mouth dropped. The guys were picking themselves off the ground and watching as the group scrambled around trying to get away from the assault.

"What the hell is this?!" One of them yelled before getting hit below the belt.

Lisa looked over at Rose who looked to the side only with her eyes and gave her a wink.

The group started running then probably faster than the disk was spinning and the guys laughed.

"That's right keep running!" Adam yelled, still laughing.

Lisa was shaking her head at what those guys are probably thinking right now after getting beat up by a flying Frisbee, or if Decker and Adam would ever stop talking about it.

"Yo did you see Josh dude he got hit right in his face dude!" Adam was on the ground holding his stomach.

The Frisbee stopped spinning and fell to the ground.

CHAPTER 20

"So what comes up when the rain comes down?" Decker asked. They were just turning the corner off the one long street.

"What?" Adam asked, thinking this was a stupid question.

"It's a riddle you idiot."

"What goes up?" Lisa thought for a moment. "Flowers? Like when the rain falls and then flowers grow?"

Decker shook his head. "Nope. Well, yes, but that's not the answer."

"Grass?" Adam suggested. "Grass grows when it rains doesn't it?

"No . . . well yes, but . . . it's a specific answer."

"Hmmm . . ." Then Adam snapped his fingers when he said, "I got it. Steam!"

"Huh?" Lisa looked at him confusedly.

"Well when the ground gets hot, steam comes up, you know cause the rain . . . comes . . . down . . . no?"

"No." Decker said.

"Well then I give up." Lisa said but then Rose said excitedly. "Oh I know! An umbrella!"

"We have a winner." Decker nodded.

"An umbrella? That's it?"

"Yep." Decker said.

"Wow." Adam shook his head.

"Looks like we were all thinking outside the box." Lisa laughed.

"Maybe you should start thinking inside the box." Decker winked at her. She got what he meant and laughed.

"What's funny?" Adam asked.

"Nothing." They both said.

Rose giggled.

CHAPTER 21

They walked to the pizza place to grab some cheese fries. Well Decker, Lisa and Rose would be grabbing cheese fries. Adam would be grabbing cheese fries, a cheese burger, some onion rings, some mozzarella sticks and a large soda. As thin as this kid was he could really eat.

"Hey guys. The usual for you right?" The owner of the pizzeria smiled at Adam and he nodded his head. "The usual with some dipping sauce."

"Damn Adam, where do you put it all man?" Decker laughed.

Adam slapped his flat stomach. "Right here."

Lisa shook her head and showed Rose to their table.

"So this is where that pizza comes from?" Rose asked, looking around.

"Yeah." Lisa laughed. "We come here every once in a while with friends, or whenever Adam wants to fill his black hole of a gut." She whispered.

"Heard that." He said from the front counter.

Rose giggled. "Oh but if you really saw what a black hole could do, trust me, you would never speak of them again without fear."

Lisa watched a documentary one time about black holes. Some scientists believe they suck you in on one end, and then spit you out through the other. Then there are some who say you would never even survive getting sucked into a black hole, you would be stretched to pieces. It gave her the shivers just thinking about it.

"See, told you." Rose laughed, noting Lisa's shiver.

The guys came back to the table after ordering. Decker pulled out a stack of their favorite card game and shuffled the deck.

He gave six cards to every person. Rose examined her cards still lying on the table. She looked quizzically at Lisa, who picked her cards up in hand, then at the guys who also picked theirs up.

"Hey Rose, I've been wondering. Remember when you told us before about non-planets?" Lisa said, laying down a card.

"Yes?"

"Well if a non-planet is something that cannot support life, then wouldn't the moon be considered a non-planet?"

The guys looked up from their decks then. Adam paused before laying down one of his cards. "You know, I never thought of that."

"Me neither. But that makes sense doesn't it? The moon can't support life. All it has is a bunch of rocks and dust." Decker said.

"You are a very clever observer Lisa, I am impressed greatly." Rose smiled. "But to answer your question, yes you are correct. Your moon is indeed a non-planet." Rose laid down a random card after watching everyone lay down their cards, but they all just sat staring at her, waiting for her to continue. The game was forgotten.

"So like . . . does that mean . . . ?"

Rose nodded. "Yes it does Adam. Your moon has been visited in the past by Drifters." She laid the rest of her cards down on the table, seeing as everyone else has. "Unfortunately it has been visited by a well-known Drifter."

"Hadrian." Lisa already knew it was him. And apparently she was right, because Rose nodded. "Yes. Years after Hadrian had escaped he was found colonizing on your moon, to the Council's absolute irritation."

"Colonizing?" Decker asked.

"The Council found an entire community built on the non-planet. His numbers have increased slightly because of this new colony, but only very little, since no living being can survive for very long on a non-planet."

"But I don't get it. How could he make a whole colony with buildings and stuff when there are no resources on non-planets?" Adam asked.

"Hadrian may not be skilled with construction, but he is extremely intelligent. According to the Council, he made trips back and forth to Earth to collect supplies. He brought materials back to the non-planet to build his colony."

"Sneaky little bastard." Decker mumbled.

"Dude, can you even do that?" Adam asked.

"It is illegal to steal from other planets, unless the people of that planet willingly give away their supplies, which is what the people of the colony told the Council was the case. However, around that time, Earth was in its early stages of development, so its people were perhaps deceived into giving Hadrian supplies."

"So hold up, how is it that he was able to build stuff if he can't build? Adam asked.

"Yeah and why were they deceived?" Decker added in.

Rose sighed. "The Council underestimated Hadrian's thinking. Somehow he convinced other Drifters to help build the colony, Drifters that were skilled in the art of crafting monuments and structures. And as for how the people of Earth were deceived . . ." She paused, a sad look on her face.

Lisa believes she might already know. If Earth was in its early stages, then that would probably take us back to—

"Around the time of scholars and writers. During that time period, your people believed completely in powerful entities that could control the impossible or "Gods", which is what the Council believes Hadrian had represented himself as to your people of that time, so that they would be willing to give him whatever he wanted."

Adam raised his eyebrows. "That's some crazy stuff right there." He picked up his deck again.

"So Hadrian created an entire colony by himself?" Lisa asked with doubt.

"No, he found a few Drifters and persuaded them to become a part of his growing colony. They were apparently very desperate for food and a home and so joined Hadrian for a little while, not caring that he was stealing from Earth. But then the High Council found out about this, and Hadrian escaped with his wife and child before the Elders could capture him, leaving the other beings to face the High Council by themselves. At first, the beings were thought to be the ones stealing form the planet, but they told the Elders that it was all Hadrian's doing. They told the entire Council that Hadrian had a few of them go to Earth despite the danger and retrieve supplies, so his face would not be so easily recognizable. The Elders believed the Drifters, and built them brand new Gift Ships so that they could leave the non-planet. And the hunt for Hadrian continued."

An employee laid their food down on the table then and the boys dug right in.

Rose looked quizzically at her cheese fries. "This is pizza?"

Lisa laughed. "No. Those are cheese fries. Try them." Lisa ate some of hers. Rose picked one cheesy fry up and bit into it, then she let it roll off her tongue.

"You might have to wait for them to cool a little." Lisa said.

They sat the rest of the day in that pizzeria playing cards and eating cheese fries.

CHAPTER 22

The next day, Lisa heard a knock at her door. It was Rose.
"Hey."
"Hey." Rose waved her small hand.
She was wearing a dark blue shirt with black jeans, and a little black hat. Lisa realized only a few days ago that Rose liked to dress with her mood. If it was a sunny day, she would dress in bright colors like forest green, purple, pink, red and black. On cloudy days she would wear dark blue, dark purple, or all black. Apparently this was one of her cloudy days.
Lisa stepped out in her socks and sat down on the step next to Rose.
"Can I talk to you about something?" Rose asked suddenly.
It caught Lisa off guard, but she said, "Yeah, of course."
Rose sighed. "Do you and Decker ever miss each other when you separate for a long time?"
Now that really caught her off guard, so much off that she didn't know what to say. She stared at Rose for a minute, then realizing she hadn't said anything yet she blurted, "Oh yeah, like all the time."
"Truly? Even when you are both very far away from each other?"
"Yeah . . ." She felt like she wanted to say more, but was busy trying to figure out why Rose was asking this.

When Rose didn't say anything else, Lisa figured she'd say, "Like, a while ago, Decker's mom tried to take him to—"
Lisa stopped herself then. Oh jeeze! Why was she suddenly talking about that? As if Rose wanted to hear about her and Decker's life stories. Jeeze . . .
"I do not mind listening, Lisa. I would very much like to her this story of yours."
Lisa almost thought for a second that Rose was reading her mind, but then she remembered she didn't have that ability.
"Trust me, you don't want to hear it, it's boring." Lisa laughed nervously.
"But I do. Please tell it to me. It will make me feel better, honestly."
Lisa felt so embarrassed she wished she never opened her big mouth. But when she looked down at the girl with her big round eyes Lisa knew she didn't have a choice now.

"I tried giving Decker a call one night because he hadn't called like he said he would. When his step father picked up the phone, he told me Decker went with his mom somewhere, and when I asked him where exactly he said he didn't know because she didn't tell him. So of course I panicked and tried to call his mom's cell phone.

After a few rings the line picked up and the only thing I could hear was arguing, loud arguing. Decker finally answered me when I kept asking for him and he told me everything would be fine, that I should go to bed and he would call me in the morning. But I didn't believe him and I made him tell me what was going on. He said his family threatened to kick him out and his mom was taking him to Philadelphia to dump him somewhere so he could find his way back home."

Rose gasped. Lisa knew it was a long time ago, but she still remembered the anxiety and pain like a fresh open cut. She was worried and scared and was so close to calling the police. Lucky for his crazy mother, Lisa got his call saying he had to swallow his pride and beg her to drive him back home, and she did. Yeah, lucky for her, because at that moment Lisa was so hurt and enraged she wanted to get her hands around the woman's neck. Never in her life had she felt such anger towards someone.

"Is this Philadelphia a far away place?" Rose asked.

"Only if you're walking back on foot."

Rose just looked at her with bewilderment.

"Yeah, but after a thousand or so of those kind of scares I guess I just learned to calm myself in those situations. I hate it when he goes home every night, back them, back to her. Sometimes I keep myself awake wondering if he's ok over there. I worry the most when he goes to sleep."

Rose put a hand on Lisa's shoulder. "But eventually you do fall asleep, because you believe in his words when he tells you that everything will be alright."

She did. Maybe it was the only way for her to keep herself together at times but Lisa did believe in Decker's promises. She always has.

"Something bothering you Rose?" Lisa finally asked the question, trying to get the conversation off of her.

Rose nodded.

"I feel that I want to tell you about my . . . what is it that you call it? The home sickness. Is that it?"

"That's it." Lisa confirmed with a smile.

"Yeah, I think I have that." Rose nodded.

Lisa smiled but nodded.

"Actually it is not so much my home as it is my betrothed. I miss him so much."

Lisa recognized that painful look in Rose's eyes. It's the same look Decker says he sees in Lisa's. He would smile and tell her that she had the "poor puppy" look, as he called it.

Lisa smiled softly at Rose. "You'll see him again. At least you don't have to worry about getting old too quickly and missing out on anything."

They both laughed. Rose looked up into the sky and caught a brown leaf that floated down into her gloved hands.

"I am here to collect data about your world, the human race. It has always been a dream of mine to visit this planet that Father adores so much and discover what it is truly about, all the life that grows and thrives here. I wish Cornelius could've traveled here with me."

Lisa smiled at the way Rose sighed when she said his name. She obviously loved him more than anything in the universe.

"I knew coming here would be a challenge. And at first I admit that I was fearful that you would not accept me into your human society upon learning that I was not human."

Lisa smiled. "That actually sounds very human."

Rose tilted her head, confused. "It does?"

"Sure. There are humans that want to fit in with other groups of humans. It's not so much about wanting to feel accepted as it is to actually *be* accepted by others. In fact, if you never told us you were an alien, we would've never guessed."

Rose grinned. "Not until I started making shoes float."

They both laughed.

Lisa looked up at the browning leaves as each one started to fall with the wind.

"I guess the only difference between aliens and humans is that you guys know everything." Lisa said.

"Believe me when I tell you this, my good friend. There is not one being in the universe that knows everything. If they did, they would be living only half a life."

Lisa looked to her then. Half a life? What did that mean?

"Everything about this world fascinates me. Father spoke true when he told me of the numerous wonders. It's all so wild, so beautiful."

"Not always. I'm sorry if I'm disappointing you by saying this Rose, but it's not always so perfect down here like it is . . . well, out there. People do hurt other people. And they hurt this planet."

Rose shrugged. "I believe there is an Earthly saying, "Every rose has its thorns.""

"Rose!" Adam waved as him and Decker came around the corner and walked up to Lisa's front porch.

"Wow, you're up early." Lisa said to Decker as he came up to give her a kiss on her forehead.

"Well Adam came by around five in the morning and woke me up." He sent a scowl over to Adam who was giving the innocent "what did I do?" look.

"Hey but Lisa at least I got him up for you."

"You got me up because you didn't want to walk to Wawa by yourself, you big wuss."

"Look man, it gets lonely walking up there by myself alright?" Lisa shook her head.

"So what do we do now?" She asked. The guys shrugged like they didn't really feel like thinking up any ideas.

"How about another walk?" Rose suggested. Lisa looked at the guys and they just shrugged again. Adam said, "Eh, why not?" So they were off on another of their usual walks around the neighborhood.

Lisa noticed as they were walking that Rose was playing with the chain of her necklace absently, probably still thinking about her boyfriend back home. Lisa thought to tell her how brave she was for actually taking such a long trip away from him, something Lisa probably wouldn't be strong enough to do, but she decided not to say anything. Maybe after a while Rose will forget about her homesickness.

"Dude, look at this guy's lawn." Adam said as they passed someone's house.

The lawn looked only half cut, like someone mowed a spiral walkway down the middle of the tall grass.

"Someone doesn't know how to cut grass."

"Why do you care?" Decker asked him.

"I don't care. I'm just saying it looks like crap. He needs to get that fixed."

"Alright Mr. OCD." Decker laughed.

"I don't got OCD!"

Lisa laughed. It did look a little odd.

"Maybe they were trying to make one of those . . . what are they called again?" Adam asked.

"What's *they*?" Decker asked dryly.

"You know man, those line things that people say pop up in their cornfields and stuff."

"You mean crop circles?" Lisa asked.

Adam snapped his fingers. "That's it! Crop circles."

Lisa remembers watching a show where they talked about the strange crop circles. But people say they're fake and really easy to make.

"Aren't there other kinds of crop circles? What about the ones that they found in rocks and canyons?"

Rose perked her head up.

"Those aren't crop circles you idiot those are just lines." Decker said.

"Yeah but dude did you ever see one of those things? They say you gotta get up real high just to see them. They're huge."

Lisa noticed Rose was no longer playing with her necklace. They all turned around when they noticed Rose had stopped walking. Her face was a bright red.

"Rose? You ok?" Lisa asked.

"Oh! I'm fine Lisa really." She laughed nervously.

She looked embarrassed for some reason. Lisa was going to ask her if she was sure she was ok but Decker beat her to it. He went over to feel her forehead. "You got a fever or something? Your face looks like its burning up." He said.

"Oh it is nothing really I assure you. May we continue on our walk?"

169

"C'mon Rose you can't fool us, you're hiding something." Adam grinned.

Rose's face turned a deeper red.

"Jeeze Adam she could just not be feeling good." Lisa said.

"Yeah man, lay off a little."

Adam put his hands up. "Hey I'm sorry alright? I just thought it was whatever we were talking about."

"Well maybe she doesn't want to talk about the alien shit all the time." Decker said.

Rose spoke up now. "No, Decker it's quite alright. Actually the truth is I am feeling most guilty about something."

Adam gave Decker the "I-told-you-so" look.

"Guilty about what?" Lisa asked.

She started playing with her pendant again. "Well, it was a very long time ago . . . I was much younger than I am today, and Cornelius had only just become a part of the High Council defense forces. One day my father took us on a trip to visit the "new" planet that they had recently discovered. He wanted to show us the amazing scenery. And it was truly amazing." She smiled at the memory. "He left us in the control room so we could view the surroundings through the large glass window, telling us he would return later after a sudden meeting that had come up with the Council Elders. We did promise him that we would behave but . . ."

Cornelius leaped into the large blue seat and laid his hand down on the control panel.

"What are you doing?" Rose asked, jumping into the seat next to him. His finger was swiping back and forth across the large touch screen panel and Rose said in horror, "Cornelius! We could get in trouble."

"He won't know, trust me. Besides, look at this system, it's absolutely amazing!" They both jumped back when the lights in the room suddenly went out and the screen lit up green. Two hands then appeared in sparkling black on the green screen and Cornelius waved his one hand to the right, the hand on the screen also moving with his.

"Simply amazing." He said in wonder.

"Cornelius, I am not so certain about what we are doing. Father will be displeased."

He ignored her words and continued playing with the green screen. A large black laser suddenly protruded from the outside bottom of the ship. They both looked out the glass to see the black metallic device aiming directly at the ground.

Before Rose could caution him further, the laser fired a long black beam straight at the ground. Cornelius ripped his hand away from the screen and the beam went out.

"What did you do?!"

"I don't know." He said. When he moved his left hand, they noticed the laser moved with his hand's movement.

He grinned and said, "I wonder . . ."

"No! No wondering! We must cease this or Father will—"

The black beam shot out again and with his left hand, Cornelius guided the device so that the beam was now carving into the soil. Rose only watched with amazement as the beam carved out the rest of the shape. It was a spider. One of the many creatures that inhabit the planet or so Father has told them.

"What do you think of my creation?" He looked down at it proudly.

She was at a loss for words. Oh they would surely, no doubt, get in huge trouble for this.

"Goodness my love, whatever must I do with you?"

He grinned. "Punish me?"

She gave him a playful push. Oh, she really shouldn't. But then . . . will they ever get this chance again?

He moved over so she could sit directly in front of the green screen. She cautiously laid her one hand down and only moved it an inch, then the beam was on the ground again.

More confident now, she moved her other hand in a circular motion and the device moved with her. She concentrated as she drew out her creation.

Cornelius laughed when she was finished. "And what is that?" He asked.

It was a stick-like figure waving.

"A being." She said. "Like us."

He smiled. "It's beautiful. Like you."

He grabbed her into his arms.

Just as he was leaning down to kiss her Marius walked through the door . . .

Adam was laughing. "Oh man! I bet your dad was pissed. Did you get in trouble?"

Rose smiled wryly. "Yes, but it wasn't for playing with the laser."

They all laughed then.

Lisa supposed that alien or not a father will always be a father. But thinking now about Earth, and remembering what Rose had told them before about the necessary cautions, Lisa had to ask, "Wait Rose, I know this sounds a little random and all but how could you be here breathing our air if it might be toxic to you?"

Decker and Adam looked like they couldn't believe they hadn't thought of that either.

"My levels were tested and compared to the planet's levels before I was sent here. There are a few spots that I must avoid, but the glasses help me to see them. They show spaces covered in red where I am forbidden to touch or enter."

"That's crazy. So what, does it light up or something?" Adam asked.

"Not exactly, the area just turns a deep red."

"But what if something actually is red and it's not toxic. How would you know?" Decker asked then.

"I would have to look at the object or area first. If it changes red before my eyes than I know it's a forbidden zone."

"Ok I get you." Adam nodded his understanding.

"So you're allowed on any planet, so long as you don't go into any red zones?" Decker asked.

Rose nodded.

Lisa didn't think she could get any more surprised after everything they've already talked about, but she was. It was true then that aliens had amazingly advanced technology, probably more advanced than our own. Of course, we also have stuff that could detect levels of toxicity, like carbon monoxide detectors. Of course now it made her start to wonder why would we have to have toxic detectors if . . . ?

Something hit her gut then, a terrible sinking feeling.

"You ok love?" Decker asked looking at her pale face.

She hesitated before saying, "Guys, you know . . . there are places on Earth that we can't touch."

They all looked at her confusingly, all but Rose, who turned her eyes away.

"What do you mean?" Adam asked.

"I mean think about it. We would die if we breathed in any kind of toxic air right?"

The boys looked at each other but nodded.

"And there is toxic air here right? Like pollution and chemicals?"

"What are you trying to say Lisa?" Decker asked, a hint of worry in his voice.

"And the cold could give us frostbit, the heat could burn us. There's disease everywhere. Think about it, if your planet matches your body levels perfectly then . . ."

Now the guy's went pale.

Adam took a step back. "You're not trying to say . . . what I think you're trying to say . . ."

It felt like everything was suddenly closing in on her, the walls getting thinner and closer. Yet now the world seemed greater. Intimidating.

"Let's just calm down a bit Lisa—"

"If a being's real planet matches accordingly to their data then it would be a perfect match right? That planet would be their home planet. But there are toxic places here on Earth that could harm us. So if that's the case then . . . wouldn't that mean that . . . Earth isn't our real planet?"

CHAPTER 23

Why didn't she put the pieces together before? Rose told them that the two beings that were found didn't make an exact match to the Council's scanner when they scanned the planet, and if those two beings were the beginning to the rest of their species then . . .

"Now hold on a second, I know we got disease and everything but toxic chemicals are manmade let's not forget."

"And where did those materials *come* from Decker?! Where did they get all those things to make those chemicals huh? Outer space?!"

"Hang on guys. I think I gotta sit for a little." Adam fell down onto the curb and put his hand on his throbbing head.

Then all eyes were on Rose. She wasn't looking at any of them, just the ground.

Decker folded his arms. "And you knew didn't you Rose?"

She didn't look up, just nodded her head. "Forgive me for withholding such information from you all but I knew it would come as a shock and so wanted to wait—"

"Wait till when? Until we got more *comfortable* with all the other crazy shit?"

She flinched at his angry voice. "Perhaps if you were to just accept it . . ."

"Oh, so you mean just go back to being sheep right? Cause that's what we all are anyway. Sleeping sheep!"

"Hey man, chill a bit."

"Why should I?" Decker yelled.

"Because there's nothing we can do about it! Man if we hadn't known all of this we would be getting on with our lives right now wouldn't we?" Adam said, his headache growing.

"So you're just going to *accept* the fact that we don't really belong here? You're just gonna take that?"

"Yeah Decker I am! What other choice do we have?!"

"And I bet that's why we got so much problems down here, cause there's a planet out there that's actually ours."

"Man, can't you just drop it already? There's nothing we can do! You want us to grow wings and *fly* there?"

Lisa pulled herself together enough to intervene. "Alright guys let it go already. There really isn't anything we can do about it so let's just let it go."

They stopped just before the punches were about to be thrown. Rose bowed her head and said to them, "My friends, please accept my apology for withholding the information, I meant no harm in any way. I was only concerned with how you would react and so I became a coward."

Lisa sighed. "You're not a coward, Rose. You were just trying to protect us."

Decker scoffed, "Some protection."

Lisa gave him a look of warning.

"Look guys, I don't know about you, but I say just move on with life. Of all the crazy shit out there that we learned about we shouldn't be losing our heads over one little thing."

Adam said, still holding his throbbing head.

"My friends, believe in me, there is much you still do not know. But if you do not wish to hear anymore, you only need to say so." Rose bowed. They all were silent as they let that sink in. There are so much more they still don't know about . . .

"Do we even wanna know?" Decker looked at her and then Adam asked, "Should we wanna know?"

Lisa shook her head. "Don't know . . . but we got each other right? I don't mean to be getting corny right now but that's the truth isn't it?"

"You know it." Adam smiled.

"Definitely." Decker said.

They continued their walk. Lisa felt the tension melt away from her shoulders. It was true that as long as they all had each other to lean on then hell, let the world fall to pieces or whatever else might happen. And she had Decker. A little ping of sadness reminded her that she wouldn't have him for long, but she ignored it, because at the moment she did.

"Hey guys, I still wanna know more about the damn crop circles."

"Sorry Adam, those are man made." Rose said, smiling.

"For real?! Aww man!"

CHAPTER 24

Lisa was sitting in the school library reading one of her favorite books. This is what she usually did during lunch period, since she didn't care much for the school food.

She really loved to read, and it was all thanks to her mom. After she got her book published her mom decided that at fifteen, Lisa was probably old enough to read her vampire romance novel. Lisa had been begging her mom for years to read it. She had never read an entire book before then, not even any of the famous Harry Potter books that her friends were really into at the time. She just got bored too quick.

She almost got bored of her mom's book too at first. Of course, it's not exactly a book for young teenagers to read, so of course it seemed boring at first. But she forced herself to read the whole thing from start to finish. It felt only right of her to do. Her mom put a long five years into making it, so Lisa felt that as her daughter she should know what her mom's book was about. The only problem was that Lisa dozed out after maybe the second paragraph of the first chapter. She thought to herself, there has to be a better way to do this. So she decided to picture every sentence in her mind like a movie, visualize what was going on and maybe she would get into it.

Sure enough it worked. Sometimes when her and her friends would talk about their favorite movies, Lisa would bring up something nobody has ever heard of before, and then she would laugh because she was actually remembering something from a book not a movie.

She got to be so good at it that every time she read a book, all of the outside world would disappear, replaced with only the sounds of "trees blowing" or "horses hooves on cobble stones" or any other descriptive sceneries. She could even hear the character's voices in her head as she read their dialogue, and picture their every movement and facial features. It was almost like jumping into an adventure. At times she would forget she was even reading a book.

Her first ever author other than her mom was Susan Carroll, author of the Bride Finder. After that trilogy she discovered Sandra Hill, a bestseller of Viking genres.

Even though she had read all four of the Twilight books, she still had to say her favorite vamp novels were written by Amanda Ashley, Lindsay Sands and Anne Rice. Of course, nobody in school knew who any of those authors were, not even some of her English teachers, so she didn't have anyone to discuss her favorite readings with besides Decker and her mom.

Maybe one day she would write her own book, so that she can talk to her fans about it and get their opinions and share ideas, thoughts and feelings. She wasn't much of a writer, but with a little more reading, maybe the skill will develop in time.

Lisa then remembered what it was that she had been trying to forget. It came back like a slice to the heart, salt on a wound. She put her head down on the table. Decker . . . Why did it always have to come up at the worst time?

"There you are, Lisa."

She brought her head back up to meet her English teacher.

"Hey Mr. O." She said weakly.

"You alright? Tired?"

She shook her head. "Nah, not really."

"Well, I saw you sitting over here and just wanted to tell you how amazed I am at your reading ability."

Wow, well, she wouldn't call it an ability, but she accepted the compliment.

"It's just a hobby of mine."

"Well it's a good hobby to have. At least you won't have to worry about writing essays when you get into college, unlike your fellow students who could use some help on simple grammar."

He chuckled. "These kids of today probably don't even know that good ol' Shakespeare invented most of the words they say today."

"Shakespeare would turn in his grave at the words kids say *today*." She said.

Mr. O laughed. "I suppose you're right."

He grabbed the seat across the table.

"Have you ever thought about being an English teacher?"

The question came out of nowhere and Lisa was a little surprised.

"I don't think I have."

"Well you should. In all my years of teaching I have never came upon a student reading the Iliad for their own enjoyment."

Lisa felt like she should at least take pride in that. She was probably the only kid in Norse High that loved reading Homer and Shakespeare.

But being a teacher meant having to work through college. Lisa gave up thinking about college a few years ago when she found out how extremely difficult it was to get into some of the best places, and all the stress and competition, not to mention the cost. But the real reason she wanted to forget about it was because she didn't know what she wanted to do. All of her teachers told her to think about what she wanted to do now, like right now, and get to it. Jump on it. And that frustrated her. She wanted to get through high school with awesome grades first and then work on college, but apparently she had to start the college stuff during high school. She felt like she was stupid because she didn't know what she wanted to do. She can't just go to college and do something she didn't like, and she didn't exactly know what she liked. But now that Mr. O brings up the English thing . . . yeah, she could do that. "I'll think about it." She told him. He got up to leave when she said, "Thanks Mr. O."

"Teaching." He said as if to remind her, and left.

She smiled and returned to her book.

CHAPTER 25

Lisa heard a knock at the door and sped through the last sentence of her chapter before closing the book.

Decker was standing in his grey hooded jacket, hands in his pockets.

She told him to wait as she ran to grab her black jacket and shoes.

"Hey love." He said when she stepped outside.

"Hey." She smiled at him and wrapped her arms around his shoulder. But she let them fall back to her sides when she saw that one of the neighbors were outside on their front porch smoking a cigarette. Even if nobody was looking it still felt weird to Lisa to hug and kiss in public, she liked it better when they were alone.

"So where's Adam at?" She asked.

"Doing homework."

"Really?" That was a shock. Adam doing homework?

"And Rose?" Decker asked her now.

Lisa shrugged. "She didn't call. She must be busy with something cause she didn't call last night either.

Decker shrugged.

They decided to sit on her porch for a bit since Lisa didn't feel like walking around. Her feet were aching after lifting bricks and spreading mulch all day in shop class at school.

"So we can't go inside today?" Decker asked after a few minutes.

Lisa shook her head. "Mom isn't feeling well, so she probably won't want anybody in the house."

He nodded in understanding. "Eh, I don't mind sitting out here and being a popsicle. As long as I get to be the cherry kind."

"Maybe I wanna be cherry." She said grinning.

"Fine then I'll be blueberry."

They both laughed.

Lisa leaned up to kiss his cheek. It still amazed her that even without a home life like Lisa's, Decker could still be such a funny and sweet guy.

It wasn't until a few months after they started dating that Lisa finally got to meet his family. They didn't greet themselves to her, but Lisa didn't think anything of it then. Decker lived with his mother, his step father, his aunt and uncle, his two younger cousins, and four step siblings. Lisa was surprised all those people managed to live in such a small house at the same time. She didn't really know too much about them, because Decker always avoided the subject of his family whenever it was brought up in conversation. She insisted that she meet them one day, and because she insisted, he said he would take her to his house.

The moment she walked in it was chaos. Kids were running around screaming and cursing at each other. His mother and step father were arguing while their huge Rottweiler barked and scrambled to get loose from his chain. Decker scooped her up into his arms and had taken her out of the mad house before things got worse, all the while the kids mocking at how the "prince carried the princess off" or something like that.

Decker didn't beg her to forgive his family or for her to forgive him for bringing her over there. He had even told her, "If you want to break up . . . I won't be upset."

She kissed him them and told him he was crazy to think that way. She assured him that she loved him and that nothing would change that.

Of course, as the years passed it became clear that Decker's family was more difficult to deal with than they had thought. His mother never bothered helping him with getting into sports in middle school. She was too busy helping his younger sister try out for her cheerleading. And she never helped him look for a college, didn't think it was necessary to "throw money away." He got into constant fist fights with his step father, while his mother threatened to kick him out of the house.

Her first and only son, the black sheep of the family.

The one that "ruined" her life because she had him at sixteen.

Lisa's mom eventually learned just what kind of people they were and told her, "If I had noticed this sooner I would've put a stop to it."

Lisa didn't get mad. She understood why her mom would think like that, after all, Decker's family was crazy. And she was only thinking about what was best for Lisa.

But there was no way in the world that Lisa could just "not" love Decker anymore. And she knew that if she married, it wouldn't be for gain of any kind. Money, title, a guy with a good job, a guy with a car and a nice house. She would marry for love, and as long as he loved her too, than that's the way it would be. She hated to see that her mom worried about her in the sense that she might have a hard life ahead of her, but Lisa didn't mind. She was happy. And she would rather be poor and happy than rich and miserable.

She felt his arm around her waist then and he pulled her onto his lap. His mouth was on her's before she could get out even a gasp. Forgetting everything she melted into his kiss and against his chest. Both his arms wrapped around her in a strong embrace. She pulled away slightly and said on a grin, "People might be watching us, you know."

"I know." He said and leaned in again.

She smiled against his lips as he whispered those words.

"I love you."

"Aww I love you too, man!" Adam's voice sounded right next to them.

Decker grumbled and released Lisa on a sigh. She laughed and gave Adam a playful slap on the arm for interrupting them.

"So where's our little alien chick at?" He asked.

"We don't know, she didn't call yet." Lisa said.

Adam sat down next to them on the porch.

They waited the rest of the day, talking about all the stuff they've learned so far, about Earth, about the universe. That night they watched the sky for shooting stars, believing them to actually be alien space ships. Adam made a comment about being ready to kick Hadrian's butt if he ever had the guts to come down here to Earth, and Decker apologized to him about being a jerk yesterday. The apology was accepted and the two were back to throwing playful insults at each other.

Rose never called.

CHAPTER 26

Lisa heard a banging on her door the next day and scrambled to get off the couch. It was Decker and Adam.

"The news." Adam said quickly when she opened the door. They ran inside and Decker grabbed the remote to turn the tv on.

"It was here at this bowling alley that ex-marine Nicolas Mays suffered what his doctors believed to be a traumatic seizer. But Mays says he has no past of epilepsy and that the seizure he had wasn't a seizure at all, but something else."

"It was the devil! I'm telling ya that's what I saw! He took the form of a little girl. He tried to possess me!" The man yelled into the camera. There were a few police officers trying to pull him away from the frightened news reporter who he was shaking and screaming, "You have to believe me! I saw it with my own two eyes!"

"Holy shit . . ." Adam said sitting down slowly on the couch.

The police finally ripped the man away from the reporter and she cleared her throat before continuing.

"Doctors believe the flashing disco lights at the bowling alley may have caused May's seizure, along with flashbacks of his traumatic experience from his years in the marines. The bowling alley will be closed due to the incident while police look into the matter. Mays insists he did not have a seizure at all, but that he was struck by an evil cast. He will be taken to St. Nobara hospital where he will receive psychiatric aid. Reporting live from—"

Lisa clicked the tv off.

They all sat there in shock, confusion and silence for the longest time.

Adam heaved out a sigh and put his head in his hands.

Lisa stood staring at the blank screen as she tried to take it all in at once.

"This is bad, guys. Like . . . really *really* bad."

"Calm down love, nothing is gonna happen." Decker said, though she could tell he was trying to tell himself that too.

"But what about Rose? What if that guy ends up talking to someone and—"

"Nothing will happen. You heard the lady. He's gonna be stuck in some mental hospital. There's no way he's getting out."

Lisa didn't want to worry but she did. Fragile little Rose. What could they really do to her if they found out she was an alien? Would they take her away to some secret base and do weird tests on her? Ask her questions? Keep her locked up until she breaks down and then . . . She had to push those thoughts aside. It was stupid to think of stuff like that anyway. That guy could be crazy for all anyone knew. Nobody would believe him . . . right?

"He was an ex soldier dude. What if he tries to talk to one of his soldier buddies and they go talk to a higher person in the army about it?"

"Dude shut up. It's not going to happen." Decker said.

Lisa decided to take a seat next to Decker on the couch. All that worry she was feeling now tripled and she was starting to get that headache back again. Rose . . .

She was just this little alien on this big planet full of humans. Greedy, selfish, crazy, in-*humane* humans that would probably torture or even kill her. People often did cruel things when they didn't understand something.

Lisa grimaced remembering a good example of cruelty and misunderstanding.

It was a long time ago, and she was almost six. Her and her other friends would ride around outside on their bicycles all the time. But one day they found this huge, ugly looking caterpillar. It was big with green fuzz on its back and black spikes. It crawled across the sidewalk, its fat body scrunching up then going back down like an accordion as it made its way toward the tree.

They thought it was gross, yet fascinating. They had never seen a bug this ugly before.

One of her friend's poked at it with a stick and it stopped moving. Lisa thought now that the poor thing was probably terrified at us poking it. After a few minutes we thought maybe it had died because it wasn't moving. Then one of Lisa's friends ran it over with her bike. Green blood squirted out, she even heard it, and it got on her bike tire. They laughed at how disgusting it was and rode away.

. She wasn't thinking that it was just some poor helpless, defenseless creature that did nothing to her and she should've just left it alone to go back to its family. She wasn't thinking about that because she was young, and curious. Is that how our government, or whoever is in charge, would treat Rose? Why would they need to anyway? Why couldn't they just talk to her, get their answers and then let her go home? But Lisa was just thinking the worst. Maybe they would let her go home, who's to say they would keep her and do stupid experiments on her just because she's an alien . . . ? An alien that they may never have another chance with again, so of course they would take the opportunity to be curious. *And isn't that what kills the cat?*

Here on Earth, Rose is the caterpillar.

"This is bad . . ." Lisa mumbled.

"She'll be alright." Decker wrapped his arm around her shoulder and Lisa leaned into him.

"Yeah, maybe she's got one of those teleporting devices or invisibility thingies." Adam said.

"Invisibility thingies?" Decker asked dryly.

"Man you know what I mean."

Lisa smiled just a bit at them trying to cheer her up.

Rose. She grabbed her phone out of her pocket and stared at the empty call box. *Where are you?*

CHAPTER 27

It's been five days since Rose has been gone and Lisa was getting more worried by the minute. It was getting harder to sleep through the night without waking up from these horrible nightmares.

Rose sitting in an empty room, white walls, and people in hazmat suits waiting on the other side of the door. She was shivering and begging for someone to help her.

Another one had Lisa and Decker on some kind of space ship. It was absolutely huge. The walls were of alabaster stone and the soft couches were made of a deep blue. The room fell dark and the long table of gears and buttons suddenly lit up a bright green, then the Earth showed up on a bigger screen on the wall just above it. Lisa moved closer toward the Earth, only to gasp when she noticed how the once green planet now dripped with red. It pooled into the sea from every continent, until the entire world was drenched in a dark red. Even the screen started to drip in red.

On the sixth night, Lisa had a dream that she was looking at Rose in a mirror. She put her hand to the glass, watching as Rose also mimicked the movement. Then she opened her mouth to speak but nothing came out. Rose smiled, but it was a sad smile. Suddenly somebody was grabbing for her shoulders and Lisa was yelling for Rose to turn around, but Rose couldn't hear her. She kept smiling as these white gloved hands yanked at her arms and wrapped around her throat, pulling her farther and farther away from the glass as Lisa banged and yelled. Then she was gone, and Lisa was all alone. She was standing on and around blackness with only an empty mirror that didn't even show her reflection. Then she saw the hands appear like out of a mist on the other side of the mirror, and Lisa backed away only to be grabbed by those hands from behind her. They dragged her away into the blackness . . .

She woke up that early morning screaming.

CHAPTER 28

Five more days passed and still no Rose.

Lisa was getting more and more worried. Hopefully if Rose tried to call her now while she was in school she would at least leave a voicemail. But she did turn it on in between classes to check for any missed calls. There were none yet.

Lisa was so worried she couldn't even focus on her writing. She felt a hand on the back of her chair and looked up to see Mr. O.

"Writer's block?"

Yeah if only it were that.

"Sort of." She replied.

He nodded. "I used to get those a lot when I was feeling impatient."

"Impatient?" Lisa asked.

"Yes, well, when I thought about how well my paper was going to turn out and the praise I would get from my teacher at how well written it would be, I started imagining the excitement I would feel and that A plus I would get. I wanted to see it done so bad that my mind wasn't focusing on what I really had to do, and that was to see that it got done."

Lisa didn't exactly know what to say but did take in what he was saying.

"The trick is to put your mind at ease and save that excitement for later, don't even think about how well it'll turn out, just think about getting it done."

If they were talking on a much more *different* topic, then Lisa would have to ask him what he expected her to do. He winked then and said, "You'll know what to do."

That night Lisa knew exactly what she would do.

"You want us to what?" Decker asked rubbing the sleep out of his eyes.

The three of them were standing in front of Decker's house in their winter coats and pajamas. It was still dark and the air was so bitter they could see each other's breath.

"If we find her ship, then we'll know if she's there or not. Then we'll know if something bad happened to her." Lisa didn't want to have to keep explaining it, she wanted them to get going while it was still dark out so nobody saw.

"But what if we can't find it?" Adam asked on a yawn.

"Does that mean you'll go with me?"

"Does that mean if we don't you'll go alone?" Decker asked her then and Lisa held her chin up in the air like she was brave enough to go by herself. And of course Decker would never let Lisa go walking around in the dark by herself.

Adam looked like he was hoping for Decker to say no so they could go back to bed.

His shoulders slumped in defeat when Decker yawned out, "I guess we could check it out. But I'm not staying out here all night."

"We should leave right now so that we have enough time to look." She said, buttoning up the rest of her coat.

"You wanna go walking around in the woods . . . in the cold . . . at two in the morning . . . to look for a space ship." Adam said dryly.

She nodded as if to say, "yeah, pretty much."

He slumped over and sighed.

They left that very moment, still dressed in their sleepwear and winter coats. Lisa led the way towards the woods, the same place Rose told them she landed her ship in. The strange thing was that Rose's ship was huge, and Lisa wasn't talking huge like a car or boat, more like a two story house. And the woods behind the football field weren't really deep at all, so how the heck did she hide the damn thing back there anyway?

Lisa insisted they split up but Decker wouldn't allow Lisa to walk around by herself. She tsked at him and told him he sounded like her father.

Really, the woods back there weren't that deep, and if she screamed they would hear her. But Decker was firm with his opinion that it wasn't a good idea, and she stubbornly let it go. All she wanted right now was to find Rose anyway.

They pushed through dangling tree branches and swatted at annoying spider webs. They leaped over huge thorn bushes and climbed over fallen tree trunks. They searched with their flashlights here and there. The lights played tricks with their minds making them think they had found the large ship when it was only a shadow of fallen leaves in a tangled mess of tree branches. High and low they looked. All in the dark. And all for nothing.

By the time they scoped out a good half of the area they were frustrated and shivering.

"This isn't getting us anywhere." Adam said through chattering teeth.

"Yeah, love. I don't think its back here."

"It has to be! Rose told me she landed it in these woods."

She expected the guys to give her a comeback but they were too cold to even think of one, what they really wanted was to go home to their warm beds.

"Maybe she moved it." Adam said.

Decker pulled his coat up over his nearly frostbitten face.

Lisa was furious, more with herself than anything else. She was so worried about Rose that she dragged the guys out here in the freeze to find an alien space ship . . . an alien space ship for goodness sakes! Jeeze what the hell was she thinking?

"Look, we got all of tomorrow to look for it. Right now I think I'm just gonna head home and hopefully get some slee-oww!"

Adam bounced back onto the ground.

"What's wrong?" Lisa asked.

"My nose . . ." He held both hands to his face, then lifted one hand off to check for blood. "What the hell man!" He sucked in a breath at the sudden pain.

"Dude, what the hell did you hit?"

"A branch?" Lisa asked.

"No man, I hit something hard."

"Well that's not very descriptive." Decker said dryly.

"I don't know dude! I bumped into it over there." He pointed over to an open area, no trees or branches, just a patch of dirt.

"What did you hit?" Decker asked.

"I.Dont.Know." He said impatiently, still holding his nose.

Decker was helping him up while Lisa walked forward a bit, slowly, in the direction Adam pointed.

There were no trees at all in this one area here. None. What could he . . . ?

Then she walked forward some more. *Clank.* She jumped back when the tip of her shoe hit something hard.

"What the hell?" She tapped her foot forward again and hit it. *Clank. Clank.*

But nothing was there.

Suddenly a whirlwind started up around them, pulling their hoods off their heads and rushing up all the dead leaves off the ground. It vibrated and sparked blue waves of electricity. Something was materializing right in front of them.

It faded and re appeared again, over and over until the whole thing came into view now, as real and solid as . . .

Decker grabbed Lisa's arm to pull her against him as the whirlwind picked up speed and the electricity sparked and blasted around them, more and more until they were all holding their ears against the loud vibrating sound that shook the dead trees and blew back branches.

Then it stopped.

She braved to look up, dared to peek. And there it was. Huge, red and shiny . . .

CHAPTER 29

They found it. They found the ship.

And it was just as Lisa had seen it that night. It's beautiful deep red color glistened against the moon's light and it sparkled. It was huge.

They all just stared at it at first, but once it registered into Lisa's mind what she was looking at she was running toward it yelling "Rose! Are you in there? Rose!"

"Lisa get back here! Get away from it!" Decker called to her but she ignored him.

"Rose!" She yelled again, banging on the hard metal.

"M-maybe she's not home at the moment . . ." Adam was still in a state of shock, no longer caring about his injury.

Lisa put her hands up against the cool metal and leaned in, trying to listen for any noises going on inside. She couldn't hear anything, but she felt her mind wander for a quick second. She was touching metal from another planet . . . It didn't feel like their metal at all. It felt solid, yet thin. If she closed her eyes she would think she was touching water, such a strange feeling. She was touching metal from space, if it was even metal at all.

She shook her head to get out of her thoughts. She moved her hands up and around as far as her arms could stretch. Then she knocked three times. No answer.

She ran all the way around to the other side of the huge ship, knocking here and there.

She knocked hard one last time, still no answer.

She leaned her head against the cool metal, feeling hopelessness and worry consume her mind all at once. If Rose wasn't here than where was she? This was her ship. This should be where she would've come back to right? Where else would she have gone? Unless she was taken . . .

"I guess she's not here." She said as though she just had to accept it.

"Maybe she can't hear you." Adam said.

"Or maybe she's not here. So before we freeze to death I suggest we all just head home."

"But Decker, it's been *days*. And if she's not here then where is she?"

"I don't know but standing around in the cold isn't going to give us anything."

"Except the flu." Adam sneezed and shivered.

"We're not gonna get any answers here. We just have to be patient, she'll turn up eventually." Decker said, putting his gloved hand on her shoulder. Lisa didn't argue. She knew Decker was right. Standing around in the cold wasn't doing them any good. Of course now there seemed to be more questions than answers. She gave in and followed the guys out of the woods, Adam still complaining about his "broken" nose. Decker looked back and she looked up at him, then he gave her one of his smiles, the one that always turns her cheeks red and makes her smile back. Maybe she should just not worry. Rose was an alien of a much higher intelligence than they were. If she knew her life was in danger she would know what to do. Right?

Lisa shook her head. Why did she have to worry so much if it only hurt? She looked back up at Decker. If she knew he was in danger she would worry too, even though it only gave her pain. But it was worth it, she thought. She loved Decker. Though now that Rose was their friend Lisa was obviously going to worry about her too. But did she have to? Well it's not like she *has* to, but she doesn't *want* to worry a lot either. Does that make her a terrible friend? Jeez how embarrassing. She was worrying about worrying.

CHAPTER 30

Still no call from Rose, and it's been two weeks. By now Lisa was starting to believe that she had really been taken. By who, she didn't know. She used the word "they" a lot when she and Decker talked about what might have happened to her, against Decker's wishes of course. He didn't want to talk about it because he knew it only upset Lisa more to think on it, but she needed to vent anyway. Seriously, they got some nerve snatching her up like that and all because she's an alien. Yeah, so? And what makes them think that? Is it true then that there're cameras on every street corner and radio devices listening in on someone's every word?

And what if Lisa announced she was an alien, would they take her too?

There she goes using that "they" word again . . .

Who exactly was "they?" Lisa remembered something Rose had said before.

"There is not one being in the universe that knows everything. If they did, they would be living only half a life."

What did she mean by that, half a life? It still nagged at Lisa's brain when she thought about it. Rose didn't even get the chance to really explain it to her.

Half a life.

So does it mean we spend half our lives . . . learning? If someone knew everything . . . then what? Then they know everything. They know what will happen next. They know their tomorrow, and their next day, and the next. They will know history, and the future. They would no longer "wonder". The word "wonder" wouldn't mean anything to them. They would just . . . live. When she really got to thinking about it the whole thing sounded crazy. Who would want to know everything? And did everything really mean *everything*?

Jeeze that would drive her crazy. She wouldn't have to go to college. She would already know everything there was to learn! She wouldn't get that adventurous feeling while reading a new book, the curiosity and excitement at finding out what was about to happen next. No longer would scientists need to study the stars, or teachers need to teach. No longer would we need to make predictions or ask questions. No longer would we need to discover.

They walked around the neighborhood, didn't talk about much, didn't really feel like talking at all. Adam had brought up how he still couldn't believe the pyramids were made by aliens. Lisa and Decker just shrugged their shoulders like it was old news. Adam just sort of left it at that and didn't say any more either. Lisa was checking her phone every few minutes to see if she might've missed any call or text from Rose. She turned the volume up on the ring just in case.

The next day they stopped at their local pizza place to get cheese fries. Decker brought the cards with them, but they stopped playing after a little while, nobody really felt like playing cards anyway. A little later that same day their friend Joe gave them a call to see if they wanted to go out since the bowling alley was open again, oh and to bring their friend Rose with them too. They told him maybe another day, if they felt like it. They just didn't feel up to bowling at the moment.

The next day looked as dreary as it felt. It started to rain later on into the afternoon, so they had to call it a night after another walk around the neighborhood. Tomorrow would be Monday and another boring week of school would continue once again. Lisa checked her phone only once that entire day.

CHAPTER 31

A few more weeks passed and still no word from Rose. Lisa began having doubts that they would ever hear from her again. The worry and uneasiness soon misted away as time went on, to her surprise. But then, she really wasn't surprised. Decker had three months before he had to move, and right now Lisa's mind was only on him and how much time they could get with each other for the remainder of their days. Funny, it sounded as though he was dying, or she was. Maybe they both were.

Adam didn't come over as often, probably figuring Lisa and Decker wanted time alone. She felt bad, but at the same time grateful that Adam understood. She knew it was probably selfish to want Decker all to herself right now and not want to be with anyone else, but she didn't care. Oh how childish she sounded. How teenager.

Was this how everyone felt when they knew the clock was ticking?

She begged her mom to let her and Decker inside for the next few days. She knew her mom would say no, because they were inside the day before and she didn't feel like having anyone inside today, but Lisa wouldn't have it. She got mad and told her mom that she lived here too, and it was still cold out and they couldn't go over to Decker's so what else were they supposed to do? Her mom told her no again flatly. Lisa yelled, "Fine! Then we're going to freeze outside and I'm going to get sick!"

The look of guilt on her mom's face tore her up and instead of waiting for her mom's response Lisa just said, "never mind," and ran out the door. She heard Decker call her name but she didn't feel like stopping. If she did all the neighbors would see her crying. She finally got to the field and had to stop to catch her breath.

"What's wrong love?" He asked as he caught up to her. She just sat down on the bench, tears falling down her face.

"Me. That's what's the matter."

What the hell was she thinking anyway, acting like that? She always respected her mom's word, when the answer was "no" it was "no", there were no "if", "ands" or "buts." How dare she . . .

How dare she do that to her mom, of all people. The one who took care of her, gave her everything, loved her to pieces. No . . . the one that *takes* care of her, *gives* her everything, and *loves* her to pieces. And she loves her too, more than anything in the world. For her to just get an attitude like that . . . and the look on her mom's face. That was what was killing her right now.

Decker sat next to her and pulled her into his arms. "Did something happen?"

She shook her head, wiping away the tears with her arm. "It was nothing."

"Doesn't look like nothing." He said.

She sniffed. "I know. Actually it was just something me and mom were talking about."

He pulled her closer against him. This was stupid, she thought. Here she was crying like a two year old when she should be apologizing to her mom right now.

That was it then, she was to stop this selfish behavior and go home right now.

Or not . . . Lisa decided perhaps now was not the time to go home right away. Her eyes were still red and puffy and if her mom saw her like that it would only make things worse. She decided to get brave and go over to Decker's house instead, even though it was probably a bad idea, but they didn't want to stand in the cold for hours.

They finally got up to the front door. Decker told her to wait out front while he went in to check the scene, make sure there were no dead bodies. It was something they had to do now every time they got desperate and needed a place to be. One time Lisa walked in and the kids were all over the place throwing crayons and lamps and globs of glue at each other.

"I'll be right out." He said before walking in. She nodded and sat on the porch step to wait for him. After some twenty minutes of what sounded like soft talking, then vulgar yelling, then voices rising, Lisa heard a loud *bang*! and she jumped up, almost stumbling off the porch. The front door swung open and she froze, but when she saw that it was only Decker she relaxed her nerves a bit.

He slammed the door shut behind him after stepping outside. When he noticed her at the bottom of the steps he immediately went over to her and lifted her into his arms. "Decker—"

"It's ok." He said, and broke into a run. She looked over his shoulder when she heard more loud arguing, half expecting someone to come dashing out of the house with a kitchen knife or something. That sounded like something his mom would do . . .

He carried her all the way to the field, and didn't let her down until they got to the very back where the woods were cut off from the gate. When he put her down next to him she asked, "What happened?"

He looked like he wanted to say, but didn't. Instead he cupped her face in his hands and kissed her. His lips were so soft and warm. How long did she have left to feel that warmth? How long did they have before he had to leave? She melted against him. How would she live?

She smiled against those warm lips and he smiled back. But then he pulled away and told her on a sigh, "I told my mom I wasn't going."

She looked up at him, confusion and hope raced through her. "You did?"

"But she told me I didn't have a choice. And we got into a fight . . ."

He shifted his stance uncomfortably as though in guilt.

"I sort of . . . broke the living room table. My step dad gripped me up by the throat and I guess I just lost it."

He sighed and ran his hand back through his hair. "Mom really loved that table. I don't even know if I should go back there for a bit."

She stared at him.

"Wasn't that the fancy table she spent your college tuition on? The one with the diamonds around the edges?"

He nodded, looking at the ground.

Suddenly she was laughing. That surprised him and he looked at her in confusion. She was laughing so hard she couldn't seem to get a hold of herself.

"What?"

"You really broke that table?" She asked.

"Yeah . . . ?"

She broke into laughter again. Jeez maybe something really was wrong with her, she thought, swiping away at her eyes.

"You alright?" He smiled wryly.

"Yeah, I'm just-" She let out a breath from laughing so hard and smiled up at him. "I'm just glad you're ok."

He still looked at her confusedly, so she walked over and wrapped her arms around his neck. She had to stand on her toes just to kiss him, he was so tall.

He closed his eyes and kissed her back, wrapping his arms around her waist.

"Hey can't you guys get a room or something?"

Adam pulled his one ear bud out of his ear and leaped up onto the second bench seat behind them.

"I'm sorry, do I know you stranger?"

Adam chuckled at Decker's joke and the two clapped hands together in greeting.

Lisa smiled. "So the video games got boring huh?"

He shrugged. "Yeah well you know. I'd rather kill zombies than be one." He laughed.

They decided to take a walk around the neighborhood, something they hadn't done for a while. Lisa liked to walk on days when the sun was slightly covered by some gray clouds, but bright enough to provide some light. The weather wasn't too hot or cold, just perfect.

After walking for about an hour and listening to the guys talk about video games, they finally got back to the field. They all sat on the benches and Adam let out a loud sigh. "Well. I'm bored."

Lisa and Decker just nodded their heads. Boring days was just something they were used to.

"So I'm guessing she didn't call yet?" Adam decided to ask.

"Not yet." Lisa said.

Adam searched through his Ipod for the next song. Her phone began to ring then and Lisa looked at the caller i.d. It was her mom.

"Hey." She answered.

"Lisa you should come home and see this you aren't going to believe it!"

"What is it?"

She listened. The guys were waiting patiently yet curiously as Lisa listened to what her mom was telling her.

"Yeah . . . yeah? What?!"

"What's she saying?" Decker asked.

"We'll be right there!" Lisa shoved the phone back into her pocket and broke into a run. The guys looked at each other then bolted into a run behind her.

"What did she say?" Decker asked quickly.

"She said to check out the news!"

"-space ship. It was supposedly found deep within the back of these woods behind me. Police are not specifying if it was indeed an alien space ship or not, but the locals who were biking through these trails Tuesday evening are convinced completely." The same news reporter from before was talking into her microphone.

"Yeah we were just zipping through where we usually go with our bikes and we see this massively huge thing and I'm just like, "What is that?!""

"So you believe it was a space ship that you found?" The reporter put the mike up to the man's face.

"Yes ma'am, it was an alien ship."

"Uh oh . . ." Adam said, slumping back against the couch, not taking his eyes off the television.

"Authorities investigating the area are not making any comments but a few of the locals have said that they recently have been hearing strange sounds coming from the woods late at night. Police have blocked off the area in order to proceed with their investigation and so far we have only gotten as close as the parking lot where police then respectively told us to turn our cameras off. Reporting live from-" The tv went blank.

"Hey Lisa I was watching that!"

"Sorry mom, finger slipped." Lisa murmured, and handed her mom the remote.

"You alright?" She asked, looking at their pale faces.

"Yeah I'm good. Guys?"

They didn't answer. They were just as stunned as she was.

"Now Lisa don't believe everything you hear. It's probably nothing to worry about." Her mom assured. "Aliens. Ha! It sounds more like that show you like to watch doesn't it? The one with the aliens in it? Doctor . . . something?"

"Yeah. Uh, mom we're gonna go outside. I got my cell on if you need me."

"Alright . . . ?"

They were out the door before her mom could question further.

They speed walked down their dead-end street until they got to the gate that separated the street from the field. Their jaws dropped at what they saw.

The whole place was packed in with police cars and big black vans. Yellow police tape was placed around the outside of the woods and football field. Of course they had to be big black vans, Lisa thought grimly. It was pretty obvious they were dealing with something different here, like *otherworldly* different.

On the farther side of the field there was a crowd of curious people standing behind a police barricade, and some reporters with their trucks and cameras.

"Damn . . ." Adam raised his hand to his head. "This shit just got real."

"What are we gonna do?" Lisa stared out in horror.

"*We* should just stay out of it, that's what I say." Decker said adamantly.

"Yeah, I'm sure Rose is fine. Maybe she knew this was gonna happen and left before it got like this."

"No." Lisa shook her head. "It's my fault, I led us back into those woods, and before we found the ship it was invisible. Nobody would've found it."

"My nose found it." Adam said dryly.

"Yeah it wasn't exactly well hidden. Someone would've found it eventually." Decker said.

The guys were right. The thing was so big it was still amazing that Rose could even fit it back in those woods with all those trees.

"So what are they gonna do with it?" Adam asked, climbing a few inches up the gate to see if he could get a better look over all the cars.

"Take it away, probably. It's an alien space ship for crying out loud, you think they'll just leave it here?"

No but now Rose is gonna be without a ride home. Does she even know about this?

Lisa suddenly felt weak in the knees. Decker caught her just in time before she fell to the ground.

"Lisa?" He asked worriedly. She grabbed his shoulder, felt her heart racing against her chest, felt that too familiar feeling. It was that nervous feeling.

"I'm just a little . . . scared."

She felt so helpless. She didn't know where Rose was and now they were taking her ship. What if they never find her? Or worse, what if the police find out that the three of them were her friends, what then? She imagined the scene as though it was playing right in front of her. Men in black suits barging into her house and taking her family away . . . taking the three of them and throwing them into cells and forcing them to talk about everything.

Decker sat down against the gate with Lisa in his arms. "Hey, don't worry alright? Rose is fine."

How do you know?

"And I'm here with you." He said soothingly and kissed her forehead. At least now her heart wasn't racing like crazy and she could breathe a little easier.

He kissed her again and said, "I love you."

"Seriously guys, this is no time for lovey dovey."

Lisa would've laughed if she knew Adam was just joking, but he sounded kind of serious.

"Dude shut up."

"You shut up, man. Do you not see what's going on right now?"
He started to walk away but Decker grabbed him by the shoulder.
"What the hell's your problem?"

"I don't have a problem!" Adam shoved his hand off. "You're the
one with the problem. All this shit is going on and you're over here
kissing!"

Decker just stared after Adam as he walked off up the hill and sat
down next to the tree.

Lisa got up to go over there with him. Of course Adam was
expecting, or wanting them to go over and ask him what was
wrong, otherwise he would've gone home. Lisa noticed this
behavior a lot with some of their other friends too. If someone was
upset and they wanted you to talk to them about it, they would
walk away, maybe sit down somewhere close by or keep walking
and expect you to follow them, but they wouldn't go home.

At least not when they wanted to talk about something, and Lisa
knew Adam was a really emotional guy. There was that one time
when they were at a backyard bonfire over at a friend's house . . .

*T*hey roasted marshmallows and told stories. Then Decker got
an angry call from his mom and he must've argued with her for at
least ten minutes. When he hung up, he said how much he hated
her and that he wished she would just leave. Now everyone knew
Decker didn't have the best home life, and for a teenager that was
hard to handle. It was actually rare that Decker ever got really mad
at his folks, he told Lisa it was because he just accepted them the
way they were and even though he wanted to get mad, he couldn't,
because that wouldn't change them, and it wouldn't change his
mother. But Adam told Decker he was being immature and that he
should be happy to have a mom.

Decker had already been fuming over the argument so he just told
Adam to butt out because he doesn't understand what it's like.

"I wish I did know! I wish she could be here to yell at me and
argue with me . . ." That's when he got up and walked over to the

patio. He pulled his hood over his head and just sat there with his hands in his front sweater pocket.

Everyone got up to go over to him, but Decker told them that he should just be the one to talk to him. Adam could be heard sobbing and sniffing as he let out all he had to say, and Decker took it like a beating. He figured he deserved it after what he said. They had been friends for years and to Decker, Adam was like his younger brother. He didn't care that Adam had emotional issues, just as Lisa didn't care that Decker had a horrible family. That night nobody else bothered to ask Adam if he was alright.

Lisa and Decker walked up the hill and sat on both sides of the tree. They didn't say anything for a little. Then they heard Adam sniff and drop his head into his knees. After a few more moments of silence Decker said, "C'mon Adam. Be a man and stop crying." Lisa didn't expect Decker to say something like that and was about to scold him for it but then Adam chuckled and said dryly, "So sue me, man."

Decker laughed then and Lisa smiled . . .

Adam lifted his head and leaned it back against the tree with a sigh and a sniff, then wiped his sleeve across his eyes.

It was then that Lisa really became aware of the annoying sounds of police car sirens rushing to the scene. As if they needed more there!

She turned her head toward the sounds of people yelling and screaming, where the growing crowd was probably still growing with curious neighbors. If their situation was different and Rose was sitting here with them, then maybe Lisa would be thinking that these people really need to chill. The only problem was that Rose was still missing and Lisa wasn't exactly *chill* herself. But now she understood why the aliens didn't want to make much contact. Looking out over the chaos that seemed to be going on down at the field, it looked like something out of a movie.

Now they were setting up tents over by the edge of the woods. Well if that wasn't odd and obvious enough that something weird was happening than she didn't know what was. Really, it seemed that people tended to overreact a lot. Then again, it is an alien ship. Lisa wondered how different everyone would think of the aliens if they had shown themselves to us a long, *long* time ago. Would we be so curious and frightened? Would we still behave the way we do? And how would our civilizations have grown then? Would we have flourished in technology and medicine, more then we already have? Would we have become such great allies with the aliens that they would've shared their wisdom and knowledge? Rose is such a sweet girl, and her dad seems like a normal guy, especially as a father. The way Rose described the High Council they seemed like sensible aliens, probably more sensible than most humans.

Lisa looked up at the graying sky. All of them. Her, Decker, Adam . . . everyone. They were all these little beings living on this planet. This planet among billions . . . maybe trillions of other planets. Maybe more than our minds could ever fathom. And here we all are. Searching, thriving, fighting, killing, being . . . How do they look at us up there? If she were an alien . . . if she were looking at them all, she would feel nothing but pity. Pity that all these beautiful and intelligent beings could separate themselves because of judgment and difference. Pity that they would even think of harming their own. Pity that their world was crumbling around them, and that only a handful are willing to pick up the broken pieces. But she couldn't just think negatively, she was probably thinking that way now because of everything that was going through her mind. She had to remind herself that there is still good out there, there are still good people. Maybe we're all good. We just . . . need a little help.

Rose.

"Do you think she left because of us?" Adam asked suddenly.

"Why? What did we do?" Decker asked.

"I don't know, I'm just saying she might've left cause she saw how pissed we were when she told us about Earth and stuff. Remember when she said Earth wasn't our planet?"

"And we freaked." Lisa finished.

It could be the reason why she left, but Lisa didn't think it sounded right. Rose wasn't like that. If she was upset, she would probably tell them, wouldn't she?

"Then it was us?" Decker asked in what could've been a hurt voice.

"No." Lisa said firmly. "Rose isn't like that. She wouldn't just up and leave all because we got mad at something she told us. She would've expected that. She's not dumb."

"I didn't say she was. I'm just saying she could've left cause she felt bad maybe that she's telling us all this stuff and—"

"No. It's not like Rose. She isn't weak like that. And we aren't either, otherwise why would she pick us?" Lisa was waiting for Adam say something but was surprised when he just sat there in silence.

Rose wouldn't do that. Lisa was sure. She wasn't the weak little girl to go running away somewhere all because *they* were upset. For goodness sakes wouldn't she have expected that? Wouldn't she have expected that when she first told them she was an alien?

She started thinking about herself then. That's right. Rose wasn't weak like that, but Lisa was. She was weak enough to go off crying when she should've stayed home and apologized to her mom.

She was weak enough to keep reminding herself that Decker was leaving and she would never see him again. She was weak enough to let it all, everything, give her grief. Well no more. It was time to get brave. It hasn't killed her yet.

Lisa stood up then. Decker and Adam got up too and followed behind as she walked away.

"Where are we going?" Decker asked.

She turned and said with determination, "We're gonna go find our friend."

CHAPTER 32

They drove to the mall to start there first.

Decker had to remind Lisa a few times to relax, especially while she was driving, and Lisa had annoyingly told him to stop trying to distract her. He just sighed and searched for another song on her music player. Lisa knew she was a new driver and that she had to be alert at all times while on the road, so it was hard for her to have to calm her growing anxiety until they got to their destination.

When they finally got to park Lisa was the first one out of the car. She was speed walking toward the double doors to the mall entrance when Decker grabbed her arm.

"Hang on, love. We can't lose our heads here. I know you're worried and all but if we don't take it one step at a time we might miss her somehow."

She knew he was right. She really had to calm down or they may never find Rose.

They walked through each store, keeping their eyes peeled. Lisa thought it might be better if they split up. Adam agreed thinking it might be easier to scope Rose out, that way it won't turn out like those cartoons where the group of people go one way while the person they're looking for goes the other way they just came from. So Adam went to look downstairs while Lisa and Decker searched upstairs. Decker didn't want Lisa walking around the mall by herself so he insisted he go with her.

The first store they checked was Hot Topic. No sign of her there. Next was Gamestop. Still nothing.

They walked around the food court, maneuvering through crowds of people, but still no Rose. They were about to throw in the towel when Decker suggested they check Build-A-Bear, remembering Rose's excitement as they walked past by the store before. Lisa thought it was worth a shot. Unfortunately Rose wasn't there either. They crossed the whole top floor from one end to the other almost five times, going back into stores they checked before just to be sure she wasn't there. Then they both slumped down on a bench, frustrated and weary from all the running around.

Almost ten minutes later, Adam joined them on the bench, also seeming frustrated and weary.

"Now what?" Decker asked, dragging his hand through his hair. Lisa shook her head, having absolutely no idea what to do now other than just keep looking. It was really all they could do.

"You checked every store downstairs Adam?" Lisa asked him.

"Every store."

Lisa sighed in defeat. It didn't look like they were getting anywhere. They didn't have a clue as to where Rose could be at this very moment. What bothered Lisa the most was that Rose hadn't even called her, not once. If she really was ok then wouldn't she have called? Unless she suddenly forgot how to use her own phone. Lisa still can't believe she even has a phone . . .

"We're usually here at my house so you can just stop over whenever you want." Lisa said one day as they were sitting out on the front porch.

"Do you not have a communication device that I can contact you with?"

"You mean like a cell phone?" Decker asked.

Rose nodded and pulled out her "cell phone." It was a rectangle shaped touch phone, or so it looked like. The edges were decked out in purple crystals and the whole back covering a sparkling black.

"Yo check this thing out!" Rose handed the phone over to Adam and he turned it in his hands. "Coolest cell ever."

"But this is the "coolest" part, I do believe." Rose tapped the screen once and a long purple beam shot up to reveal a wide picture of the solar system right above their heads. It was amazing . . . Like they were really looking up into space. The guys stood back up slowly after crouching down from the explosion of stars. All the planets spinned and glowed as though it were really happening. Then Rose smiled and told them, "It is. What you are seeing my friends, is the universe in motion. Whatever is happening up there, you are seeing."

Lisa almost laughed, but she was so entranced in the projection she couldn't do anything but stare.

Apparently aliens have cell phones. Who knew?

Then Lisa remembered something. She snapped her fingers. "The bookstore!"

Of course! Why hadn't she thought of that in the first place? Rose would most likely be at the bookstore than the mall, she absolutely loved it when they took her there . . .

$\mathcal{R}$ose gazed around in incredulity when they entered the bookstore. She walked over to the one shelf of new books just brought into the store and grazed her fingertips along the spines. The guys went over to the electronic book section while Lisa followed Rose as she continued her exploration.

"This is amazing. I have never seen such a place." She walked over to a shelf and pulled a book carefully out of its place between all the other ones. She opened the cover like it was an ancient piece of writing that could crumble in her hands at any moment.

"This parchment is much different than the kind my father showed me."

That had Lisa curious. "Your father?"

"He showed me something that was not exactly pieced together such as this, but it was written beautifully."

"Really?"

"Yes indeed. Oh Lisa if you could've only seen it. The language, the artistry. I believe it was a poem of some sort. A long poem about a man who traveled for twelve years, and he battled evil monsters and spoke to gods and . . . Oh it was truly a magnificent story. Mother would often read it to me when I was little."

"Sounds familiar. You still have it?" Lisa asked, picking up a book.

"Actually yes, I still have it, though I do not dare open it less the parchment turn to dust at my touch." She laughed. "Father told me he received the story as a gift from a man he had come across while visiting your planet many years ago."

"He got it from Earth?"

"Yes. He said that the man was not well known among his people, but he was a brilliant writer, truly he was. My father may have broken a rule or two by giving the man a sleeping potion for his insomnia, such a great writer he was that his mind kept him up so late at night thinking of stories. But he was very grateful, so he gifted my father with his first piece of writing. Father kindly refused, not wanting to take something this man had worked so hard on for so long, but the man insisted, assuring my father that he would make more stories like that one."

Lisa smiled. "Guess it's really special huh?"

Rose also smiled. "Indeed. Perhaps one day I may read it to the next generation of children of the Council."

Lisa returned the book she was skimming through back to the shelf and turned to another.

"So what's it called? The poem?"

"The Odyssey." Rose answered. The book in Lisa's hands fell to the floor . . .

That was an experience Lisa is sure she won't be forgetting. The guys followed her out of the mall in a quick pace to the car.

The bookstore was only right across the street from the mall so it took them not even a minute to get there. They parked and leaped out of the car. This time, Lisa told them all that they should split up again, this time each one of them should take a different section of the store. Lisa had the front, Decker the back, and Adam had the middle isles and magazine sections. The store wasn't as big as the mall of course, so it should be easier to spot Rose if she was here.

After about half an hour, all three of them ran into each other empty handed at the store's café. Asking them, "Any luck?" would've been a stupid question to ask since it was obvious they didn't find her.

Decker came up with another place to look then. The bowling alley. It would take them twenty minutes to get there from where they were at now, and Lisa didn't like wasting mom and dad's gas on a trip that would probably be a waste of time. Really, why would Rose be at the bowling alley without them? That was what her logical mind was asking, but the other part was telling the logical part to shut up so she could just get in the damn car and go check it out anyway. So off they went.

She should've listened to the logical part of her brain. Rose wasn't at the bowling alley. No surprise. So now they were right back where they started. Literally. When they got home they decided to take a walk toward the end of the street to see if all those police cars were still there. And yep, they were all still there, and Lisa thought the place couldn't get any more crowded with vehicles. Somehow it had.

She texted her two friend's Syl and Britt, but they replied saying Rose wasn't with them and they hadn't seen her.

"So what, are they gonna take her ship or something?"

"No Adam, they're just gonna leave it in the woods."

He scowled at Decker's sarcasm.

Lisa sighed and leaned back against the tree. If Rose's ship was gone then that means she won't have a way back home, and worse, now they're probably going to be looking for her. Lisa wondered if our DNA experts would be able to pick up on something that didn't look normal, or rather, didn't look human. Of course, having Rose's DNA wouldn't get them anywhere, because it's not like she's registered into our government's system or anything. But now she had no way to get back home. Lisa tilted her head up at the still-gray sky, now seeming to grow darker with heavy thunder clouds rolling in.

What would her dad do if he realized his daughter wasn't coming home? Lisa just then realized that she was using the word "home." Rose told them she didn't have a home, at least not yet. The High Council Ship was where she and her father stayed. But did that mean that he would come to earth to look for her? Where would he begin? And how?

Lisa then remembered Rose telling her about her boyfriend who was waiting back at the ship for her. What would he think? No doubt if it were Decker he would make his way to Earth and wipe out everything until he found her.

She sighed, looking over at Decker, who was sitting next to her with Adam on his right. The two were talking about their zombie video game they loved to play so much and Decker was arguing that Adam got killed more than he did so Decker was the better player. Adam snapped that he was the one who finished the game faster and with all the weapons.

She shook her head. All this crazy stuff was happening and these two are talking about video games.

She smiled and put her hand on top of Decker's hand. He looked over at her, smiled, then lifted her hand to his lips. He then went right back to arguing with Adam.

Lisa laughed.

Oh how she would miss this. Their walks, their fun, their conversations, their company. Decker would be moving away in only two months. Then they would all graduate. Lisa wondered if

Decker's mom would even let him come over to her house for her graduation party.

The woman would probably refuse to let him come over simply because it would be rude of him to leave the house when they were also throwing him a graduation party. Lisa rolled her eyes. Yeah, a graduation party his mom just "sprang" up as though she forgot to mention it to him when he told them he would be over Lisa's house that day.

Decker told his mom that he didn't want a party, but she wasn't letting him off that easy. She guilt him with the old, "You're growing older every day and I remember when you were just a baby in my arms." Pff! More like a baby in your *sister's* arms. Decker's mom was only sixteen when she had him, so of course she didn't want to be stuck home every day with a newborn when she could be out partying with friends. Decker's aunt told his mom that she would watch Decker while his mom went out, since she was young and "didn't deserve to be shackled at home with a baby." If Lisa had it her way she would go right up to that woman and tell her exactly what she thought of her. She would tell her that she was nothing but a selfish, no good, lazy bi—

"Lisa, which one of us do you think is better at killing zombies?" Decker asked her.

Lisa blinked at the question.

"I get all the weapons in every stage." Adam boasted.

"Yeah but I always get the headshots." Decker countered.

They both looked at her then, waiting for her answer.

She just laughed and put her hands on both their heads, ruffling their hair to their protest.

"You both are."

They didn't seem satisfied with two winners.

Lisa smiled softly. Well, the truth was that she might not like the woman, but she can't criticize her for being a teen mom. If she hadn't, Decker wouldn't be here. So maybe Lisa doesn't hate her as much as she thought. Maybe she's even a little grateful.

CHAPTER 33

Another week passed. Maybe two. She couldn't tell. To Lisa, it felt like time was going faster yet slower at the same time, if that made any sense. Actually it felt more like eternity. She thought it funny how she always read in her romance books how not having seen someone for so long felt like "eternity." Maybe she should come up with a different word. "Eternity" was used too much. "Forever?" That was used a lot too. An endless infinity. She supposed that would work.

Lisa remembered the first time they met Rose, and how they freaked out when she told them that she was an alien. Then all that turned into curiosity and excitement when they started asking her questions. The things she told them . . . that "wow" feeling when they learned about the planet, and the Bermuda triangle, and the pyramids.

These were things nobody else on Earth knew. Just them. Three teenagers. They weren't scientists who have dedicated their lives to finding the answers to the world's toughest questions, or scholars with the genius minds of Einstein, or theoretical physicists. They were just three ordinary teenagers.

In a way it made Lisa feel kind of special. Nobody else on Earth . . . well except the government of course, and the MIB . . . and all the people at Area 51 . . . She'll say a mass majority of people didn't know all the things they knew.

When Rose told them about Area 51, Lisa was sure she had heard it all then . . .

"*A*nd so we allowed for only some of your people to know of our existence, in case another species should pass by or land on your planet. The Council would much rather keep track of what Hadrian is doing and where he is rather than worry about any other aliens, so if a species should land on your planet, we have left it up to your people to handle the situation."

They were sitting at the pizza shop eating away at cheese fries and garlic bread. The guys were in their third round of Uno.

"Everyone already knows that Area 51 has aliens." Decker said.

"And why do you think that is? After all, if they did not want everyone to believe they were harboring extra-terrestrial intelligence and information, why wouldn't they simply make it difficult for people to assume such?"

"Ok, you kinda lost me at extra-terrestrial." Adam lay down another card. Decker was irritated that he had to pick up another four cards.

"Well why is it that when people hear Area 51 they think aliens?" Rose asked.

"Because they're so secret about it all. I mean c'mon, they got a sign that says they're ready to shoot anyone that trespasses." Decker said.

"True. But what do aliens have to do with it all?" Rose delved deeper into her question, trying to get them to think about it.

The guys shrugged, too into their game to really come up with an answer.

"Maybe because they want us to assume . . ."

Rose clapped her hands. "Excellent Lisa! Well thought."

"But why would they want people to assume that Area 51 has aliens? Don't they even know that people get curious about those kinds of things? Some even wonder if our own government is hiding aliens from us."

"Better to be curious than scared." Rose said.

"What do you mean?" Adam asked, looking up from his cards.

"I mean there are humans that get frightened very easily, and in mass amounts of groups it would only take a few people to cause a chain panic reaction. The more people who believe in aliens, the less frightened they will be if ever the Earth should encounter such a thing. And it has. Of course, the Council did not want to interfere as much with your human world, in fact, they stopped shortly after they noticed how intelligent humans were starting to evolve and so did not feel it necessary to aid them anymore. But eventually the humans started to discover what they called "strange" things like Stone Hendge and mysterious carvings on cave walls. They started to wonder, and that arose questions that many were too scared to ask, because the very thought of something out there being much larger than they were and probably dangerous was terrifying."

The guys were listening now, all their cards on the table.

"Our interference produced both positive and negative effects. The humans did indeed need our help or their species would've died off, but the gap between the time there and the time of discovery left unusual questions with no answers."

Adam absently picked up one of Decker's cheese fries off his plate to which Decker snatched a fry off of Adam's plate.

Rose continued. "As life on this planet developed more and more, so did the way the humans craved for independence and diversity. Some felt that they were more intelligent than others. More wealthy or more unique. Eventually the humans began to group themselves based on similar looks, gender, lifestyles and beliefs. And one of those many groups held a strong belief that only they should know about extraterrestrial beings."

"So how long ago was this again?" Adam asked, gnawing on his half eaten sandwich.

Rose seemed to have to think about this. "Well I could not give you an exact time period only because we were not so focused on tracking your time, but I could tell you that they're way of living was much different than today's. Females wore large dresses and head coverings. They even carried small umbrellas with them even when the weather was dry. Males did not wear the colorful attire that the females wore, rather they were clothed in mostly brown, grey or black suits with similar colored leg wear. The people did not travel in metal cars, only wagons pulled by horses. Their electricity was flame and their medicines were herbs. Indeed it was a much different time."

But Lisa had to ask, "How is it that they knew about aliens?"

"Many knew. Others convinced them that what they saw were only figments of their imagination, so that only they could hold such knowledge and consider themselves unique. The Council believes that a species of alien must've traveled to Earth in some way that the humans saw as strange. However it happened, the Council does not know, but they suspect that Hadrian had something to do with it. By now he was beginning to gather more and more allies."

"So he's getting some other aliens to do shit for him? That's messed up, man." Adam said.

"But why doesn't he just do it himself like he did before? He would've been able to control everyone and make them think he was some kind of god or something couldn't he?"

Rose shook her head. "Around this time the humans were becoming more monotheistic, meaning that they believed in only one god. Hadrian is indeed intelligent. If for some reason he is not able to travel to Earth by himself then he would have no choice but to send someone else and the humans would see that he is not the only "god." He wanted to stay as invisible to your people as possible. The only reason he succeeded in doing it himself before was because the humans were easily led, and their numbers were not so great."

"So he got other aliens to go to Earth to collect needed materials." Lisa realized.

"Exactly." Rose nodded.

"But if he wasn't living on the moon anymore, then where was he?" Decker asked.

"We don't know, but it couldn't have been very far. We've had beings tell us that they saw his ship just along the outer ring of a nearby planet."

"So like, what does this have to do with area 51?" Adam asked, stealing another fry absently from Decker's plate.

"With the knowledge that Hadrian may be sending aliens down to Earth, the Council had decided to intervene in the human's world once again. Not only was Hadrian putting other beings in danger but the humans as well. These beings may have been brainwashed by Hadrian to despise the humans as much as he has, so any accidental encounter could be dangerous."

Adam and Decker were chewing down their cheese fries like they were at the movie theaters watching a suspenseful film.

"Father built indestructible Tracer ships for the Elders, since the Council Ship was much too large to travel to Earth in, and they didn't want to cause a commotion. Once they landed, the Elders sought out the humans who believed in their existence. Among them were perhaps the most intelligent human beings the Council had ever met. They were not frightened when the Elders approached them. A pact was made that if the humans could conceal the existence of aliens from their own then the Elders would grant them with supreme knowledge, knowledge that no other human would ever know of.

But the humans were not interested in supreme knowledge, they wanted material things. So each Elder present gifted the humans with what they believed to be decent gifts. A communications device, an invisibility cloak, and indestructible armor. The humans accepted these gifts and the pact was complete. Many years passed. When the Elders reached out to the humans once again, they learned that the group had grown in numbers, and they were enhancing the gifts that were given to them to their own advantage. The humans had also moved the group to an isolated location so that they could work on these devices in secret away from the mass population."

The guy's mouths were hanging down to the table. Lisa was so overwhelmed with this info she actually went to go take a sip of her soda and spilled it all over her pants . . .

Lisa just got done putting more water into Gustav's bowl when her cell phone began to ring inside her pocket. She picked it up, not even bothering to check the caller i.d. since Adam said he would call once he got to Decker's house.

"Yeah guys?" She answered.

"Lisa?"

She froze, recognizing that female voice.

It couldn't be . . . There was no way—

"Rose . . . ?"

"Oh thank goodness I could finally reach you! I have been trying to call for such a long time."

"Rose where are you?!" She asked, expecting the worst. All her nerves were standing on end now.

"I'm-" She heard static. There was some mumbling and the sound was changing from low to high.

"Rose? Rose?!"

"-here with—at the sc . . ."

"Rose!"

Lisa tried to focus on what she was saying through the static that was growing louder and louder, and then a loud beeping sounded and the phone was saying, "We're sorry, but your call was disconnected."

"Damn!" Lisa pressed the end button and looked up her "Received calls" panel.

Rose called her alright, but it wasn't from *her* cell. This was a random number Lisa didn't know, which didn't help at all.

She tried calling it back but it only rang once before the phone said, to Lisa's annoyance, "Your call has been forwarded to an automated voice messaging system."

"You gotta be kidding me!" So she dialed for Adam's cell.

"Yeah." Adam answered.

"Guys you won't believe this but Rose just called me, just now!"

"What?!" She heard Adam and Decker both say.

"Yeah but the call got all static-y and I lost it."

"Hang on we'll be right over." Then they hung up. Lisa couldn't believe she had just heard Rose's voice, after all the time she had been gone! Was she hurt? Was she in danger? Was she ill? Lisa had to mentally slap herself to keep it together. She was thinking the worst when she shouldn't. Rose didn't sound hurt or ill, actually she sounded relieved.

"I've never seen that number before so I couldn't tell ya." Adam was examining Lisa's phone.

The guys ran over immediately after getting Lisa's call. Adam tried using his phone to call the number but couldn't get a single ring. Lisa felt adrenaline rushing through her. At least Rose was still alive, for now. So they had to find her before it was too late. She felt guilty that they had stopped looking for her a while ago, but now there was hope that they would finally find her.

"She was about to say she was somewhere, but I couldn't get what it was."

"What did it sound like?" Decker asked.

"Umm . . . she said something with an "S." That's what it sounded like anyway."

"An S?" Adam asked, thinking that clearly wasn't enough to go by. They were all sounding out places that started with an S.

"S . . . skate park?" Decker suggested.

But there weren't any skate parks around here.

"Shop?" Lisa didn't think so, Rose would've specified better.

"Sandiego?"

"Dude why would she be all the way over in Sandiego?" Decker asked Adam dryly.

"I don't know man! I can't think of anything with an S."

"S . . . Soccer field?" Lisa suggested then.

"The only soccer field around here is the one next to the football field, and that's surrounded by police."

Lisa felt her hopes break down. "Then . . . . she really was captured?"

Is that it then? Did Rose somehow return to her ship for whatever reason and find herself being taken away by government officials? Did Lisa really hear Rose's last words?

She thought about Rose's father, what would he think if he found out something had happened to his precious daughter? And her mother and sister?

And Cornelius. How would he be, knowing the love of his life was lost forever, possibly being tortured or kept away?

"Hang on, what about school? School stars with an S." Decker said.

"The school? Ours?" Adam asked.

"Why there?" Lisa asked.

"Don't know, but I'd rather check there than the field."

It was worth a shot, even if Rose wasn't there, at least they could say they tried. Lisa thought about how she wished there was a way to contact her family in case they never found her, or if they found out something bad happened to her and just wanted to let them know. Although Lisa doubted she could tell them straightly, she would be an absolute mess.

How would they take that news? Lisa knew what she would be like if it were Decker. Her being a complete mess is an understatement. She would feel like someone ripped out a part of her soul, leaving a big bloody hole in her chest, never to heal. Lisa grimaced at her descriptive mind. To anyone else, it might sound as if she was being way over dramatic, but it's really the only feeling she could describe if she ever lost Decker. Then that awful sinking feeling dropped into her stomach when she remembered Decker was going to move to Florida.

She felt her body stiffen. *Six months left . . .*

"Lisa?" Decker put his hands on her shoulders like she was going to faint. Maybe she was . . .

He was leaning over her and saying something but she couldn't really understand. She tried to focus but her mind was a blur, or maybe that was just her eyes.

"Lisa! What is it? What's the matter?"

She wanted to say something. *Say something!* But she couldn't. She felt numb and lightheaded.

"Lisa?"

"I'm fine Decker. Really."

"No you're not fine. What's wrong?"

Adam was looking at her with concern. "You alright?"

She couldn't stop the tears then. Rose was still missing. Decker was leaving . . . It felt like her whole world was breaking away from her.

She remembered when she first met him.

She stopped wearing those black, baggy clothes. She started to talk a little more. She pushed her hair out of her face. She stood taller. He was trying to tilt her chin up so he could look into her eyes, but she looked away, feeling like an idiot for getting so upset. Then he wrapped his arms around her, leaning his cheek down on her head. "Lisa . . . my Analisa." He kissed the top of her head.

He knew. *He always did.*

"I'll come back to you. Just think about that. Don't think about anything else."

She leaned further into his embrace. He tilted her chin up and kissed her.

It wasn't one of his gentle kisses. He was showing her he was serious. He was trying to show her that she didn't have to cry. He wasn't going to be gone forever.

"I promise." He said to her.

And she believed him. It wasn't because she didn't have a choice, she wanted to believe it.

"Hey guys, I don't mean to get in the way and all but we should probably check out the school right away." Adam said.

Lisa swiped at her eyes. "Alright. Let's go."

CHAPTER 34

They drove to the school and parked in the outside parking lot. Thankfully the gates were open so they could get through, but they looked to be the only ones there.

"You sure about this?" Decker asked her when they stopped the car.

Honestly, she didn't know. Were they really going to break into the school? Rose might not even be here. They were really taking a risk on this. For one, Lisa could kiss her perfect school record goodbye, and her parents would hit the roof if they found out she was doing something like this, then what would she tell them? "Oh yeah mom we were just looking for our alien friend." She would never see the light of day again.

"I don't know about this you guys. What if someone finds us?"

"If we make this quick then we won't have to worry about getting caught." Decker unlocked his seatbelt.

"You say that now and the next thing we know we're sitting in the back of a police car. Damn, man my dad would kill me!"

They snuck around the first building away from the parking lot in case they had to make a bolt back to the car. Decker pulled at the doors but they were locked.

Ducking further into the main campus entrance, they made their way toward the farther, longer building. Lisa snapped her head from side to side as she followed close behind Decker, keeping an eye out for Rose but also for anyone else. That would just be their luck for a security guard to stumble upon them trying to break into the school, and they haven't been having much good luck lately. They all took to the three different doors on all sides of the long building.

All locked. Big surprise there.

Lisa sighed thinking maybe this was just a waste of time. And a really stupid idea. Maybe Rose really wasn't here. Why would she be at the school anyway? But then something off the corner of Lisa's eye grabbed her attention.

She yelled for the guys to get over to where she was and they came running.

"Look over there." She pointed toward the other parking lot by the next farthest building.

Adam shaded his eyes from the sun with his hand to see. "A car?"

"Shit." Decker said in a panic.

They all scrambled to get behind the building.

Lisa poked her head out first.

"Man, its Saturday! I should be home right now, playing some Xbox and killing zombies." Adam complained. Decker shushed him.

After a few minutes of hiding they decided to cautiously move out from behind the building so they could get a better look at the far away car.

"Probably a teacher." Decker said, squinting his eyes.

Probably, but it didn't ease Lisa's nerves. So now Rose wasn't here at the school either. Her hopes were fired up after receiving that phone call earlier, only to be thrown into an icy river of disappointment. But then, Rose never said she was at the school, she just said she was somewhere that started with an S.

Jeeze, why did everything have to be so complicated?

"Let's go check it out." Decker said suddenly walking away from them.

"You want to go check out a car?" Adam asked dryly.

Decker just gave him a "you-know-what-I-mean" look.

Adam threw his arms in the air. "This is so stupid. Can't we just go home and call it a day? She obviously isn't here."

They ignored him and went to check out the car.

"Hey isn't this Mr. O's car?" Adam said when they got up to the blue dodge charger.

Decker circled around the car, looking into the passenger window and noticing the Shakespeare bobble head on the dashboard he confirmed, "Yep, definitely Mr. O's."

"What's he doing here though? He told us during class that he had errands to run, and that's the reason why he cancelled the book club for today." Lisa said.

They moved past the car to the small building across from the parking lot. It was Mr. O's classroom.

Lisa tried turning the door handle, then noticing it was locked she tried knocking.

No answer.

She moved over to the windows and knocked again on the glass.

"Mr. O? You here?" She put her head up to the glass to see if she could hear anything. But there was nothing.

The shades covered the windows and there didn't seem to be any lights on inside the room.

"Maybe he's in another building." Adam said.

"Then why would he park here?" Lisa asked.

The guys shrugged.

Lisa didn't know what to make of it either, but whatever it was it really might be none of their business. Maybe he was just here for teacher things. They really shouldn't be nosing around. Actually, they shouldn't be here at all. Maybe they should just leave . . .

Fainted noises sounded from inside the room and Lisa leaned her head back up against the window. Mumbling . . . and rustling . . . someone was talking.

"Guys listen . . ." Adam and Decker leaned their ears up to the glass. There was so more rustling. Like paper.

"I hear it." Decker said. "Someone's in there."

"Mr. O.?" Lisa knocked again on the window. Nobody answered so she walked over to the door to knock a second time.

This time however, the door creaked open. They all tensed up and looked at one another. Nobody moved.

Adam nodded with a gulp that he was ready. Lisa and Decker nodded too, and they all walked into the dark room together.

"Mr.—"

The lights flashed on. Lisa nearly jumped out of her skin and felt the guys both flinch next to her.

Mr. O. was standing over by the light switch.

"Well if it isn't my three favorite students." The teacher said with a grin.

They were all too startled to speak.

"What brings you all here? It is Saturday you know. Shouldn't you be at home relaxing?"

"Yes!" Adam said in frustration, the blood returning to his face.

"Actually uhh . . . we were kinda . . . looking for someone." Lisa admitted guiltily.

"Oh? And who would that be?" Mr. O asked suspiciously.

"Just a friend." Decker said plainly.

"Ah. Small? About maybe . . . this high?" He measured up to his waist. "Blonde hair? Glasses?"

"Yeah . . . ? Adam said.

"Yes. Rose." Lisa said firmly, seeing as how they were already caught.

"Yes?" A light voice called from the closet door . . . *the closet door?*

Then she stepped out in her short dark blue skirt with black chains crisscrossing from one pocket to the other, black striped. Her black, long sleeved shirt hugging her small frame and her dark blue and black winter hat covering her head, the long black ties dangling down to her knees.

Lisa couldn't believe it.

And neither could the guys. Their mouths dropped open in shock. Then Lisa muttered out, barely audible, "Rose . . . ?"

Her face lit up when her eyes landed on the three and she yelled out in joy, "Lisa!" And she ran into Lisa's arms.

"Oh! I am so happy to see you, my beloved friends. I have missed you all so sorely."

She then ran up to Decker to give him a hug, having to leap up to meet his height. Then she ran to hug Adam, who was in such shock, or was that emotion? He couldn't even hug her back in greeting. Or was it reunion?

Lisa finally regained enough composure to understand what she was looking at, or rather *who* she was looking at, and she smiled. It was Rose. She was alive.

"Wooooaaa hold up! How is it that you could be here . . . when we were . . . and you-but we—"

"Oh Adam! My humorous friend. How I have missed you the most!" She threw herself into his arms again and he nearly tripped backwards trying to catch her.

"So you were here this whole time?" Decker asked when she finally released Adam from her death hug and he was gasping for breath.

"Yes, I've been here with Ragar."

"Ragar??" All three of them asked.

"Ragar" put up his one hand in greeting.

"Mr O?!" Adam exclaimed.

"Shit, I think my brain just overheated." Decker put his hand to his throbbing head and leaned on one of the desks for support.

Lisa was looking back and forth from Rose to Mr. O. *"Ragar."* What the hell?!

Everyone was silent. Lisa didn't even know how she knew the room was silent because her mind was racing all over the place. Mr. O.—"Ragar" cleared his throat to speak. "I believe there is much to be explained here Ms. Rosalind."

Rose nodded and turned to the three of them. She began by bowing her head saying, "I am very sorry for disappearing from the three of you these last few weeks, but Ragar had called me about something very important that had to be brought to my attention." Oh great, something else to add to all this craziness.

"Wait hold up, before we get into it and all . . . so you're not upset about before?" Adam had to ask. Rose tilted her head at him in confusion.

"You know. That time you told us about Earth and how it wasn't really our planet and all, and we got all upset and stuff. We thought maybe that was why you left . . . cause you thought we were mad." Rose smiled softly at him. "You were worried about me?" She asked when she got up close to him.

Adam blushed and scratched his head, not knowing what to say at first, but then he smiled and stumbled out, "Well you know . . . you're our friend and all. Ah, what am I saying! Of course we were worried about you!"

Lisa smiled when Rose started to laugh and grab Adam in for another death hug, to Adam's protest. "Can I ask why you were in the closet?" Decker figured he'd ask. "Oh. Of course." Rose walked over to the closet and turned the doorknob a few times. Right to left, left again, right again. Then she pushed it in, and the small room inside started to turn, rotate. The "closet" turned into this huge silver room with black shiny gadgets displayed in rows along the walls. There was also a big black screen sitting in the very back, and a long silver table circling around it. "I have been trying to make contact with the High Council ship for days now. This phone device of mine does not function as properly as I thought it would. But it is a good thing Ragar has had this sec ret communications room built in just in case such a dilemma should arise." She smiled. The guys had their mouths hanging open. "Dude are you seeing this . . . ?" Adam mumbled to Decker, still mesmerized at what he was looking at.

Mr. O. walked over to pull down the projector screen hanging above the chalkboard. When Rose finally let go of Adam she walked over to the screen and nodded for Mr. O to turn it on, her happy face replaced by a more serious look now.

The whole screen lit up with a three dimensional picture of the solar system, *our* solar system. It looked like the exact same one they saw before when Rose showed them from her cell phone. There was the sun, and all the planets. Even the moons looked amazingly realistic. It was all up there, like someone had taken a picture of it from space. Star dust hovered over the outer parts of the picture, and you could literally see every spec. Beautiful colors of pink, blue and purple stretched around the globes like strokes of paint in water.

It all looked so real, like no drawing or "possible" figurative photo ever seen in a science or history book. This was the real thing.

"The High Council has taken this photo only a few Earth days ago. I was ordered to inform Ms. Rosalind immediately upon receiving it."

He threw Rose a laser pointer.

"Something was detected here." She was pointing to an area close to Earth. *Very* close to Earth, Lisa realized with a sudden lump of fear in her throat. The guys went up to the screen to get a better look, their eyes widening and Decker mumbling, "Damn."

Lisa joined them, equally shocked when she saw what it was. Nobody said a word. They just stared at the frightening black figure as it shadowed the darker half of Earth, sitting ominously to the side.

"The Council believes it is Hadrian's ship."

That's Hadrian? It was all that played through Lisa's mind as she stared at the picture. It definitely looked like a space ship, and it looked huge, probably bigger than Rose's ship. Lisa felt shivers run up her spine. Jeez . . . this was taken only days ago?

"So then he's here . . . ?" Decker was still staring at the picture. "This is it . . . ?"

"Shit dude. This can't be the end, it can't! I-I haven't finished school, man! I just got my license. I got my whole life ahead of me. I can't die now—"

"Nobody is going to die!"

Rose's voice broke the ringing in Lisa's ears.

They all looked at her then. She was gripping the laser pointer in her small hand.

"I promise. I promise to you all that I will not let anything happen to Earth. *We* will not let anything happen to you."

Adam walked over to the window, his hands in his hair and his chest visibly heaving in and out like he was having a panic attack, but he didn't take his eyes off of Rose. Neither of them did.

"We have protected this planet since the beginning and we will continue to protect it. We may not have the power to save you from your own kind, but we *will* defend you from *us*."

Lisa suddenly realized she was seeing a completely different side to Rose. This shy, giddy little girl had more spunk to her than Lisa thought. They might not have known her long, but ever since the first day they became friends Lisa felt her life change. They didn't really make a lot of friends, after all. Not a lot of good ones anyway. It almost felt like they had known her forever.

Lisa remembers when her and Decker made the agreement that they would always be with each other, just the two of them. They always thought they didn't need anyone else. But the truth was they wanted to have others. They wanted friends. Even if they had each other, they could still get lonely. They liked to go out and have fun, and sometimes it just wasn't fun without anyone else.

Lisa always thought it was silly, since all they really needed was each other. Decker wasn't just Lisa's boyfriend, he was her best friend. So why then did it feel lonely sometimes when it was just the two of them? Maybe it was because they were like one whole person. Or maybe they were actually more social than they thought. Whatever it was, Lisa was just glad to have friends like Rose and Adam. And Syl and Britt. And she was glad to have her mom, dad and brother. Even little Gustav. In this big world . . . she knew she wasn't alone.

"Ms. Rosalind speaks true." Mr. O. said. "The High Council took the responsibility of protecting this planet long ago. Not only that, but they had been searching for Hadrian's ship for centuries. This is the opportunity they had been desperately waiting for. Now perhaps they will finally capture him."

"Oh snap . . . uh . . . speaking of space ship . . ." Adam looked nervously over at Decker and Lisa. Realization dawned on them both and they exchanged troubled looks.

Rose tilted her head in confusion.

Might as well spill the beans. "Um . . . Rose, there's something we gotta tell you about your—"

"Adam knocked into your ship in the woods and broke its invisibility thing." Decker said and Adam snapped, "Hey! It wasn't my fault I didn't *see* the damn thing! Besides we all agreed that anyone could've bumped into it cause it was right *there*. It was an accident!"

Rose came up and put a reassuring hand on his shoulder. "Adam, its ok. I'm sure it was an accident. Oh dear, but this may be a problem." She sighed.

"I'm really sorry Rose. I'll make this up to ya somehow."

"Adam it's ok, really. I'm not mad at you. Though I suspect someone has surely found it by now and has given it over to authorities yes?"

They all nodded and were relieved they didn't have to go into how big the whole "finding an alien ship" blew up in the media and all. Rose sighed. "Father told me strictly not to let the humans see me or the ship. He will no doubt be extremely disappointed. I had just recently received my authorization pass to fly it too."

Then she started chuckling.

This threw Lisa off to say, as though Rose didn't quite understand the predicament she may be in, "There were a lot of police cars and big black vans and stuff. They probably took your ship—"

"Not to worry Lisa." Rose winked and motioned everyone with her finger to follow her outside.

She told them to stop after they walked out about ten feet from the door.

Then she walked out away from the group, putting herself a good distance from them. They all stared awkwardly after her as she then pulled out a red glove. They watched as she laid the glove carefully on the top of her right hand, and in an instant the glove melted around her skin, molding into something that would be confused with thick leather, changing from its original elastic texture. It enveloped around her entire hand, leaving only her fingers free.

What the . . . ?

They all gaped, mouths open at what they were seeing.

The diamond-like shape on her palm and on the top of her hand started to glow a bright white, and she fisted her hand, as though grabbing for something.

"You might want to stand back some more . . ." Ragar warned and they moved with him over to the corner of the building.

Rose released her clenched fist and a ball of white and blue flashed out of her palm and revolved around her small hand and up her arm in little waves of blue electricity. Lisa and the others had to shield their eyes from the light's intensity. Booming sounds erupted through their ears like someone was blasting a cannon right next to them. Then they heard sparks. Lisa could see the light dim behind her eye lids and squinted out to see what was happening.

And then they saw it. Rose's space ship. Big, red and shiny. Sitting before them, gleaming in the sun's light like polished metal.

And not a scratch on it.

"Now that's what I'm talking about." Lisa heard Adam gasp out next to her.

The memory of the first time she laid her eyes on the large ship flashed across Lisa's mind then. That night the moon's blue glow glossed over the beautiful red ship, and it sparkled like snow sparkles in the evening.

Rose used her other hand to wave it lightly over the top of her right hand and the glove melted off the same way it melted on.

Lisa was the first to get the feeling back in her legs to move closer towards the great ship and the guys followed.

"Woa . . ." Decker and Adam both said in awe.

Rose ran her hand over the cool metal of her ship and sighed in relief, probably glad to know that nothing bad had happened to it. She turned to the three of them and said with a chuckle, "Go ahead, you can touch it you know."

The guys exchanged looks of "you go first" but then they both shrugged and went over to touch the large ship.

"It's cold." Adam shivered but grinned, amazed that he was actually touching something from space.

"Yeah. Like it was sitting in ice." Decker said, retrieving his hand and looking at it.

Lisa walked up to the ship in absolute amazement. She had seen it before when they found it in the woods, and she touched it then. It felt so surreal seeing it before her again right now.

She was surprised nothing had happened to it while it was in the government's care. She would've thought they would want to start taking it apart to examine its technology. But here it was. She wondered what those government people were saying right now. It was actually kind of funny to imagine their shocked faces at seeing the thing disappear from their sight, and probably right before they were about to check it out.

Lisa saw her reflection in the shiny red metal. She reached her hand out and shivered at the coolness she felt under her fingertips. The same coolness she felt before.

This is just amazing . . .

They all jumped back when the door to the ship suddenly started coming down. Rose turned to them all with a sad smile on her face.

"Rose?" Adam asked.

She was biting her lower lip as though to hold back tears.

"My friends, I will miss you all."

"You're leaving?" Lisa was surprised to hear some emotion in Decker's voice, but then, he had come to love Rose just as much as the rest of them.

Rose nodded her head. "I'm deeply saddened to say that my mission is now over. Father warned me that if a situation such as this should ever arise that I take my leave immediately so as not to draw any more attention."

Decker gave Adam a hard shove then.

"Man if you hadn't knocked into her ship-!"

"No! Please Decker. It is not anyone's fault. Actually I blame myself for not taking the necessary precautions. But as my mother always told me, "You live to make mistakes and learn from them." I do not regret coming here. Not at all."

Lisa heard Adam sniff behind her.

"This has been the most wonderful adventure of my life." She went up and gave Decker a hug first. Then she went over to Adam, who was trying to cover up his tears with his hood.

"I will never have another one like it, and you have all taught me so much."

Then she went to Lisa. "I will never forget any of you."

Lisa smiled. Rose was like the little sister she never had, and even though it felt like they had always known her, now that she was leaving, it didn't seem long enough.

"So . . ." Adam said, dragging his sleeve across his wet face. "The Bermuda triangle huh?"

Decker had to smile too. "Pretty crazy stuff."

Lisa smiled faintly.

Mr. O. came up to put both his hands on the guy's shoulders. Adam laughed and said to him, "Man, I can't believe all this time you were an alien."

"Yeah what gives Mr. O?" Decker grinned.

The teacher smiled and said, "There are a lot of things you might have missed while sleeping in my class boys." Then Decker mentioned something about knowing all along Mr. O was an alien and Adam laughed in his face saying that he had a clue way before Decker did, in fact, he had a feeling a lot of their other teachers were aliens and started naming them off, starting with Mr. Derbell.

Lisa smiled and turned back to Rose who started saying to her, "I hope you all can forgive my absence for so long, it's just when Ragar informed me of the message he received I had no choice but to go to him at once."

"Don't worry about it. Besides, we're just happy you're ok. I was like a nut wondering what could've happened to you."

Rose laughed. "Well I suppose I may have also been a "nut" as you say when I realized how long it had been since I contacted you."

That was definitely something Lisa was wondering about. "So how come you never called?"

Rose took out her phone and tapped her fingers against the glass screen. "My communications device somehow malfunctioned and I was unable to call you. Luckily, Ragar remembered he also had a device and allowed me to use it, but the frequency here at the school is not so strong."

Lisa laughed. So really she was worrying herself to death for nothing. Rose was never in any danger after all. And it turns out that Mr. O was like her guardian to watch out for her while she was here. Figures one of her favorite teachers in the world had to be an alien. She wondered how long it would take for the three of them to get over *that* one. He would probably be leaving with Rose no doubt.

Actually, Lisa was almost relieved that Rose was going home. At least she'll be safer up there with her father and the High

Council then down here on Earth. Lisa thought about that for a moment. Safer. It was really a shame to think that living up in space might be safer than living down here on Earth. With all the crazy things that happen around this world it doesn't surprise Lisa that she would think that way.

She hugged Rose then, knowing that even though Rose would be far away, at least she would remember them, and they would remember her too. Which suddenly brought up a question in Lisa's mind that she should've asked a long time ago.

"Hey Rose. Why did you really pick us?"

Rose just looked at her with those big green eyes, eyes that have seen more than Lisa will ever understand in her lifetime, eyes that were showing guilt and longing. For some reason that gave Lisa a weird feeling in her stomach. *Why?* "What I mean is . . . why did you really tell us all that stuff? About Earth and space and . . ." Rose was smiling softly. She shook her head with a sigh and said to Lisa, "I hope I never have to tell you.," Lisa was silent then.

"Oh! That reminds me, would you like to meet them?" Rose said suddenly, and grabbed Lisa's wrist.

"Wait hang on Rose-! Meet who?!"

"My family. Oh I cannot believe I almost forgot to show you. You must see them Lisa, you simply must."

Lisa looked back at the guys who were now running to catch up to them as Rose pulled her towards the ship.

"What's going on?" Decker asked when they boarded the stairway. Lisa finally grabbed her hand free. "Wait Rose, you don't mean we're going back with you to space do you?"

"What?!" Both the guys said at once.

The lights inside the ship flashed on when Rose pushed a button on the side wall. The whole room sparkled white save for the big black screen on the far end and the black sofas that sat in a circle inside this gaping hole in the floor. There was even red carpeting on the bottom of the hole. The ceiling and lights were white with red rims. Lisa looked across the large room at the far wall where there was a red door knob, but no door. Actually, she remembered coming in and seeing a few other red door knobs on the walls, but she didn't see any outlines of doors.

Adam was practically clawing at the door to get out. Then he turned around and looked like he had just entered a whole other world.

Lisa had heard of luxurious cruise ships and five stare airlines, but a luxurious alien space ship? Well that was all that she could really describe it as.

They followed Rose to this huge screen. Rose grabbed for her red glove and let it melt into her skin like it had last time. Lisa gawked at the way the thing formed around her hand like a second skin, and then grew in texture like a real glove. She raised her hand up in front of her and a blue panel blinked on.

"How did you do that?" Adam asked, looking back and forth from the glove to the screen.

Rose waved her gloved hand and winked. "Magic."

She moved her hand over the black glass screen. It looked like suddenly they were looking into space because the black lit up with billions of bright stars and swirls of colored space dust. And they were moving.

"Uh Rose . . . where the hell are we?!" Adam asked, backing up against the wall again.

She laughed. "Don't worry Adam. This is just a decorative paneling. My father made it for me so I wouldn't feel the home sickness. Lovely isn't it?"

Adam didn't laugh. He stayed plastered against the wall.

Something started to pixilate on the big screen. It was a picture of a man with long silver hair and a mustache. He looked strong and intelligent, like a clever warrior.

"This is my father." Rose told them, looking admiringly up at the picture.

"He is the wisest person I know."

Lisa could see a little resemblance. The man grinned the same way Rose would smile and he looked like he had a strong will, and a determined spirit.

"Hey wait a minute. How come we can look at his eyes?" Adam asked.

"I changed the color of the irises so that you can all view them safely." Rose said, tabbing again on the bottom black screen.

The picture faded and another soon popped up in its place, this time it was a young girl. She had short curly blonde hair and a wide toothy smile. She looked to be about five or six.

"This is my sister Elizabeth." Rose said, but Lisa already knew who she was before Rose even said the name. Her and her sister looked like twins, only Rose had a more mature look about her of course, being the oldest and all. The young girl looked like she was just full of life, full of youth. Her skin was creamy and her eyes sparkled a forest green. Lisa was a little disappointed she couldn't see the girl's actual eyes. How bright do they actually shine? Lisa could imagine. She looked like beautiful flower. Like a rose.

Then another picture came up on the screen. It was a young woman with long blonde hair and a soft smile, Rose's smile.

Lisa heard a low break in Rose's voice when she told them, "And this is my mother."

Lisa saw that the guys must've caught the hint to, but she offered a compliment anyway.

"She's beautiful Rose. You look just like her." Lisa smiled softly. Rose smiled back, but it was a sad smile.

"Yes. She was always receiving compliments on her beauty. So much so that often times Father would get a little jealous." She laughed a little. "She was always reminding him that only his compliments meant the most."

Lisa frowned. She didn't want to ask, but couldn't stop herself. "What happened to her?"

Rose put a hand up to the black screen gently, a look of regret and sadness washing over her face. "She died while giving birth to my second sister."

The guys just stared at the screen, not really knowing what to say, but wishing they did. Lisa felt her eyes mist. Poor Rose. She never told them . . .

How it must've felt, losing her mother and new baby sister after they survived all that time on the non-planet. Lisa could imagine what her father had gone through, having to hold together the responsibility of not only his job as a High Council member but as a single parent of two young girls.

"Sorry for your mom Rose . . ." Adam said, pulling his hood over his head.

Rose looked over at him and smiled softly. "My Father told me that she will always be with me, so if I ever feel lonely all I have to do is think of her."

He nodded and sucked in a broken breath saying, "Yeah you know . . . You just gotta remember all the good times you had with her and . . ." Decker put a hand on Adam's back.

Lisa looked back up at the picture, thinking how grateful she was to still have her mother with her. She couldn't even imagine . . .

No, she really couldn't. Lisa would never be able to have the strength to ever be herself again if something were to happen to her mom, the person who she can always count on to be there, to love her and encourage her and give her guidance. Her world would never be the same.

But Adam and Rose are strong, stronger than Lisa, no doubt. They still smile and laugh and live. They still find a purpose to be themselves and be happy. Thinking back now Lisa regrets not being there for Adam more. Her and Decker would just take it for granted that Adam just had another side to him that wasn't always laughing, that side of him that still felt the loss of his mom like a fresh open wound, and often masked it away. They knew he would always get back up on his feet, and they let him get back up alone.

What kind of friend is that anyway? Nobody should have to go through that kind of tragedy alone. Nobody should have to relive the pain by themselves.

They walked off the ship down its long silver platform walkway.

Rose and Ragar stood at the front entrance to the door.

"Mr. O! You leaving us too?" Decker asked, but with a grin.

"I'm afraid so. Farewell to all of you. Oh and boys, do be sure to finish that essay for the substitute by next Friday." He winked.

They all waved their goodbye as the ship lifted lightly off the ground. Lisa watched with tears in her eyes as Rose and Ragar walked through the large metal door.

Rose looked back just before it closed and waved.

Lisa waved back.

Goodbye.

The ship flew straight up into the sky like a rocket, its blue lightning streaking behind it, leaving a faded trail from the ground. The wind from the take-off hit them with such force it felt like someone had opened a door to a tornado, but it was brief. They lowered their raised arms to shield from the blast and looked up into the sky.

No clouds, no planes, just a star.

EPILOGUE

3 months later . . .

Lisa sat with her mom in the bedroom watching the local news. Anchors on every channel were talking about leaked info on how the supposed "alien space ship" they recently discovered suddenly vanished without a trace. Nobody was saying how they had obtained this info or who it was they heard it from, only that it was making its way around the internet. Neighbors around the area are still convinced that there really was a space ship sitting in the woods, even though the two bikers that apparently stumbled upon it are now saying that what they saw was actually a car, not a space ship.

The very next day after the news went to air, all of the police cars and black vans left the field.

Now people are saying there never was a ship, and that it was only a hoax.

"A hoax. Can you believe it?" Lisa's mom said in disappointment. Lisa just shook her head, keeping her eyes on her handheld game and not on the news. "Nope. Can't believe it."

The pain in Lisa's chest hadn't disappeared like she thought it would. It had only been three months but to Lisa it felt like years had passed. Her heart felt like it had shards of broken glass stuck in it, and it was trying to heal but couldn't.

Unfortunately Decker's mom didn't feel like waiting for his
graduation to move them all away. He told Lisa his mom felt that
it was a burden on the family and a "selfish" thing to have them all
wait for *him* to graduate. So she decided it was best to leave early,
so that they can all get going right away like they wanted to.
She wasn't prepared for that one. Lisa had to actually fight the
urge to walk herself over to his house and give his "loving mother"
what for and how.
They both spent the last few hours that day in each other's arms.
They cried. They kissed. They talked. They even got an hour's
nap in, which Decker regretted because he didn't want to waste a
minute not kissing Lisa or looking into her "beautiful angel eyes."
Lisa felt like the rest of the world didn't exist at that moment. It
was just her and Decker. When she looked at the clock, however,
and saw that it was the time his mother had told him to come home
by, she was thrown back into cold reality. Decker was leaving . . .

"I'm gonna head to bed." Lisa said to her mom, looking up at the
clock and seeing it was already eleven thirty.
Her mom yawned and said, "Yeah, me too. I'm tired."
Lisa gave Gustav another pat on the head and he yawned his
doggie yawn. She was about to open the door when her mom
called her, "Oh and Lisa?"
"Yeah?"
"I have to run to the food store tomorrow. You wanna come help
me out?"
"Of course." Lisa smiled, and closed the door behind her.
　　　Lisa put the bowl of cereal she finished in the sink and
headed for her room. She crawled into bed and grabbed up the
covers. They felt cold, something she figured she better start
getting used to.
She closed her eyes and slept the way she slept every night since
Decker left. She lay on her side, imagining him lying next to
her . . .

Lisa felt something on her bed. Gustav again. The little pup has made it a habit of pushing his way through her slightly closed door and jumping up to crawl his way toward the end of her bed. He started doing it ever since Decker left. Guess he knew she was feeling down. Lisa read somewhere that dogs had a sixth sense type of thing, and they knew what their owners were feeling like by the vibes they gave off. It sounded like a bunch of bologna to Lisa, but the way Gustav has been acting with her lately, she might be a believer.

She moved to prop herself up on her elbows to greet the little rascal. But then she felt something on her shoulders. Then her lips. Sirens went off in her head like an alarm and she nearly leaped out of her covers when she saw who it was that was kissing her . . .

It was Decker.

"What—?"

His lips covered hers again before she could get out what she was going to say.

He parted away from her long enough to whisper, "I told you I'd come back." Then he was kissing her again. Lisa's mind was in a frenzy trying to understand what was happening. This wasn't a dream was it?

She blinked her eyes again and again but he was still there. She mumbled a confused and dazed, "Decker?" And he was still there. He didn't fade away like all her other dreams did. He was sitting in front of her smiling that warm smile he only gives her. Her eyes misted with tears and she leaped into his arms. So warm, like they were waiting for her. He held her tight against him, and she melted into his embrace. She needed this, she needed him. It had only been three months and already she had begun to feel like an addict in relapse. And as strange as that sounded it was the truth. She craved his touch, his kiss, his voice. She didn't know how much longer she would've gone before she was back to her old ways again. She could see herself now dressing in all black baggy clothes, walking around with headphones on listening to her rock music, not giving a damn about friends calling or social parties. Would she really go back to that? When Decker pulled her down gently next to him and wrapped his arms around her waist she knew then.

No.

She wouldn't go back to that. Even if Decker was gone forever, she wouldn't go back to that. He changed her. He was the first guy, other than her father of course, to tell her that she was beautiful. Just that little compliment had changed the way she looked at herself. She didn't need to wear baggy clothes to hide anything. Decker loved her for who she was. He didn't care what she wore or how she wore it. No longer did she need . . . Or rather no longer did she *want* to be that shy, low self-esteemed little teenager anymore. She was Analisa.

A cool breeze swept through the room and Lisa then noticed that the window was open. She sat up out of her covers and asked what had really been playing through her mind the second she saw that it was him.

"How did you get here . . . ?"

"Magic." He winked.